JOURNEYS ON A DIME

JOURNEYS ON A DIME

SELECTED STORIES

TOBY OLSON

grand
IOTA

Published by
grand**IOTA**

2 Shoreline, St Margaret's Rd, St Leonards TN37 6FB
&
37 Downsway, North Woodingdean, Brighton BN2 6BD

www.grandiota.co.uk

First edition 2021
Copyright © Toby Olson, 2021. All rights reserved.

Typesetting & book design by Reality Street

A catalogue record for this book is available from the British Library

ISBN: 978-1-874400-80-6

Some of these stories have appeared in *Conjunctions, Dispatches from the Poetry Wars, Fiction International, Gargoyle, Golden Handcuffs Review, New Review of Literature* and *The Philadelphia Inquirer Magazine*. "Reading" appeared in the anthology *Journeys* and was published as a limited edition book by the Friends of Typography, in Madison, Wisconsin. "Calavera" can be found in slightly different form in the author's novel *Tampico*.

Contents

Preface to *Journeys on a Dime*

THE PUBLICATION IN 1969 of Robert Coover's collection of short stories, *Pricksongs & Descants*, included a statement on the book's jacket which can be seen as a signpost towards the way in which that world of narrative was going to be so central to the development of the fictional realities in the work of Toby Olson:

> These "fictions" exemplify the best in narrative art, using the fabulous to probe beyond appearance, beyond randomly perceived events, beyond mere history, to challenge the assumptions of the age.

In 2006, nearly forty years after the publication of Coover's short stories, Olson was interviewed by Jaclyn Cole and Jason Macey for the autumn issue of *Golden Handcuffs Review*. After talking about his method of writing the 1976 novel *The Life of Jesus,* Olson commented on what Macey had termed the "discontinuous in its often short, choppy sections":

> *The Life of Jesus* started out with two poems. When I wrote them, they were very odd poems for me, I didn't know what they were all about, and I didn't know they were about Jesus when I wrote them. Then I wrote a short story called "Walking", and there's a section in that where Jesus and St Peter are in a boat, and they're in close to the land and all that is about being in Arizona as a child, and about the principal of my

high school and desert rabbits and other things and memories from that time.

The novel itself came together as "a bunch of short stories", work that was pieced together, and Olson went on to point out that it was at about this time that he first came across Coover's *Pricksongs & Descants*:

> I was so taken with that book and so taken with the gravity of it that I thought, if I were ever to write fiction, that's the kind of fiction I'd like to write.

Olson's comments proceeded to highlight the manner in which Coover's re-telling of the Grimm fairytale concerning an abandoned brother and sister, "Hansel and Gretel", was presented in sections, a story told in a piecemeal fashion:

> He writes of the two walking along the trail. Then there's a section when he tells that part again from a different point of view and again from another point of view.

Coover's "The Gingerbread House" had merged its sense of the world of childhood and a world of intense menace in a deeply disquieting fashion before it concluded with a picture that was certainly not suggestive of a destined return of two lost children to their home. At the end of Coover's story there are no welcoming open arms from a deeply regretful father and there is no removal of either a wicked witch nor a jealous stepmother:

> The children approach the gingerbread house through a garden of candied fruits and all-day suckers, hopping along on flagstones of variegated wafers. They sample the gingerbread weatherboarding with its

caramel coating, lick at the meringue on the windowsills, kiss each other's sweetened lips. The boy climbs up on the chocolate roof to break off a peppermint-stick chimney, comes sliding down into a rain-barrel full of vanilla pudding.

The repetition of inescapable sweetness here and the emphasis upon its consumption ("suckers", "sample", "lick", "kiss"), constructs an architecture of the near-nauseous, and one can almost hear the click of the trap shutting as the girl reaches out to catch her brother in his fall from that roof and "slips on a sugarplum" before tumbling "into a sticky rock garden of candied chestnuts". The children catch their breath as they find themselves confronted by a door:

> It is heart-shaped and blood-stone-red, its burnished surface gleaming in the sunlight. Oh, what a thing is that door! Shining like a ruby, like hard cherry candy, and pulsing softly, radiantly. Yes, marvelous! delicious! insuperable! but beyond: what is that sound of black rags flapping?

The witch who "flicks and flutters through the blackened forest" with her eyes "like glowing coals" and "her black rags" flapping loosely has arrived and there was to be no going home in that version of the story!

Moving from that to a reading of "The Sister and the Cistern", the second tale in this compelling new collection of Toby Olson's stories, one is immediately confronted with the enormous influence Coover's writing has had upon Olson's fiction. When Sister Mary Grace (note the use of a name that could well belong in a fairytale) is "just two years out of the convent in Guadalajara", she teaches mathematics to high school seniors at Saint Lois Catholic School:

> Saint Lois was not really a saint, but the grandmother
> of one, Timothy, whom she had instructed. Grand-
> mothers are always sainted. This sister was only a few
> years older than her students.

It is the confident assertion concerning grandmothers
always being saints that alerts us to an echo of a storyline
that goes back to the classical world of Pausanias before it
became most popularly re-told by Charles Perrault as "Little Red Riding Hood". The curiosity and innocence of Sister Mary Grace is destined to make her the victim of Father
John the Baptist Esposito, the sexual predator she is going
to meet. Sister Mary Grace is excited by the "energy of the
young, and yes, their sexuality":

> She was feeling it, this late adolescent randiness, and
> she recognized she'd never had an adolescence of her
> own. When she came to America, she noticed that
> many nuns were out of habit and were like ordinary
> women, and this frightened her, so she quickly
> decided that she would always wear her habit, slightly
> refined, of course, and she did.

In Bruno Bettelheim's *The Uses of Enchantment*, his 1975
account of the meaning and importance of fairytales, he
wrote about the Little Red Riding Hood story and, referring to the Grandma's transformation into an ogre, he
wondered how someone who had been so very kind and
who brought presents and a sense of trust could suddenly
act in such a radically different fashion:

> Unable to see any congruence between the different
> manifestations, the child truly experiences Grandma
> as two separate entities – the loving and the threaten-
> ing. She is indeed Grandma *and* the wolf. By dividing

her up, so to speak, the child can preserve his image of the good grandmother. If she changes into a wolf – well, that's certainly scary, but he need not compromise his vision of Grandma's benevolence. And in any case, as the story tells him, the wolf is a passing manifestation – Grandma will return triumphant.

However, a little like that sound of black rags flapping at the end of Coover's tale, the sexual predator in "A Sister and a Cistern", the wolf in priest's clothing, pulls Mary Grace towards him, "kissed her stony lips, then pushed her back over and into the cistern". Like Hansel's fall from the roof there is going to be no escape here.

Robert Coover's collection of stories had opened with "The Door: A Prologue of Sorts" in which he had suggested that "I have veils to lift and tales to tell" and it is with a nod of recognition in that direction that *Journeys on a Dime* pulls the curtains apart with "Reading". The act of reading is itself like peering through a rent in the world, a gazing through doors and curtains which open onto threads of pathway, and Olson's selection of short stories begins with a sense of immediacy in a railway station with the narrator telling us that "To travel is *like* a story, like reading one in a book: being some place where you aren't and yet being someplace." This is an appropriate prologue to a collection of tales in which the world of imaginative reality offers a mirror to a world founded upon a close knowledge of the ordinary:

I was sitting in a train station, in a city, somewhere in a country. It was midday, and across the large, half-empty room a woman sat, reading a book. Her legs were crossed, the book's spine rested on her knee, and she was gazing intently into the pages, as if she'd just opened a Christmas gift, a box holding an intricate quilt, and she was discovering what was there.

The exciting prospect of newness, the opening of a series of journeys, is caught in this photographic moment as the intent gaze at the pages of a book is described in terms of the opening of a Christmas gift. As a reader of these fictions we are asked to recognise how much they provide a mirror held up to our own faces and to what extent we are compelled to acknowledge an understanding of ourselves in what we read. As the retired academic scientist in "Burial of the Red Squirrel" wonders, "Am I a participant or only a witness?" It is the sort of question that might well have occurred to Aphrodite, the narrator of Toby Olson's recently published novel *Walking, a love story* (Occidental Square Books, Seattle), as she walks out of the oppression of one space into the relative freedom of another. Her comments towards the end of that terrifying and uplifting novel question the nature of our own identity within the contours of our own journeys:

> Maybe we are all walking, from place to place, comings and goings, always working to get there. But how many of us are aware? Do we mark the passage with sight, or hear the changing sounds surrounding us as we make our way?

Uniting this new collection of tales is a firmly-held sense that wherever we travel we take ourselves with us and we can only see with our own eyes. Pascal's famous *pensée* had suggested that all of the problems facing humanity seemed to stem from man's inability to sit quietly in a room alone, and in this sense *Journeys on a Dime* is a destination, the conclusion to a voyage: "It's a way to go somewhere and stay put at the same time", reminding us perhaps of Durer's 1514 engraving of the study of St Jerome, the patron saint of libraries.

In *Walking,* Aphrodite had set out to escape the preda-
tory eyes of her father and throughout the novel she is in
almost constant motion, "getting nowhere, while the bus
took me somewhere". Reading as an act of travelling might
be compared to the pacing of a prison cell or the claustro-
phobic circularity of Van Gogh's 1890 painting, *Prisoners
Exercising*. Or, more imaginatively, it could bring to mind
the 1794 publication by Xavier de Maistre, "A Journey
Around My Room", in which a young official imprisoned in
Turin for six weeks undertook a journey round his cell:

> I rarely follow a straight line: I go from the table
> towards a picture hanging in a corner; from there, I
> set out obliquely towards the door; but even though,
> when I begin, it really is my intention to go there, if I
> happen to meet my armchair *en route,* I don't think
> twice about it, and settle in it without further ado.

As de Maistre concluded, "What more flattering delight is
there than being able thus to expand the soul's existence?
Is it not man's eternal, insatiable desire to augment his
strength and faculties, to be where he is not, to recall the
past, and live in the future?" It is the insatiable desire of
the storyteller to tell tales and the narrator of Olson's
"Reading" offers us a picture of the writer waiting to write:

> When I travel alone like this and sit in train stations, I
> feel that I'm nowhere. I've left my life, the encum-
> brances of its textures and responsibilities, the matrix
> of threads that make it real, and I've not yet arrived at
> some other place, with its own textures, the place I
> call my final destination, so I can return home from it.
> I might say I was in that city once, just passing
> through, but it was only a train station, much like all
> the others, and though I might make a list of places,

brag about a broad experience of travel, it's only a story.

The desire of the storyteller is only matched by the insatiable desire of the audience who wishes to hear the tales, and the narrator in the railway station watches a young couple who are sitting with their children. She is reading and so are the children:

> ... thin, colourful books, with pictures on their covers, as if the covers were the outskirts, and opening the book was to enter into the city itself.

Realities can come to the surface in reading, and as Olson suggests there are differences between cover and content, appearance and what lies beneath:

> But a woman can be a man, men can be children, and the old who read in soft, safe houses in Florida can be all of them. It has something to do with imagination, with food, and with memory.

Many of the poems Toby Olson included in his 2019 collection *Death Sentences* (Shearsman Books) were addressed to his wife Miriam, who died in 2014 having suffered for years from Alzheimer's disease. The poems often prompt memory to bring to the surface images and ideas that have seemingly been buried by time, and as with a palimpsest a former reality can be detected lying beneath the immediacy of the present. In "Standard-18, *There Will Never Be Another You*", the messages of the dead become "written into the skins of the living", and a later poem, "Etudes", bears the dedication *For Miriam, in memory*, permitting us to see how the "literal was transcribed / and the story arrived at midpoint". Toby Olson the historian, the story-teller, creates a picture for the reader:

> we found ourselves in a new city
> pining for those earlier days
> in which what's left behind is prelude
> that remains still in memory
> of all those figures haunting us
> until in darkness and this city's lights
> were harbingers
> of what I would be following
> into these calm adventures

However, although much of the art of Olson's storytelling lies in his penetrating ability to perceive what lies beneath a surface and what tracks and pathways may be discovered by the imaginative reader peering through those rents made in the surface of reality, he also knows full well that the removal of a surface does not simply bring to light the existence of a past that has long gone. In "Plastic Surgery" Norman realises that what his wife Natasha has undergone is not a "going back to a time when one was younger" but as if "a thin sheet of polyester film had been tightly affixed there, to provide a certain youthfulness that, though apparent at a distance, was on closer examination no more than a subtle covering of the actual". They had met at a gallery opening, "a strange and compelling showing of enhanced photographs of women's faces", and when they began the early stages of their six-month courtship their meeting in a park is described in a language of sentimental inflation in which a fairytale description glosses over what should have been a serious recognition of each other's personality and needs:

And so it was that they met again, in a park beside a

giant maple tree encircled by a bench, the boards of which were dappled by sunlight and warmed and cushioned their bodies as they leaned back against them, sweet scent of the tree's bark and the twitter of sparrows invisible among the branches and leaves about. The faint, cheerful voices of children in the distance and the gurgle of a fountain provided background music for their casual talk, softly punctuating the cool stillness of the day.

We almost seem to be immersed in the witch's house made of sweets and cake that Coover had presented us with in "The Gingerbread House". Rather like the merging of the stepmother and the witch in the Grimm tale of "Hansel and Gretel", where a smile disguises betrayal and deceit, Norman comes to recognise what the effect of plastic surgery really is:

Now he saw clearly what he had imagined he'd seen before. The warm voices and graceful gestures of such women were the same as they had been, though somewhat aggressive now, or mildly strident. Often they seemed subtly ventriloquized. When they spoke, their words might be sweet or angry or simply fed up, but they floated on a soft red slide, which was the tongue, and their deliverance was fragrant and of cold, hard thinking and of deep understanding. This even while yelling.

Norman also comes to recognise how the eyes, those windows to the soul, offer a glimpse into a reality that lies beneath the surface. Looking through a shop window at another woman who has had plastic surgery, he sees a "thin, beautiful, mask", but as he gazes on the two realities which seem to step forward at one moment only to retreat the next, the coarse mundanity of the real world shatters the image. He had inherited five million dollars from his cousin's uncle and Natasha had of course known about this fortune in advance of their brief courtship. Now, as he is compelled to recognise something about the differences between appearance and reality, he hears the voice of his aggrieved, steroid-abusing cousin Fred, who is standing behind him in the street and about to beat him up:

> "I shoulda got the fuckin' money. He was my uncle,
> not yours!"

Toby Olson is a storyteller, a man who recognises the inter-woven connections between narrative and travel, and *Journeys on a Dime* is an imaginative symbolic act in which the telling of stories becomes the quintessential form in which reality can present itself to the human mind. The title story presents us with a man who is a walker in the city. Although he has a lot of money, "more money than he could ever spend", the possession he values most is the pair of shoes purchased "at the end of a flea-market Saturday, when the prices fell drastically, for one thin dime". The shoes open up new worlds for him by directing his travel and "he was sure they would deliver him wherever he wanted to go, at any time":

> Of course, they were magic shoes. Well, not magic,
> actually. They didn't do anything. And yet at times
> they did seem to have a mind of their own, taking him
> places without his conscious volition involved

When his shoes are stolen he sits on a bed and "is nothing, might as well be among the dead, but should he move or should his mind move, he'd come alive in a story, experi-enced or lived through or thought about, which is the only living to be counted on". The tone of voice here echoes that of Thoreau's *Walden* in which the saunterer, the man *sans terre*, sees the mass of men leading "lives of quiet desperation" and watches the insane ambition of nations "to perpetuate the memory of themselves by the amount of hammered stone they leave". Journeying on a dime's worth of shoes, the man from the city goes to Italy:

> He'd never been to Italy, and he supposed he could
> walk into something new there. So here he comes.

Ian Brinton

For Robert Coover and Richard Wiley
and in memory of Walter Hamady

Reading

I WAS SITTING in a train station, in a city, somewhere in a country. It was midday, and across the large, half-empty room a woman sat, reading a book. Her legs were crossed, the book's spine rested on her knee, and she was gazing intently into the pages, as if she'd just opened a Christmas gift, a box holding an intricate quilt, and she was discovering what was there.

But it was August. We were in a southern city I knew, and as I watched her reading I imagined colorful clothing, limp and humid figures moving like reading threads sewn into the various fabrics of the city's streets, its outskirts beyond the air-conditioned room. I thought she might be reading something about that, her mind in some story in the tropics, while she rested in cool comfort somewhere else. She lifted the book up from her knee then, and I saw her smile.

When I travel alone like this and sit in train stations, I feel that I'm nowhere. I've left my life, the encumbrances of its textures and responsibilities, the matrix of threads that make it real, and I've not yet arrived at some other place, with its own textures, the place I call my final destination, so I can return home from it. I might say I was in that city once, just passing through, but it was only a train station, much like all the others, and though I might make a list of places, brag about a broad experience of travel, it's only a story. To travel is *like* a story, like reading one in a book: being some place where you aren't and yet being someplace.

Sitting in a train station, I often feel I could get right up and walk out of my life. I could cross the half-empty room, throw away my wallet, the labels in my clothing, even my fingerprints. Just walk into the outskirts of this foreign city, to begin again. That's why I often bring a book along when I travel, and sit in train stations, and read like that woman. It's a way to go somewhere and stay put at the same time.

I can't tell the woman's age or guess at her occupation, her "story", at this distance, but I can see her attentiveness in her posture. She's turned many pages while I've been watching, and I remember standing in front of a classroom, reading from a book, when I was a child. I can almost hear the teacher calling out softly from her seat, "posture, posture". Then I'd lost my place, something about Florida, houses and humidity.

I have an aunt who is in her nineties but still travels. When she goes someplace, then comes back, she measures where she's been by shopping centers. Shopping centers are like train stations in cities, but she doesn't see it that way. This *good* place has a fine one, but *that* place has nothing to speak of and is therefore suspect. She travels because most of her friends have moved to Florida; they live in condoms down there.

She means condominiums, of course, and she knows she's made that mistake. She's said it often in my talks with her, a twinkle in her eye, and now the mistake has become part of her story. Hearing her is like reading a book, over and over, and in the meantime anticipating reading it, because it is so good. I mean, the image of that. Her friends live very close to shopping centers, and I can see their postures as they crawl into the pink tubes of their thin rubber homes. She means condominiums, like a book says one thing but means another when you read it.

A young couple with two small children sit close to the woman now, but she doesn't seem to notice them. She's reading, and so are the children – thin, colorful books with pictures on their covers, as if the covers were the outskirts, and opening the book was to enter into the city itself. The parents have gathered suitcases and overflowing paper bags around them. There's food, toys, pieces of clothing, all forming a low wall, containing them in a kind of house, at their wooden bench. This is a traveling family that has brought its life along, I think, a life that holds even the stories in the children's books, fantastic ones I'm sure: talking animals, purple trees, small homes as pink, pliable and safe as those rubber ones, near shopping centers my aunt visits, in Florida. Even the parents are reading now, leaning back on the bench, as if they sat in a soft couch, that one in their living room at home.

Not once has the woman reading the book looked up from it and seen me watching her. My own book rests on the wooden bench beside me, and I realize I have two choices. I can take up the book and go somewhere in it, or I can get up and do that other thing, forget my train and my life, head for the door, just walk out into the humid and foreign city and become someone else. Those are the choices, and thinking about them, my head down now in concentration, is like reading about them. They both become real.

I look up again and discover I'm in a shopping center. It's something I'd not noticed, that row of colorful stores behind the woman and the family, people my aunt's age moving in and out of them. Some are looking in at the windows; others head for the door to the limpid city, thinking of home, images of those houses on the outskirts, soft pink, and yet safe in their pliable minds. None of this has been true.

There was no woman reading, no family, no dank and foreign city. That train station was a local stop and I was riding the express, reading a book, never looking up, even as we slid through the city's dark tunnel and the lights in the coach came on, a kindness of the railroad, so that no one would lose their place. Only my aunt was real, and though I have never been to Florida, I can see the homes her friends now live in quite clearly.

Still, the woman looked up finally from her book, closing it, and where the man had sat there was another man, or a woman, or parts of a newspaper hanging from the edge of the wooden bench, discarded, to be picked up by someone else who needed some reading. In her story, the man might have risen and gone out into the humid, foreign city; he might have discovered he'd left home prematurely and walked across the station to the telephone; he might have crossed to where she was, sat down beside her and introduced himself. I don't know.

I was on the train, reading about her, a book about a woman who had never been to Florida but had plenty of imagination, a constantly expanding mind, and who read a lot. Some thought her lonely, bookish, disconnected from real life, but it was clear in the book that it was *they* who were that. They were not readers, and because of that had no powerful focus through which to see her clearly.

But a woman can be a man, men can be children, and the old who read in soft, safe houses in Florida can be all of them. It has something to do with imagination, with food, and with memory.

The train came out of the dark tunnel and into the sunlight just as I finished the last page. I put the book down on the seat beside me and looked out the window. Trees were passing, then a river. Then we came to the first houses at the outskirts of a new city. They were row houses, condominiums, and because of the sun's slant I could see into their pink windows clearly as the train slowed, approaching the station.

People sat in chairs, on couches, reclined on beds, all reading books. And I saw a woman standing at a window. She was looking out and watching the train I was in pass by. She'd been reading, but now held the book like a fragile and prized possession, open, as one might hold up a quilt for warmth near a draughty window, against her chest.

Still, it was August, I was headed for home, and even as I saw her she became an image in the mind only, though just as vivid that way, after she was out of sight.

I was smiling. The train eased into the station, but it was not yet mine, and I could stay put. So I reached down for the book I'd just finished reading, lifted it up into the light, and began again.

The Sister and the Cistern

DEVOUT PRINCESS OF the May, you might say, but there were a few problems. She was flirty. And she had a way with pleats and draping. She even washed her starched white wimple, that stiff half-moon wafer covering most of her chest, in some substance that gave it a third dimension. Still white, but if you lowered your gaze from her beautiful face, her crisp white bandeau dressing her forehead like a bandana worn by a sorcerer, you would find you were seeing deep into some unearthly presence of dark clouds and rain. And at night you might even see stars.

Sister Mary Grace, just two years out of the convent in Guadalajara, Mexico, now teaching mathematics to high school seniors at Saint Lois Catholic School. Saint Lois was not really a saint, but the grandmother of one, Timothy, whom she had instructed. Grandmothers are always sainted. This sister was only a few years older than her students.

And she was excited by them, the energy of the young, and yes, their sexuality. She was feeling it, this late adolescent randiness, and she recognized she'd never had an adolescence of her own. When she came to America, she noticed that many nuns were out of habit and were like ordinary women, and this frightened her, so she quickly decided that she would always wear her habit, slightly refined, of course, and she did.

In the convent dormitory, the nuns were goofing around, playing grabass, farting to excessive laughter, generally on the loose. It had been May Day at the school, little teaching, but a good deal of policing, keeping the kids corralled and out of trouble. An exhausting eight hours, and now habits had been shed, and the six sisters were romping around in their underwear. The seventh sister, Mary Grace, was not among them, but was ensconced in her small room, a cell really, preparing for her appointment. The first and the last time, she thought. Just this once. I've never ...

First her cotton underwear and black stockings, then her long black dress, which she had hemmed so that her shoes, a little higher of heel than the usual, would show. Her woven belt, the rosary, then a good deal of time spent with her coif, her bandeau, and the black veil flowing down her back. Then her wimple, of course, freshly washed and treated, so that this time ghostly figures, very much like tortured saints, danced in the gloom. What clichés, she thought. Just this once. Just this once. She wasn't looking for love.

Mary Grace grew up on a farm far from the city of Merida, on the Yucatan peninsula, and so she was comfortable in the town where she taught, since it was surrounded by farmland, woods and low hills. On her father's farm she'd worked the crops and was home-schooled. The work was hard, but her father was a kind man, and she had plenty of time for her carving, those small sainted figures she had fashioned even as a small child, learning the technique from a Mayan worker her father employed to help with the harvesting.

And she was very good at it, producing a series of saints that dressed the shelves and mantle in their farmhouse. These would be given as gifts to those her father did business with. They were always delighted with the craftsmanship. And she had continued with this endeavor when older, carving the figures of people she knew, nuns at the convent where she had taken her vows, prizes given to those American students who excelled on various tests and oral presentations, here, in her new life.

Now she slipped the small carved figure into the pocket of her dress. She was ready. It was seven o'clock, and not quite dark, and she left the convent dorm to the frolicking nuns and set out for her rendezvous.

Father John the Baptist Esposito, known throughout the parish as Johnny E, had become a raconteur, though he had started out as a saintly presence, taking on the task of teaching disabled children when all others shunned them. He'd been sweet and dignified, and everyone, including the young parish mothers, loved him.

He was forty-two years old now. He told entertaining stories and jokes, drank a good deal, gambled at the Seminole casino a few towns away, and had an eye for the ladies, at times, it was rumored, taking their love for him quite literally and acting upon it. Somewhere, deep in his head or his loins or his conscience, he may have regretted what he had become, shameful, hardly a real priest at all, but he was unaware of this and felt it was right to enjoy the life he had chosen for himself. He seldom prayed any more, and when he said Mass the words came only from memory, not devotion. He had no place in his heart for Jesus.

And so it was that he found pleasure in the face and figure of Sister Mary Grace, the nun he saw often in his perambulations at the high school. He taught Bible studies there, a required course that the students had little taste for and neither did he. He knew his Bible, but he was no longer interested in it, and his teaching was little more than rote.

They spoke a few times, the good sister querying him

about Biblical matters and he taking in her beauty. And after a while their talk moved on to secular subjects, movies she had never seen, the pleasure of alcoholic beverages, current fashions in women's clothing. There was a beautiful place in the hills outside of town, he told her, smiling a little lasciviously. She might enjoy it. They could meet there. He would bring something to eat and some wine.

And so it was that Sister Mary Grace headed into the hills on a well-worn path as daylight faded and the stars came out. There was no breeze, and a bright sliver of moon hung in the clear sky.

And Johnny E was waiting there, sitting on the smooth concrete edge of the large cistern that provided rainwater for irrigation of the fields below. The cistern was full, the deep dark water rising almost to the lip of the low rectangular wall that contained it.

She sat down beside him, her black dress rising a little to reveal her slim, perfectly formed calves. He touched her fingers as he handed her a glass of wine, which she sipped with little pleasure, though she enjoyed the few cold shrimps he presented on a glass plate over a thin bed of Boston lettuce. There were nuts too, just a few, and pita bread. They ate and talked, and he looked into her dark, inviting eyes, and just as he was preparing to move closer, to possibly kiss her to get things started, she reached into her dress pocket and presented him with the small carved figure she had fashioned.

It was him, the man he once was, as seen through her innocent eyes, this beautiful nun. And it accused him. The figure's head was lowered in profound prayer, and a rosary fell from its delicately carved fingers. My fingers, he thought, my losses.

He knew he couldn't go back, couldn't be the real priest he had once been. Though he still wore the clothing of his order, it was only a disguise. He was a charlatan.

But what to do? She was here now, smiling at him. Beckoning him? No, he thought, for in her eyes he saw her purity of spirit, her saintliness. She had been tempted, perhaps by the devil, but she had found energy and peace in her virginity. Now it was locked up tight, beyond any soiling or violation. Yet he knew he wanted her, and this want was yet another reminder of what he had become. She was the object of his evil desires, and he knew he must rid himself of her.

He pulled her toward him, kissed her stony lips, then pushed her back over and into the cistern.

There had been no lakes or ponds or other watering holes on the Yucatan farm where she had been raised, and she had never learned to swim, but for a while she managed to stay afloat, to look up at him in this baptism, her eyes aglow in her faith and the saintly figures on her wimple accusing him. Then she slipped below the surface, followed by her veil. It floated on the water for a long moment, then went under with her.

He sat there for a while, considering what he'd done. Then he stood up, danced in place for a moment, settling his genitals, and headed down the path with the remaining foodstuffs. The miniature rendering floated on the surface above the dear sister.

She had been his nemesis, his shocking reminder of what had been and was now gone. She had been no saint. He was sure of that. But she had been a very good girl.

Burial of the Red Squirrel

HE HAD BEEN having what he perceived as problems with the red squirrels, who were known to eat into houses, there to create havoc in a man's walls and belongings. They seemed intelligent, but then all animals seem intelligent to those who come into close proximity to them and watch them, even bees, though they are not, properly speaking, animals. The goldfinch pecks delicately at the thistle feeder, an eye out for the stray cat that might leap up to catch and devour it; the lowly vole, only a baby, he saw nibbling at the cheese carefully in the set trap; obviously, the coyote. There were a few too many coyotes around these days, seldom seen, though he had seen one in the early morning, at first light, staring back at him knowingly in the side yard.

He was a scientist of some sort, a retired academic, very specialized, and only a few others understood his work, and these he saw as competitors and avoided them. Thus, he was alone when it came to talk about what for him were serious things. Recently his wife had passed away, or died as he chose to think of it, and he had mourned her, though he didn't think he missed her. She had become little more than an irritant to him late in their marriage. She was buried just a short distance away, near this summer home she had loved but had spent little time in until she fell ill, being on the road a good deal. He seldom visited her grave with flowers, as was the custom. "It was as if she just closed up shop," he'd often said, aware that he couldn't really know that, having retreated into his study for work as she wasted away, tended by the various nurses he had provided for her. Actually, her death had occurred two years ago, in the city, and had come to mean little to the man these days. It might just as well have been ten years or more.

His study door faced a small wooded glade, pine trees the lower branches of which were denuded of needles because the thick canopy above prevented enough light for sustenance. The study itself was its own building, a few yards from the main house and facing away from it, away from his wife when she was among the living, when many phoned but few came to visit, though some did from time to time. His daughter did, but no one visited his study, until the squirrels came.

The squirrels looked good. They were small and compact, a dusky red; their fluffy tails stood tall and vibrated when they paused on a limb for reconnoitering or the dismantling of some nut or cone gripped between forefeet or in tough little jaws. They were, he supposed, cute in their boldness, pausing to look hard at him as he strolled out for work in the mornings, but he thought they had evil intentions. And they made a racket, often interrupting his concentration, which had often been interrupted enough recently by any number of random thoughts and sounds, he supposed because of the complex difficulty of his current project. He'd hear the squirrels scampering across the study roof, and he had seen them leap athletically from the peak to the small balcony outside the second-floor bedroom of the main house, the bedroom in which he had found his wife dead, almost two years ago now, though it seemed much longer and in another kind of life entirely.

There was no evidence of their presence inside the

house, at least he didn't think there was. But animals *had* gotten in, mouse droppings at the backs of drawers and in cabinets, and a few desiccated bodies in traps in the pantry when the house was opened for the season, before the cleaners came through. And he had found a ragged edge of clapboard near the rear door, a chunk gnawed away, teeth-marks, he thought. The house was tight, but it was no fortress, and there were recesses below porches and decks at the stone foundation where he had not checked and felt he had no convenient way to do so. He had been handy when his wife was alive, but he had given up on most out-door work now, leaving it to others. Some were efficient, but none as meticulous and careful as he had been.

The house was called a farm, Gay Farm, his wife had named it well before the term was suggestive, but there was no farming. It was one of a number of places set on land that had once been a farm, long ago, before it was divided up into five-acre parcels, he thought in the 1940s, though it could have been earlier. They'd bought it in the '50s, then had watched as other "estates" had grown up around them, houses with garages made to look like barns, manicured lawns. No academics, but professional men and their families from the city, there only for weekends, which suited him just fine. They'd spent their long summers there for over forty years, and now it was half the year, and in the last two that had grown to be an even longer time. He hardly remembered their winter apartment when he was away from it.

He'd tried the few things others had suggested, a Hava-hart trap, cayenne pepper, the hottest grade, even a brutal rat trap. He'd placed the Havahart in sight of his study, and a squirrel had indeed entered it, only to carefully lift the nuts from where he'd stuck them down on the trip-switch with peanut butter. When its mouth was full, it gave him what seemed a cynical grin, then made its exit with the spoils. They had ignored the rat trap completely, and though he'd sneezed and his eyes had watered when he'd mixed the cayenne with bird seed and poured a mound on the flat bed of the feeder, only the birds had gone away, while the squirrels ate copiously to no effect.

So he bought a gun. It was not a real gun, weapons of that kind were not allowed, but a Crosman Air Rifle, a Model 2200A Magnum, not a toy the literature said in its for-use warnings. A can of Beeman Ram Jet silhouette pellets came with it, "shoot safely, be careful" printed in small lettering on the metal cover, .22 caliber. The rear sight had "windage and elevation adjustment screws" and the front one was described as something special, a glowing green tube, minuscule, sighting through which accuracy would be enhanced. Though a teacher of physics, he had never in his life shot a gun, and so he studied the literature carefully, taking account of every warning and schematic. Then he put the weapon aside, unloaded and with the safety on, leaning against the wall near his study door. The days or weeks went by, and he continued with his studies and scribblings, and before he knew it, it was late June and warmer and the few red squirrels in residence had grown into a larger number. He thought there were smaller ones now, possibly young offspring, though they were as loud and raucous as were the adults. And they stared at him and clacked in the same way as he entered his study each morning, and one morning, his work not going well at all, he decided it was time to try to shoot them.

They were out there, scampering along horizontal limbs, pausing at times to work at nuts and cones, their tails vibrating, mouths open when they clicked out those irritating calls from deep in their narrow throats, and he went to the door and closed it against the screen, then lifted the weapon and loaded a Beeman Ram Jet pellet into the port and shot the bolt. He lowered the forearm and began to pump. Ten pumps maximum the literature said, so he counted six, a muzzle velocity of between four and five hundred feet per second. He had tried to calculate the effectiveness of those numbers, had the figures but no idea of their meaning when it came to accuracy and flesh penetration. And how will I ever hit them, he had thought, they're so small.

He opened the door quietly, then pushed open the screen and stepped out slowly onto the path fronting his study. A squirrel was looking at him, sitting on a limb, suddenly tense, about thirty feet away. It barked out its ratcheting call, a warning to others, or an accusation, he thought, at his presence there. He lifted the rifle, pushed off the safety and sighted through the glowing green tube and fired, surprised that there was little sound and no kick, only a pop when he pulled the trigger.

I've missed, he thought. The squirrel scampered along the limb. But it paused for a moment, then fell like a stone, landing in last year's leaves and matted brush, half hidden by weeds under shadows the limbs cast down. He could see the downy white fur on its chest and belly, like a cat's, he thought. They'd had a few cats over the years. And he could see the rapid pumping, as if a small desperate engine were inside of it. And there was, its heart or lungs. Then the pumping stopped and it lay still. He watched it for a few moments more, then clicked the safety on again and turned and went back into his study, stood the rifle in its place, and closed the door.

He had thought to move it, take it further out into his

property and cast it away, once its body had cooled and stiffened into rigor mortis, not wanting to touch it when it was still warm. Do squirrels go into rigor? He didn't know. But every morning when he came out to his study for work it was still there, possibly a little shrunken. He would sniff for the smell, but there was none, and he left it there. Then on the fourth day, or was it the fifth, it was gone. He looked hard at the spot where it had rested, thinking it might have altered in color in death and be difficult to see. And he looked too at other spots near that one, in case he had mistaken the location. He stepped closer, moving beyond the path and into the wood, but he found nothing. It was gone. Probably some foraging animal, larger than it was, a raccoon or a skunk, even a stealthy coyote, had taken it away for food. Then, after a few days, as one might only finally become aware of the silence of a periodic bell, he noticed an absence of sound and realized that all the squirrels were gone. He stepped out to the study path, stood still and listened. In the past, when they had left the wood temporarily, for an hour or two, he'd been able to hear their chattering at a distance, but there was nothing now. He could hear the soothing warbles of birds, even a faint groan of traffic from the distant highway, but no squirrels. Were they somehow aware of him and the weapon he had used to kill one of their kind? It seemed a very intelligent thing for them to have done, going away like this, since the weapon, only an air rifle, and the killing itself had been almost silent, and he had seen no others watching the event. He went back into his study and tried to work again, but it wasn't a very good day for that, so he retreated into the house to catch the first evening news program, but that wasn't there either. It was only two in the afternoon. Perhaps the clock in his study had gone haywire.

It was mid-July. Summer was in full bloom, and he thought he was probably finished with a piece of research and had written it up, so he decided to take a good long morning walk around his property, to see how things were going out there, something he remembered he had not done for a long time. Years ago, he had cut various paths through the acreage, a thing his wife had wished for, but that he had put off, not intentionally, until she was too infirm to make use of them. Now they were grown over, almost invisible, and even when he walked to where he remembered them being, he found nothing. But what he did find, near sunset, near the base of a locust tree among other trees, in a shallow valley, as if built there by fairies, was a grave. And he thought immediately, standing over it, that it must be the squirrel's grave.

It lay in shadow at his feet, but it seemed clear, even seen through shadow, that it had been tended. Acorns and green pinecones edged the small oval, and dull purple buds had been sprinkled across the mound. He thought they were pale asters, forgetting that they bloomed only in the fall. My wife's grave should look so good, he thought, there in the old cemetery nearby, that he had not visited for a long time, though he was unable to feel guilt about this neglect. Jenevive had been her name, an architect until she fell ill. Could it have been a neighbor who found the desiccated corpse and buried it here? But people, unlike animals, did not trespass in this enclave of small gentleman farms that were farms no longer. Maybe it had been a child, the burial of a cat or small dog. He remembered the way his daughter had buried a kitten when she was that age, how awkwardly sincere she had been. He had fashioned a small white cross to stand at the grave head. But here the burial and tending had been meticulous. There was no cross, but then squirrels are not Christians, he thought. He wanted to dig the grave up, to be sure, but the sun was failing and it was time to get back.

The next day after a troubling morning of fruitless work, he went back again, but had trouble finding the spot, and it was mid-afternoon before he located the stand of locust. The grave was the same, though the pale purple buds had opened into flowers then quickly wilted. He lingered there for an hour, looking down at the small graceful mound, and before he left found a large dead branch and worked it into the ground beyond the miniature forest's brink as a guide-post. It isn't even a grave, he thought, as he ambled back through the acreage toward his study, so deep in musing that he lost his way and only came to himself again when he was standing at the blank rear wall of a neighbor's garage, one of those designed to look like a small barn.

Sitting in his study two days later, after two hours of work and few notes, he thought of his long life and of the squirrel's shorter one that by another species' measure might well have been as long as his. Gathering cones and nuts and information, building small houses in the trees as he had built theories and composed papers. His wife too had built houses, among other things. How similar our lives might have been, he thought, even had I not killed him; or maybe it was a her I shot down, he suddenly real-ized. And the next afternoon he took a folding director's chair, a gathering of flowers and a tall drink of bourbon in his hand, and headed out again, finding that his feet had made a path over time and that, though its way was cir-cuitous, it led him back to the grave without detour.

After brushing away the fallen twigs and leaves, he cut the green stems with his pocketknife then arranged the flower blossoms, of various colors, around the small mounded oval. Then he went into the trees and gathered white and gray stones and used them to form an enigmatic figure, possibly a physics formula, on the mound itself, and after he had pulled a few weeds that seemed too close and was satisfied with his work, he sat down in the chair just a few feet away and sipped at his drink and gave thought to the squirrel's gone life again, and to his own. The thoughts were random, many forgotten soon after their mental articulation, though a few drifted away then returned again. What is it I want here? Is life so precious? If I don't remember this squirrel, who will? That pumping of its chest or lungs, then stillness. Am I a participant or only a witness? Did the squirrels really do this?

And over and over again he went back, taking seeds, a trowel, his lunch, a notebook, at one point a sleeping bag, his liquor, even the Crosman air rifle, only to laugh when he discovered it leaning against a tree. It's of no use here at all, he thought. He brought a few miniature pots containing single flowers he'd planted in them back at the house, and a garden rake to clear the area more thoroughly. He left the director's chair among the trees, rather than lugging it back and forth. And he dressed the grave with meticulous care each time, having cleared a space around it so that weeds would not penetrate its inviolate space. It became sacred to him, though he didn't think he was religious in any way. And it became quite beautiful too, like an elegant formula beckoning him to that study desk where he was spending little time these days. He slept on the ground overnight, then sipped from the thermos of warm coffee he had prepared before coming. At dawn, the grave with its stone and flower dressing glimmered in the early light, and he imagined himself kneeling in the dew, praying softly for the one he had so recently killed.

The days went by, and one day his daughter called and left a message, and the following evening, listening to the message again and hearing her voice, he realized how much he missed her, so he called back and spoke to her.

"Why don't you come out. It's getting on to August and the flowers are in bloom."

"It's September," she said. "Where have you been?"

He thought for a moment. "In my study, of course, working."

She drove out from the city the next day, arriving in time for lunch, which she had organized and packed up before leaving. A seafood salad and fresh lettuce and avocado, and a baguette. He seemed quite hungry, eating every morsel quickly. Then she made coffee and they sat at the kitchen table, sipping from their stoneware mugs.

"Why don't you come back home?" she said at last. "It's getting late. Soon it's going to get cold, and besides that you're all alone out here."

"Home," he said.

"And the children miss you. So do I."

"Come with me," he said, knowing vaguely that the argument he had in mind was no good argument at all, then rose from his seat and headed for the coat rack near the kitchen door. "I want to show you something."

They passed his study and headed down under the bare pine limbs. There was a slight chill in the air, but the wind shifted and the breeze was warm. She walked at his elbow, glancing up at him from time to time, her light coat open, and when they came in sight of the locust stand, he quickened his pace and she had to quicken hers to keep up. Where is he taking me? she thought.

"Over here," he said, when they had entered in among the trees.

"What is it?" she said. He was looking down near the base of a locust tree, but there was nothing there, only fallen leaves and twigs and a few white and gray stones scattered on the ground. He looked around for his chair, but that too was gone. Who? he thought. They must have taken it away. Surely it's the right tree. He bent over slightly, looking for any evidence that he might find, but there seemed to be none, nothing but leaves and stones and a few flower petals blown here on the wind. He knew enough to be slightly embarrassed.

"It's a beautiful spot, isn't it? I wanted you to see it."

They lingered for a while, for as long as seemed appropriate, just standing there and looking around and listening to the warm breeze shushing in the branches and leaves above. Then she took his arm and tugged lightly at his sleeve and they set off back to the house.

The next morning, after a fitful night, she suggested that they go to the cemetery to see her mother's grave, and after breakfast she got his old car out of the garage.

They drove there in silence, parked in the small lot, and then set out walking among the gravestones. It was an old cemetery, their plot off in a far corner, one of the last to be sold. Much like the last reservation available at some venerable hotel, he had often mused. They stepped among trees, then came to the brief clearing and paused.

"Why, it looks just beautiful," his daughter said.

Weeds had been pulled out at the rectangular perimeter, and in their place sat low pots spilling with petunias, vinca, and portulaca. At the head of the grave itself, which had been raked of leaves and twigs, mounds of colorful stones, nature's pinecones and picture-book acorns were placed carefully below the broad granite marker. And to the side of her mother's grave, at the foot of which they now stood, the second reserved spot had been weeded and raked too, prepared with a similar care.

"Jenevive," her father said softly.

"Yes?" said his daughter, standing close at his side.

He thought for a moment before speaking.

"Your mother, of course," he whispered. "Beatrice, my wife."

"She's gone," his daughter said.

But he was not listening. He was looking around, searching for something. A chair, he thought. Then he saw it. It had blown away and now rested on its side against the rough stone wall at the cemetery's perimeter, just a few yards from where they stood, from which vantage he was now vacantly gazing. This place is prepared for another, he mused, after a time. And that time came in only a few weeks that could just as well have been years. Then he too was gone, without noting his own gradual passage.

They held a graveside service, his daughter, her husband, and their four children. At the side of the stone and her mother's name, fresh lettering had been cut, his name, and below it the words Scientist and Teacher, Loving Husband and Father. Under her name was only the one word, Architect, which was quite enough, for she had been a woman of some renown.

When Jenevive and her family returned to the house and stood forlornly in the kitchen where he had made his morning coffee, they heard a cacophonous chatter in the distance beyond her father's study but didn't know what it was. "Just mockingbirds," her husband said, but it was not that. It was the red squirrels, who had returned again now that he was gone.

They were scampering along the bare limbs and branches, chattering, ripping at cones and nuts, making those sharp warbling sounds deep in their narrow throats. And they were calling out to each other in their foreign language. It was as if at times they were laughing at his name, among the last to know of it. But that, of course, is ridiculous. They were only squirrels, after all.

Plastic Surgery

THE FIRST TIME he saw Natasha he was taken by her tall, statuesque figure and her Russian beauty. She had been a model (well, she still was then), and he found her awkward English and their brief conversation quite charming. They had met at a gallery opening, a strange and compelling showing of enhanced photographs of women's faces, and though he admired the faces of women, he found that he was unmoved by these depictions.

He was a salesman for Barrett and Johnson insurance company, indeed the Salesman of the Year (1983), and he was out on the town, still basking in the glory of that honor. Once they had spoken their few words, she was swallowed up by a crowd of admirers, and he had left and gone to a bar in which he sat on a stool, a whisky close at hand, and thought about her and the inheritance he had just received, five million dollars from his cousin's uncle on the mother's side. He'd never met the man and had no idea as to why he'd become the recipient of such wealth. His name was Norman.

And so it was that they met again, in a park beside a giant maple tree encircled by a bench, the boards of which were dappled by sunlight and warmed and cushioned their bodies as they leaned back against them, sweet scent of the tree's bark and the twitter of sparrows invisible among the branches and leaves above. The faint, cheerful voices of children in the distance and the gurgle of a fountain provided background music for their casual talk, softly punctuating the cool stillness of the day.

And that was it. A dozen or so dates, dinner and movies, six months, and they were married.

And things were just fine in the beginning. In their new life, they spoke often, but briefly, and very entertainingly. She was a wonderful cook, preparing, with great fanfare, various Russian dishes. She wore her model clothing around the apartment, a condominium that he had purchased a few years before, and he often noticed her posing before large mirrors, ones she had brought with her into their marriage. She had brought other things as well, expensive modern furniture, fancy lamps, bed linens. She'd pushed his utilitarian stuff aside or had gotten rid of it. He didn't mind these losses, nor the ones having to do with his clothing. She dressed him in designer stuff, up from shorts and jeans all the way to a tux for fancy parties, the ones they never attended now that she was struggling with her career.

Then she had plastic surgery. She'd said she needed it in order to get those now elusive modeling jobs. He understood this, and he was fine with it, noticing no changes of expression when she came home, hid in her room, then appeared one day in her new face. They were both forty-three years old. The jobs were few and far between, and she grew increasingly frustrated and angry about that. For some reason, angry at him as well.

For expecting it of me to cook only!? Lookit at me, this face! Still is beautiful? Why no jobs then? It is you, I think. Holding me preventing. All times stupid! I say, lookit at me!

But he was not looking at her. He sat at his neat desk most evening, studying actuarial tables, settling claims, examining his new investments. And so her anger increased. He was five foot seven, and she would bang into his stomach with her hip, then stride off, as if she were moving down some fashion-week runway. Occasionally she whacked him on the back of his head with her open palm or a wooden spoon. She worked out, pilates, weights, miles on her station-ary bike. She was six foot three, and that in her stocking feet.

Norman had often wondered about plastic surgery, especially that designed to improve the faces of women. It was never some returning, going back to a time when one was younger, though that seemed most often to be the intent. What was it then?

He was thinking these things on his three-mile walk, heading back home from the office, his only exercise, which he accomplished at a good pace, though on this day he could be seen limping slightly, from behind, his bowed legs more prominent that usual. He had felt blood on the back of his left knee upon awaking. She had leaned down and stabbed him there when he had approached too close while she was filleting the striped bass last night. *Get away you!* she had yelled at him. He thought she might have inter-fered with some tendon or ligament back there. The wound was quite painful.

But these women, he was thinking. In some of the worse cases, and some of the better ones too, he had seen a sheen, a glowing of the skin that made it seem as if a thin sheet of polyester film had been tightly affixed there, to provide a certain youthfulness that, though apparent at a distance, was on closer examination no more than a subtle covering of the actual. Some of the women seemed to know this as a bit of fakery and would look away. But this was perception only, Norman understood, a metaphor, and he knew the reality was quite different from that.

Walking. His leg aching. Limping. The small rise of the hump on his back more prominent as he motored slowly along. His natural tonsure, his scalp, glistening with sweat. Two more miles. What was it that Natasha had seen in him? What did he see in her?

He knew that their marriage was nearing its final stage, that he no longer loved her, nor she him. In the beginning, and for a long while, it had been her beauty, her stature and presence. For her, he thought, it had been his money, then his honor, Salesman of the Year after all, though she had seemed a bit jealous at his success. She wasn't working, hadn't been for a long while now. Though she was still beautiful, she was too old, and the plastic surgery hadn't helped. She was enraged all the time now, and the brutality she inflicted upon him was, in reality, an attack on her own body. She felt she was falling apart and wished only that he would join her. These were deep understandings, as he trundled along, thinking of his leg and the ways in which he seemed to be losing the structures of his life.

He'd always been a man who valued order, both in his doings and in his person, but recently his client lists had fallen into a shambles. He was no longer out on the road visiting prospects, something other high-level executives at Barrett and Johnson had never done. He'd been thought of as a wonder salesman, someone who stayed close to his clients, got down in the dirt with them. Kindly yet shrewd, he managed to set records in lowering payoffs that otherwise might have been astronomical.

And then there was his dress and grooming. He'd stopped shaving every day and would appear at work with a shadow of hair on his face. Some thought it was a style matter, the scruffy look, yet most were aware of some difficulty. His unkempt fringe of hair, his soiled and wrinkled clothing. Often, he worked at home, in his study, and didn't make it to work at all. The top boss was watching him, cognizant of the facts and that he might be in serious trouble. Salesman of the Year was well behind him now. It no longer carried much weight.

He was passing a row of stores now in his slow peram-bulation, a gourmet food shop, its delectable wares, cheeses and prepared dishes, on shelves facing the win-dow; a fancy fish store; a gift shop, various greeting cards, glass paperweights, display cases full of expensive soaps garishly packaged, tumblers, small ceramic frogs; and at the end of the row, a women's clothing boutique.

He paused, his knee was aching, and he was tired. And through the large plate-glass window he spied a woman who stood out from the other customers and elegantly dressed sales staff. She was tall and slim and wore a fine linen sheath dress and had moved to a floor-length free-standing mirror that faced away from the window outside of which Norman stood. She was facing him, examining herself, and he could see her clearly. Perhaps forty years old, he thought, beautiful, and she had been touched by the surgeon's knife.

He had seen many women who'd had their faces profes-sionally carved, and even looking at this one, whose opera-tion had been of a very high quality and was for the most part invisible, he could tell that work had been done. He could see it in a tightness at the edge of her eye, an eleva-tion of her cheeks, and the way she lifted her chin in order to display, even to herself now, her new neck.

Now he saw clearly what he had imagined he'd seen before. The warm voices and graceful gestures of such women were the same as they had been, though somewhat aggressive now, or mildly strident. Often they seemed subtly ventriloquized. When they spoke, their words might be sweet or angry or simply fed up, but they floated on a soft red slide, which was the tongue, and their deliverance was fragrant and of cold, hard thinking and of deep understanding. This even while yelling.

And then he saw what he knew was the most important things: the eyes and the two faces. She was there in the window, and she saw him, and she looked at him. Maybe it was his injury or his exhaustion. Maybe it was the coolness of the early fall day. Her eyes blinked once, then stared at him. And in their deep blue pools, hardly perceptible at first, he could see through to the other eye. He lowered his gaze to her face, and there, in it or through it or behind it, he saw the other, deeper face. The surface was a thin, beautiful mask, and the vaguely seen though strong and relaxed presence behind it was who she was, or not quite, for it was she who had wanted this improvement and was now both the mask and the spirit.

He felt he could speak to her, imagined that he had, and the more he looked and looked, the image of the one he was speaking to came forward and the mask became just that, something to see through. He'd been speaking to, and was now looking at, the spirit behind the mask, the controller. There came a moment in their reverse movements when the two faces came together. And there was the beautiful, fully integrated woman. Then the two faces separated and the spirit took over again.

"I shoulda got the fuckin' money. He was my uncle, not yours!"

He turned, and there was his cousin Fred, that bulky guy, a weightlifter who dabbled in cage fighting. And Norman could see that he was back on steroids once again. He was almost vibrating. He said nothing more, then lunged at him and began punching him in the face and body. It hurt like hell, and even though Fred came to his senses quickly, the damage had been done. A crushed cheekbone, a fracture of the patella on the opposite side of his damaged leg, his nose broken and pushed dramatically to the side.

And so it was that he was staggering up the stairs to his apartment on the second floor. He'd tried to wipe the blood away with his shirt, but it had coagulated and was sticky and close to impossible to rub off. He reached the landing, then opened the door and entered into the living room, only to find her once again examining herself in one of her mirrors. She glimpsed his reflection to the side of her shoulder and turned.

My Got! What is happening to you? You are one big mess!

Her words were delivered out of kindness, he thought. But as she approached, a look of concern upon her face, he saw what he had seen in the shop window, the mask, and below it the character of the controller. She was there, the real Natasha, that face and those eyes that she had manipulated so successfully in the time of their marriage before plastic surgery. Now the manipulation was on the surface, and her real face had relaxed into the person she really was. It was a face of pure evil. He saw it in her burning eyes, in the blood rising in her cheeks.

She crossed the room, staring at him, smiling now, and reached down and lifted him up into her arms. Then she moved to the closed window, paused, and threw him into the glass.

They were only on the second floor, and he landed in a dumpster full of garbage bags that cushioned his fall. He was lucky to get away with only a cracked hip and a broken ankle, and these, added to his other injuries, made it necessary that an ambulance be called. His downstairs neighbor took care of this. Natasha was nowhere to be seen.

He was in the hospital close to a month, and his cousin Fred, still profusely apologetic about the beating, sat by his bedside every day as he recovered, and when he left the hospital it was Fred who drove him to the studio apartment that he had arranged for.

It was a small but nice enough place, and Fred went to the apartment with a rental truck and gathered what was left of Norman's furniture.

"She didn't say a thing. Not anything. What happened?"

And Norman told him the story that he had told the police. He had stumbled and his bum leg has given out and he had crashed through the window.

Fred was suspicious, as the police had been, but Norman stuck to the story, and in the end his version of the event was accepted.

He got a lawyer, then he contacted a plastic surgeon, and before long he had a new face, was back at work, and had organized his affairs. He settled one million dollars on Fred. Natasha received two million and the apartment, and he was left with what remained, enough for a new condominium, a two-bedroom in a highrise closer to work, and anything he might desire, a car, clothing, travel. He desired very little, just his work, a fine single malt scotch, a little TV, and a good book for bedtime reading.

He knew the two faces were there now, but he never spent time before mirrors, and in a while he figured that the two had fused together, the controller had come to the surface.

And so it was that others began to notice the openness of his new expression. They saw it as welcoming, in no way dissembling, and sincere. He acquired new friends, went dancing with a small graceful woman, vacationed in Cabo San Lucas. His smile was contagious. He became light on his feet.

He has seen me from behind my face, so out window. Crack hip, broking ankle. Not much.

This man Norman husband was fool. I put up all years! Some time I had wish for sledgit hammer!

Yes, was money. Now I have. Two million coming from uncle of cousin on other side.

I have it my apartment, my Beemer, my model stuff clothings, my best furnitures. I have it not stupid fuck Norman.

I have it also my mirrors.

There I am now. Lookit at me.

I am so pretty!

Sweet Georgia Brown

I MET THE family that lived at the Holiday Inn on old Route 20 North on a spring day that was the hottest we'd had in years. I went there, dressed in shorts and T-shirt only, to set up, wire and plumb the kitchen unit. I'm a licensed electrician but handy in some other trades as well. They were the first to move in.

The old man was sitting in a metal chair on the narrow second-floor walkway, fanning himself with a newspaper.

"Hot," I said, as I passed him in my tool belt, lugging the bucket of BX cable, connectors and the other gear.

"You got that right," he said, not looking up. He was watching the four children who were splashing around in the pool below. They waved hello to me when I looked over. There were a couple of station wagons far down the line, fishermen I thought, but that was about it.

When the new highway came in, Route 20 got a little ghostly, and the Holiday Inn began catering almost exclusively to fishermen. Then the pollution came in, both to the big lake and the two smaller ones fed by it. Fishing dropped off dramatically, only the river and its few trout then, and the Inn got rid of the manager and hired an Indian couple to live in and run the place. The man held a full-time job in women's clothing in the city, and his wife took care of the Inn business, what little there was of it. Eighty rooms, but they retained only one chambermaid, Lupe, who I'd passed a few words with from time to time.

When you went into the office you could smell curry brewing in the room beyond.

The Inn was getting ready to close down completely when the township got wind of it. Over the years, the politicians had been remiss when it came to welfare housing; there was almost none, and now national funding was in jeopardy. The Inn was a good distance from any shopping, as if it were in the country now that the old highway had for the most part closed down, but this didn't seem to bother the politicians. They forced a deal on the Holiday Inn parent company. Eighty rooms would make for at least forty apartments, and if the company balked there'd be repercussions in the press not good for the national business. The Inn could rent the remaining rooms at will, as welfare occupancy moved slowly along. Most of the few takers were fishermen.

I'd been working for the Holiday Inn on an on-call contract for a number of years, so there were no surprises waiting for me when I entered the room, which was neat as a pin and had been cleaned with something having a faint oleander scent that was not like the bolder smelling cleaner Lupe had a penchant for. The drapes had been closed against the sun, and a woman sat hunched over in a chair at the formica desk, almost in darkness but for the dim bulb in a gooseneck lamp that was not part of the Holiday Inn decor. I thought she was an old woman, but when she heard me and got to her feet and went to the drapes and pulled the cord, I saw, blinking in the new light, how young she was, perhaps thirty I thought then.

"I'm the electrician," I said.

"I gots that," she said, looking me over. "Belt-n-bucket."

The steel kitchen unit – sink, stove and refrigerator all in one – had been removed from the shipping box, which was nowhere in sight.

"Thought ta gitit ready," she said, stepped out of the sun at the window. Then I could see her better.

She wore a loose flowered dress, and her hair was tied up in a rag; tall and a little thin, with skin like dusty cocoa of the kind that like a stone found on the beach then dipped in water turns black when it's wet; a slight overbite and full lips. I thought she was beautiful.

She watched me, hands on hips, as I hooked up the unit and worked it into the tight space between the bathroom and the closet wall. There was little else in the room beyond the usual, the long low dresser, the TV, the desk she had been sitting at, two chairs, the queen-sized bed, and the small open closet in which cardboard boxes had been stacked up tight to the ceiling. Out of the way while cleaning, I thought. Not until I was finished did she speak again.

"What ifit gits brokes?" she said.

Brokes? I thought. That's not right.

"You can call the office," I said. "I work for both Holiday Inn and the township."

"I knows that," she said. "You gotsa card?"

"Better to call the office," I answered.

"So you says. What about that card?"

I wiped the sweat from my hands, pulled one out and gave it to her, then left.

I lived in a big old ramshackle farmhouse not far away that had once been something to brag about. It had been in the family for a long time, and Wendy's father had given it to us as a wedding present, together with the thirty acres of property attached. It had been built in the 19th century when there was money in the family, occupied then as a showplace and retreat. The land itself was stony, unfit for farming, though it did look beautiful on the surface. It was only a year after our marriage, when Wendy was pregnant, that the water was tested and found wanting, the same pollution that has since virtually killed the lakes and the fishing. Though high up on a hill, the house was still lower than the foothills of the rolling mountains where, sometime in the past, there had been toxic waste dumped. Just after Wendy died in childbirth, taking the baby with her, the EPA got wind of the issue and began tying things up in red tape in the way of most government agencies. I saw to the installation of the water tanks and the trucking in, then began the serious drinking.

I went out to the bars, got drunk and chased drunken women and caught some, seldom remembering what had transpired when I woke up beside one of them in our room at the Holiday Inn. This went on for a year after Wendy's death and then it stopped, I don't know why, to be replaced by years of work on the house. I was rehired by the electrical company that had fired me, but soon went off on my own, spending all my free time getting the necessary repair work done. Then I started work on restoration, on the outside when the weather was good, on the inside when it wasn't. It became clear early on that this might be a lifetime job. The house had three stories, seven bedrooms and a bunch of other little rooms, and what had been formal spaces on the ground floor, a large dining room, a study big enough to be a small ballroom, an extensive kitchen with walk-in pantry, a living room and a few cubbies. There were elegant bays and bowed windows, and the foyer, big as a bedroom, opened onto a broad, covered veranda, complete with hardwood and pillars that meandered around three sides. Wainscoting, brass fixtures, leaded glass, and a number of other sophisticated appurtenances, all of which needed extensive and careful work, all of which I enjoyed doing, so that even when the pain of Wendy's leaving had for the most part left me, the work no longer therapy, I continued on with it.

A few days later, just as I got home from a day's work of rewiring at the prison, the phone rang.

"Hello?" I said.

"Can ya come Georgia house?" There was static on the line and I thought it must be a cell or payphone. The woman's voice came out of a cave.

"What?" I said.

"Over Holiday Inn. Where you done put in a kitchen that don' work."

"Oh," I said. "What's wrong?"

"Don' work what's wrong."

"Okay, okay," I said. "I'll be there in an hour."

"How 'bout a half," she said and hung up.

When I got there she was waiting in the doorway. It was six-thirty and a little cooler now that the sun was beginning to sink away. She was wearing that same loose flowered dress, but the rag was gone, and tight black curls fell at the sides of her neck, covering her ears.

"Sorry," I said as I approached.

"Sorry's good," she said, turning to head in through the door. "But it don' cook dinner."

It was a small problem really. An electrical connection I'd made had come loose. I had it fixed in a jiffy. Then I worked the unit back into its place again, rose up and faced her.

"There you go," I said. "Call again with any problem." I smiled at her.

"Thanks, I'm sure," she said, smiling back, and showed

me to the door. I stepped out on the narrow walkway, then turned.

"How's it going so far?" I said. "I mean with your children sleeping in the other room." There was no adjoining door, and they had to go outside to where I stood to get to the other room and their mother.

"Hell. The chirren don' mind a bit. Hear 'em gigglin' over there? Gots freedom now they think."

"How about the old man, your father?"

"Really ain't your bidness, you know, but I'll tell youens anyway. Yas, my father, and yas we done been sleepin' in this here bed together. I gots ta hold an eye on him. He wanders. May well'a did that now. Could head out jest about anywheres and has done so. But I got me a tether. To my leg. I'm a heavy sleeper. How's that? Is youens satisfied?"

"Yes," I said. "I was just wondering."

"Gotsta gittat my victuals," she said, smiled again and closed the door in my face.

I saw her from time to time that month of June, when I was called over to handle electrical malfunctions, more than usual because of the overloads in the continuing heat. Then, on a day that was a real scorcher, I saw her down at poolside when I went there to work at the central air-conditioning unit. I had it up and running again in an hour, clocked the time and started back to my truck. She was still there, in that same flowered dress, watching her children playing in the water. There was an empty chair beside her at pool's edge, and I thought, what the hell, and strolled over, dropped the bucket, and sat down. The chair collapsed immediately, and I tumbled into the pool to the complete delight of her children, who were whooping and laughing loudly when I surfaced, my soaked leather tool belt pulling at my pants, threatening to lower them.

"Good Lordie!" she said above me. "*That* some greetin'! I cain't ..." but she couldn't continue. The laughter had her and it joined the children's. She was looking down at me, her dark eyes glistening with tears.

I'd lost my cap and my hair was draining water down into my face, and my soaked T-shirt felt like a second skin, though a refreshingly cool one. I grinned up at her.

"Come on in," I said. "The water's fine."

And she did. She got right up and stepped over the edge, to the joy of her children who were already quite joyful about my flop. Her loose dress spread out over the surface like a huge lilypad, and I saw the stems of her long dark legs, modest white panties, before she rose up into it again, water streaming from her hair and face. We stood there, grinning at one another, a couple of soaked puppies. Then she turned, causing little waves to rise and wash my elbows, and addressed my attention to the children.

"Now thet you done joined 'em, you best meet 'em," she said. "That giggly one be Laticia, she six. Boy aside her be Ahmed, he eight. An' the good lookin' one, she twelve-year-ol' Beauty. An' that there my first born. He Paul. I don' know why. He thirteen. They father picked out they names." The children nodded and grinned and the little ones giggled again, and they watched us closely as we climbed back out of the pool.

I found another chair, tested it in detail and with fake seriousness, which made her laugh again, then settled into it, facing her, my tool belt on the pool's deck tile beside me. We were both soaked, sitting in the sun there, and the hot air seemed a little cooler as a light breeze came in from the north and began to dry us out.

After she'd pointed out and named the children, who were still splashing around in the pool, though keeping an eye on us, we said nothing for a while. Then she leaned back, raising her arms above her head, which elevated her small breasts, distinct through the wet fabric.

"That was extremely refreshing," she said. "I suppose I should swim more often."

"Gotcha," I said, and when she lowered her arms and looked at me again, I could tell she knew exactly what I meant. She smiled and tossed it off.

"It's what's expected, you know. We darkies from down south? Funny how it helps at the Welfare Office, talking that way. Ignorant? I guess they think that's it. The best ones take you under their wings. It helps. And it helps with other whites too, even the nasty ones."

"Does that mean I'm not one of them?"

"Maybe," she said. "What's your name?"

"Matt," I said. "Matthew Dean Gregory."

"I'm Georgia Brown."

Then the words just came right out of me.

"Well, then. I was wondering, Miss Brown, would you care to go out to dinner one evening, and a movie?"

"Oh, my!" she said. "Do you know what you're getting into, Matt Dean?"

"Not yet," I said.

There was an Ingmar Bergman retrospective running at an arts theater in the city, and I took her there to see *The Virgin Spring*, which may have been a risk and a downer given the darkness of that film. But over dinner at a little Italian place she couldn't stop talking about it, how very fine she thought it was. "That Max von Sydow? He gets you where you live!" She was wearing stockings and low heels below a deep purple cotton-knit dress that, though worn, conformed nicely to her thin body. Her hair was up with pins and combs, just a little makeup on her dusty cheeks. Good God, I thought, do I deserve this?

On our second date she told me her story and on the third she brought her father along. His name was Emmory Brown. She called him Dad and sometimes Em, and I called him Mister.

"This is a very nice place, indeed," he said, while we were eating ice cream sundaes at the local parlor after the Beethoven concert in the city. "And the music," he said. "That was fine, fine."

"You like Beethoven?" I asked.

"I favor the late quartets. But that concerto was well played, I thought. The violin was a little too careful for my taste, but it's a difficult piece to negotiate without being careful, and the man had the orchestra going rightly."

"Em plays the violin himself," Georgia said.

"Used to."

"I'd like to hear you play sometime."

"Won't," he said.

He pulled me aside when we passed each other on visits to the bathroom.

"You're getting it on with my daughter?" he said.

"Not yet," I said.

"Well, go to it, sonny. You have my blessing. She needs something decent after than lame son-of-a-bitch she married."

"Yes, Sir," I said.

"Call me Em," he said, and I began to wonder if she'd been pulling my leg about the tether and his wandering.

The children had watched him on our second date and had watched themselves when the three of us were out together. There was not a sound from their room when we got back close to midnight, but their grandfather stepped down the walkway to look in on them, and I took the opportunity to lay the first kiss on Georgia Brown, more than a peck on the cheeks, but modest nonetheless.

"Good night," she whispered, squeezing my arm.

They came north from Macon, Georgia, only after her husband had been incarcerated on a two-and-a-half-year term for beating a man half to death in a restaurant for looking at her. He was a white man, and it had taken all her father's savings and whatever other money could be scraped together to get a plea bargain, down from aggravated assault with intent to simple assault. He'd had a violent past leading to a few earlier arrests, and he had beat her, slapped the children around when he felt like it, and had even threatened her father. "I was twenty-six, had a high school education and a clerical job when I met him. I can't imagine how I came to marry him. He was very jealous and possessive from the start, and I guess I liked being possessed. He told us we better damn well be there when he got out. He had friends as nasty as he was to keep an eye on us." Then she must be closing on forty, I thought, not in her early thirties, which was my age.

They had an old car and they packed up in the night and headed out, she, the children and her father. When they got to Chicago and looked up the distant relatives they'd been in contact with, there was sickness in the house, and they weren't taken in. They had a few dollars only, enough for a couple of months in fleabag hotels. So they headed east and further north, and after a year of constant displacement in which she took up various menial night jobs, washing dishes and cleaning in office buildings, leaving Paul who was just past eleven to look after the younger children and her father as best he was able, they arrived exhausted in the nearby city where their car quit finally, then found their way to this small town, social services and the Holiday Inn.

She said she'd tried to stop them a few times, to get a real job and settle in. Neither the children nor her father was handling the moving around too well. "He did play his violin for us some evenings, and that was soothing." But it wasn't fair to burden Paul in the way she had. He was just a child too. And then, of course, there was schooling, which wasn't happening. Almost by default, they were underground. She and the children had taken back her maiden name, which was a common enough name. "His name is Dennis Davis, and he's due out in about a year. I'm sure he knows we're long gone. He'll try, but he won't find us. There's a year and a half and too many miles between."

"So, you're still married," I said.

"In name," she said.

Early in the next month, two more families took up residence in the Holiday Inn, a young woman named Bertha Beal with two children, Donny and Bitty, who were close to the ages of Laticia and Ahmed, and an old couple, the Onces, and their pregnant granddaughter, Opel Shots, with a one-year-old boy still in diapers named Jason. Carl Once was Emmory's age, and his wife Amble was charming and very good looking at seventy-five. There were no other husbands around. Bertha's had died in a non-Union construction accident near Littleton, New Hampshire, Opel's from heart failure before he was thirty down south in Louisiana.

There had been survivor benefits, but in both states political nonsense had quickly put limits on that.

I fixed up their kitchens and corrected some faulty wiring, and with the help of Georgia's friendliness toward me, quickly allayed their suspicions and got to know them. The three women laid smiles and curious eyes on me, quickly getting the drift. The grandfather, Carl Once, sat out on the narrow walkway and talked with Emmory. The women, in part because of the children, became friends, and the three cramped apartments opened their doors, making for a larger expansive apartment in which daily commerce was easy and frequent. The bus was almost a mile's walk away, and at times I scheduled my jobs so I could drive them into town for shopping and visits to the Welfare Office. It was July and still blisteringly hot. Then somebody got the idea for a cookout and pool party. I checked with the Indian couple who ran the place, and both Manu and Inder smiled from behind the counter and said "Sure, why not? Can we come too?" and on the chosen day I piled five kids, cozy under the cap in the bed of my pickup truck, and headed out for fruit. Beauty was back there keeping an eye on the younger ones, and Paul, the oldest at thirteen, rode in the passenger seat beside me.

"Are we gonna get ice cream too?" he said. "The young children would go for that."

"I'll bet they would," I said, and after we'd gathered a crate of peaches and a few pears and plums at a farm stand down the road, I drove to the little town ice cream parlor, hearing the kids squeal behind me when I parked and they saw the sign. Paul and Beauty kept an eye on them until I came out with two gallons in quart containers, neapolitan, rocky road, and tutifruity.

When we got back, I parked in shade under trees edging

the utility lot and could see from there that long wooden picnic tables had been pulled up to form a half-moon curve in grass near the pool's tiles, and when I opened the door I caught a whiff of something good cooking and saw that beyond the second-floor walkway all the doors stood open and the women were coming out of them and going into other apartments. The pregnant Opel was leaning back a little, her belly well ahead of her, and she and her grand-mother had to spend a little time negotiating passage. Then I saw Georgia step out through her door. She saw us down below and gave a little wave before ducking into the Beal's apartment. Then the kids piled out of the back and ran squealing toward the stairs, all but Beauty, who saw such hysteria as unseemly, and strolled quite casually toward the building, while Paul helped me unload the ice cream and fruit. It was a heavy load, and we moved slowly past Carl Once and Emmory, who were sitting side by side before the two charcoal cookers, waiting for the pyramids of briquettes to turn ashen and be ready. Each would bar-becue his batch of ribs then in his special sauce, something I'd heard them talk about earlier, not in any way competi-tively, each seriously interested in the other's eventual product and the taste of it. As Paul and I moved past, lug-ging our load, we heard them speaking of something else.

"I hear you play the violin."

"Not much anymore. The fingers, you know?"

"Well, I can play the jew's-harp a little."

"Deep country music."

"Perhaps we can find us a washboard."

"A couple'a spoons," Emmory said. "We can behave like old darkies near the bayou."

"*That's* the ticket," said Carl. "But what exactly is a bayou?"

The women were frying chicken in big black skillets,

and I saw that all the elements were red hot as I parceled out ice cream into the freezers of three small refrigerators. Breakers might go, I thought, then realized I was here saying that and that I could fix anything that went bad quickly. When I got to Georgia's apartment, I took a peek into the bubbling oil, the parts already turning a crispy golden brown.

"Watch your nose, Matt Dean. The oil's hot!" said Georgia, plucking at my sleeve to pull me away. Beauty was cutting tomatoes into thin even slices on newspaper at the formica desk, and she gave us one of her long-suffering looks, indulging us in our childish play.

There was this chicken and the ribs, Amble's Kentucky Mountain coleslaw, and Bertha Beal had made use of the Jalla's oven to bake her cornbread and biscuits. Then there were a variety of fresh vegetables mixed in salad bowls, a bowl of okra, and one of seared apple slices crusty with melted brown sugar. Large glass pitchers of lemonade, thick with lemon slices and ice, sweated on the redwood tables. Inder and Manu Jalla arrived with a massive bowl heaped high with her special tabouli, and a couple of fishermen who had rented rooms on the far side approached hesitantly, carrying a folded motel blanket between them on which rested over newspaper a dozen freshly-gutted trout. *Not* from the polluted lakes, they let us know immediately, but from that swift river posted as safe. Emmory and Carl greeted them with their actions, making room beside the ribs, then wiping and oiling the fish and resting them tenderly over the few coals at the edge so they could cook slowly. It was hot as hell again, and before eating most everyone took a dip in the pool, even the fishermen in their skivvies, and the children stayed in until the last minute, when, to the pleasure of all, the hot sun began to sink away and a light, almost cool sunset breeze dried up the water and sweat so we could dig into the fine victuals in relative comfort. Manu went back to the office to throw the switch and the pool lights came on turning the rectangular surface to a lime-green glow that washed over the lip and bathed our feet and legs in that color and gave, along with the oil lantern on each table, enough light so we could see each other and the food on platters and in deep bowls between us.

"My, my," said Georgia. She was sitting beside me in her white one-piece swimsuit, and I could feel her damp leg pressing against mine below my shorts. We had all eaten our fill and were now sipping lemonade and picking at the leavings. I'd taken a piece of trout and when I lifted it on my fork I smiled and nodded my pleasure to the fisherman down the table from me. He was a burly old gent and had an open, accepting face.

"The last time I remember eating like this was when Mamma was alive. That time when your daddy had gone off somewhere and we picnicked in the park? It was chicken then too and Mamma's hushpuppies. Do you remember, Paul?"

"I don't remember," Emmory said. "I must have been back home, sawing on the violin." He was sitting beside Beauty, teasing her from time to time with his fingers.

"I can play the jew's-harp," Carl said, from Georgia's off side.

"I *got* that," Emmory laughed.

"I remember," said Laticia, and Georgia and Paul laughed and Beauty smirked. She was slapping at her grandfather's hand, trying hard not to laugh. Her chin was parked on her palm, completely bored by it all, yet ready for that boredom to be captured by some handsome photographer who was sensitive enough to see the state of loveliness in it.

"Laticia, you *can't* remember," said Paul gently. "You weren't born yet."

"And yet I *do* remember," she said, and everyone at the table laughed lightly, and when the laughter drifted away Bertha Beal spoke up. She was sitting at the other table, together with Ahmed, her son Donny, the pregnant Opal and her baby Jason, and the Jallas. Bitty had crept over to sit beside Laticia, and the two were constantly giggling and whispering things to each other. Amble and the other fisherman sat at the table's end, talking about the preparation of all kinds of fish.

"It was after my husband died and I'd gotten a job waitressing. I had people watching the kids here, but that wasn't working out. Both little Bitty and Donny here weren't having any of it. I'd been home all the time looking after them before Aberham passed on, and they just couldn't seem to abide anyone else in the house. My, did they scream and holler, didn't you boy? And before long I had to just up and quit. The social services workfare got wind of that right away and said they'd cut off the home care money, that I was fit and able, and if I didn't take up a job the welfare and the food stamps would be gone too. That's what got me out of New Hampshire and over here where we are now. But that's not the thing.

"The thing was that for a short while I had my tips and my last week's salary, and one day all three of us headed out into the woods and down to the river where they had tables and grills and a nice walking path.

"You have to understand that my husband had been in the army, stationed for a while in France, and he used to fix up French meals for us from time to time. So I went to the French store he knew about in the city and got a mess of stuff for us to picnic on as we once did, though this time he wouldn't be there with us. Lord, I remember it all quite vividly, how sad it was and yet how good the food was as we ate it and thought about him and the fun we'd had.

"We had *cornichons*, a fine *sucisson sec*, a very dry hunk of cheese, they call it *crotin*, what they call *crudité*, that's carrot and celery sticks, and those fine long radishes which are sweet rather than tangy. We also had a crusty *baguette* and sweet cream butter. The children drank only chilled water, all they had wanted, and I had a split of Côte du Rhône. We finished off with *crème caramel* and little sugar cookies.

"Now I know these fancy French words might make it seem I'm putting on airs, but, really, I'm not doing that. It's a matter of me remembering my husband speaking about them with great relish when we were shopping for those other picnics when he was alive. I need to taste them on my tongue from time to time and taste him in my mouth and in my body memory when I say them."

We were all quiet for a while, even the younger children caught up in the feel of adult contemplations of various past events. It was night now, our place at poolside rendered as isolated from the night by the pool's light and that from the oil lanterns washing over our hands at table's edge and our leavings too, evidence of a recent story we had not told but had lived through. Georgia searched out my hand under the table and pressed it down on her bare knee. Then Opel Shots was weeping, her head slowly bobbing over that huge belly around which little Jason worked to get his thin arms as he hugged her, infected by these keening private sounds that had nothing to do with him and threatened to leave him there alone. We could hear some snuffling from the other children, who had caught the infection too. Amble Once rose to comfort her granddaughter, and Inder Jalla got to her feet too, but then Opel's hand was patting little Jason on the back, the other one in the air, waving them away as her weeping turned to light laughter, and we heard Bertha Beal laughing too.

"Good Lord, sister. We've certainly managed to put a damper on the evening's activities, I'd say, the both of us."

"You got that," Amble said, choking and chuckling. She looked over at Carl. "Come on, grandad. We could use a little help here."

"Well, I *was* thinking," Carl said. "But you know the story."

"Never mind that," Opel said. "Let's hear it."

"Well, okay then. It was down south, where they held the regional hog barbecue contest for the first time in our little town. There must have been posters and announcements, but I hadn't seen them. But my nose told me about it anyway, so it's no matter. I was sitting on the porch after dark and the breeze blew it in, that scent of pork cooking, and I went in and got your grandmother here and we headed up the road, guided by that beautiful smell, meeting other neighbors on the way and people we didn't know. My, we were like in one of those science fiction movies, you know, where people head for some gathering, half-hypnotized by a sound or something, gazing into the darkness and walking slowly like those mummies risen from the dead.

"We all converged at the park near the river, where lights flickered from a good fifty or seventy encampments. There were campers and pickup trucks and open tents, and at the rear end of most of the vehicles were those unhitched big barrel-like cookers, all very fancified, with large letters painted on them in the palmer method, or in the cursive, names, and pictures of dancing pigs and other things too, as well as what they call pin striping, and flames as well. I remember the Dark Brothers, Bubba's Hog, Flame Fresh Andy. Smoke was rising into the night, spewed out from stacks, and under the open tents there were big vats that were getting stirred regularly by men, women and boys, snapper soup, she-crab stew, things like that. And these things were offered in little plastic bowls to all comers. You could move around and get your fill. And you could get talk too. About recipes, winks about secret ingredients. 'You got a whole hog in there?' I remember a young kid asking. 'Hell, we got *two!*' the man answered. 'In line on a spit.' And you could get brochures that told of catering costs for lawn wedding receptions, birthdays, whatever occasion you had in mind. Seems they'd just hitch up the cooker with the fancy paintings, then park the thing at your house overnight. They'd provide the tables, probably like the ones we're sitting at right now. All the other stuff too. You and your guests would just show up and dig in.

"But this commercial business is not the point of this story. It's what happened next day that is the corker. We had nothing to do, so we went to the contest itself. The hogs had been cooking all night by then, and around noon a bell was rung, and we followed some of the judges around. Tables had been set up for them at each little pavilion, bowls of slaw and such to the side of stacks of china plates and forks and knives sticking up from glass containers. Stacks of cloth napkins as well. I guess presentation was felt to be important. There were covered garbage cans set discreetly to the side and young boys standing in attendance beside them. These were for spitting out the chewed pork, the boys there to lift the lids, then close them down after. These judges had a few hours of judging ahead of them, at least sixty hogs to be tested, and they had to watch themselves. As it ended up, the attendants had little work. Most judges just picked at the pork, some served in slabs and hunks, others shredded, and it was comical to see this prissy picking when it came to barbecue. At one point the word got round that one of the judges had to drop out. Rumor was he'd sampled the slaw and salads, never spit out a morsel, and was now under the care of some doctor, flat on his back in the judge's tent.

"Anyway, okay. When the judging was done, around 2.00pm, the judges conferred until around three. Then we all gathered on bleachers that had been set up on two sides of an elevated platform on which a bunch of tall trophies were lined up on a table. Names were then called out over the PA, and there was plenty of whoops and hollers when the winners in various categories skipped up grinning to shake hands, say a few words about things like tradition and hog quality and give thanks to members of the family, without whom they couldn't have possibly done this well or done anything at all for that matter. Then family cameras clicked as the winners were handed their trophies. I suspect the resultant pictures found their way into brand new brochures pretty quickly.

"Well that was it, the show over, and the spectators, must have been a hundred at least, got ready to get going. But then the PA came on again, and I could tell what was said had been said before, at other contests. It was the way he said it, for sure a prepared speech.

"'Okay, folks. Thank you very much for coming. There's only one more thing. Maybe you can help us out with a problem. We got all these hogs left, thousands'a pounds of barbecue that's now gonna go to waste. You could solve the problem for us iffen you would just dig in and eat it. We got drinks too and plenty'a slaw.'

"Now Opal, you know your grandmother is a big eater. I've seen her put away quantities that would shame a truck driver starved after the long haul ..."

"Watch it now, old man," said Amble, smiling.

"But all this was even too much for her, not to mention me, who you know is a picky eater."

Opal's belly shook with laughter.

"We must have gotten through only a dozen or so plates, pulled pork, pork shredded and stirred into various sauces for sandwiches, ribs, tenderloin, you name it. It was the prize-winning stuff we stuck to, a mercy that those pavilions were crowded, else we'd have had no time at all for a little digestion and would never have gotten even that far.

"And it was all so good that I believe that everyone there, who had come from miles around and didn't really know each other too well, if they knew each other at all, were gathered up by this goodness and became a kind of community. People laughed and smiled at each other and there was no pushing at the tables. I believe we all felt we could have gone off somewhere and started one of those communes you hear about, or remember, from the 1960s. It was a great two days and a great event.

"But I'll tell you something. All that she-crab stew, that snapper, all that prize-winning hog, it can't hold a candle to what we've just finished eating here tonight. I can't stop picking. I'm speaking of Emmory's ribs, hoping my own might have held up a little and, good God, the three tastes of that fried chicken, each fixed up by a woman who knew just what she was doing, and the trout, of course, can't forget that, and Inder's delicious tabouli salad, and the tomatoes and the slaw, the corn bread and biscuits and even the lemonade, just enough sugar to keep you sipping. I'm full as a tick. But there seems a little room still in this tick's swollen belly, and I'm guessing the same might be true for all of us. So what do you say to a little of that ice cream? Myself, I could go for the tutifruity. Matt Dean Gregory? Maybe you and Paul can haul it out?"

I had to take her somewhere before I took her to see the house, not only because I now found myself in love with her and was a little nervous about showing her the way I lived, but because there was history in the place, Wendy and I, and I was concerned about that interference in what, for me at least, was a delicate matter. We'd lined up Amble Once to look out for the children, and I'd taken her aside and said we might be quite late.

"Make sure it's late enough," she'd said, smiling and winking at me.

I took Georgia to one of the polluted lakes, which was quite beautiful in the evening, even with the pollution in mind, and we sat in my truck looking out across it at the smoky trees on the far shore. Then I took her to dinner in our little town, where we ate only salad, since we were still working to rid ourselves of the barbecue feast two evenings before.

"Boy, that was some night," I said. "You remember when ..."

"Matt," she said. "Get on off it. You're stalling me."

She seemed to like the house, and we took our time going through it, starting on the ground floor, then skipping the second and looking into the top floor rooms, those that I'd not gotten to yet in my repairs and renovations.

Then we went down a flight and after glancing into other bedrooms, closets and bathrooms, wound up in my room, where all the work was completed. It's a large room with nice bay windows, a walk-in closet and a big bathroom with separate shower and tub, double sink, and a toilet off in a little room by itself.

"This is wonderful," she said, touching my arm. "Big enough for a whole family. I mean to *live* in."

I started to say something in reply, but never got there, for she had turned toward me, and all I wanted to do was get the clothes off her, to reach parts of that dusty, cocoa skin I'd not yet seen. I hoped to get it wet with sweat in the humid night, to see it turn black under the table lamp's dim glow. We were naked on the bed before I knew it, and then for hours on end I knew a lot of things I hadn't known before. Maybe she did too.

We got back around 2.00am. Amble was sleeping in a chair on the narrow walkway between the two rooms. Georgia touched her on the shoulder gently to wake her, and she stretched and yawned and smiled up at both of us.

"Have a nice time?" she asked, and we both laughed like teenagers.

"Uh huh," she said, then got up, smiled again, and headed for her own apartment. I kissed Georgia deeply then and held her tight, then saw her in and headed down the stairway to my truck, thinking all the way of going right back again.

It was two days later that the rabid coons showed up and shortly after their arrival the Animal Police and the social service people. The first one bitten was Manu Jalla, attacked when he was taking trash out to the dumpster.

Then a big one got hold of Ahmed's little leg. He was climbing out of the pool and saw it just standing there, and when he tried to shoo it away, it scampered boldly up and got him. Both had to go in for the dreadful shots, and Georgia and Inder were beside themselves, suffering the pain along with the two victims. Everyone else was shook up too and kept themselves and the children in, though the weather continued to be extremely hot and the pool kept beckoning. Georgia called me from the pay phone in the lobby, and when I got there I saw the Animal Police truck parked at the building's end and heard voices on the far side where the Holiday Inn backed into woods and lowland swamp. I saw a coon, its fiery eyes staring directly at me from the parking lot's edge, and I had to climb across to the passenger side to get out. Then I moved as quickly as seemed reasonable to the stairway leading to the second floor. I was barely through the door when I heard footsteps approaching. It was one of the Animal Policemen in his green uniform, carrying a long stick and a sturdy net, both of which he leaned against the outside wall before asking if he might come in. Inder Jalla was sitting in a chair inside Georgia and Emmory's room. The two were there, as well as Carl Once, his granddaughter and Bertha Beal.

"I'll tell ya what," the policeman said, turning to speak to all of us. "We figure there's a good size bunch out in the back, big ones and little ones too. I doubt we'll be able to catch all of them, but we're gonna try. It's best to stay up here or inside for a while. We'll let ya know when it's safe enough. I wouldn't count on anything though."

They stayed inside for a few days. The Animal Police were there most of the time, and I came and went, kept a careful watch and brought back provisions.

"Still at it," the policeman reported on the fourth day,

and on the fifth the social services people arrived, more than enough I thought. There were five of them, and it was clear to us early on who the boss was, a heavy, middle-aged black woman named Janella Lemonjuice. We got a laugh out of that name, just a little one, since we were in no mood for jollity.

Ms Lemonjuice seemed a decent enough sort, and after she'd sent the others off to examine the children and the living conditions in the apartments, she got my name and what my business was there, jotted the information down on her pad, and went off to see the Jallas. Manu was in bed recovering from the first round of rabies shots, and Inder told us later she'd sat at his bedside questioning him gently, then stayed on for a while for commiseration and a cup of tea. When she came back, she looked in on little Ahmed, even pulled a few pieces of sweet candy from her pocket and gave it to him.

We stood out on the walkway and watched them all conversing in their van for a while. Then they drove off, only to return again in two days. The families were still housebound when they drove up. The Animal Police had been there daily, for most of each day, but seemed to have accomplished little. Their spokesman had come to Georgia's apartment, which had become our meeting place, from time to time. There was little news, though he spoke of desperate measures, like universal spraying and tree cutting, but it seemed that was still in the future.

One of the Lemonjuice helpers got use of a room down the line and put a little sign on the door. Then another told us the boss would like to speak with all the tenants down there in fifteen minutes. The Jallas were informed as well, but only Inder was able to come.

"Can this boy come along too?" Carl Once asked.

"The boss didn't say, but if he has any part in this that should be okay."

"He has," said Georgia.

Then we were all pressed tight together in the hot little room, all but Amble Once and little Ahmed, whose bedside she was sitting by. He'd been a tough little customer, bearing up under the rabies shots with stoic resolve.

"Well, then," Janella Lemonjuice said, looking quite cool in her cotton knit suit and tied-up hair. "I'm afraid you folks aren't going to be able to stay here."

There were groans from the children and a few from the adults as well.

"Now, now," she said, "It won't be all that bad. We've found rooms in town, only a single for each family I'm afraid. There's no air conditioning, but the summer will soon be gone, and we'll have cooler weather. The place is clean and tidy. Bathroom down the hall I have to say. But there's shopping around there, and the neighborhood isn't too bad."

"Is there a pool?" Paul asked, knowing the answer.

"No. No pool."

"What about the schools?" I said. "That time's coming."

"You're right there," she said. "There aren't any close by. But a bus is available, just a half mile's walk away." She paused for a few moments, looking around the room at dour faces. "Any more questions?"

There were none, though of course there were plenty. But the die seemed cast. Nice as this woman was, it was clear there was no questioning of the decision, and when the five left again, everyone went hang-dog back to their places. Then I took Georgia down to my truck, holding her by the arm and watching out for rabid coons, and we drove into town for an ice cream sundae and had a good long talk, and the next morning I called Janella Lemonjuice at her office and made an appointment.

She was dubious about my business, but I had prepared myself and had answers ready for her many objections and questions. It took me an hour to convince her to at least come out and have a look at the place, and when she agreed to that and I asked when it would be convenient, she said "right now," got up and grabbed her purse and a yellow pad and headed for the door. Trying to catch me unprepared, I thought, moving along quickly behind her.

When we got to the house, she didn't tarry, but set out immediately to walk around it. In the back she saw the two-thousand-gallon water tanks on the I-beam rack I'd constructed. The house backed up into a steep hill, and I'd wanted them high enough so that gravity would bring the water down, just a little electricity necessary for pumps when they got close to empty.

"Explain that," she said, and I did, telling her about the testing and the groundwater pollution. She jotted down the information, nodding, then said she'd have to look into that. Then she went into the house and looked into every one of the rooms, checking for peeling paint, vermin I guess, and God knows what else. She was very thorough, and we were there for a good two hours, and she spoke just a little on the way back. "I'd have to send others out to have a look. It's a nice house, but I'd need cover." I brightened at those last words. Maybe I have her, I thought. Back in her office we worked at the deal, all of it contingent on final approval.

"But I can tell you approval doesn't go much higher than right here," she said, eyeballing me across her desk.

"What do you want?" I asked.

"For starters and enders both, I want them off welfare in four months."

"How about six?" I said.

"Okay," she said, with no hesitation. "Now what is it that you want?"

"I want the medical for Opal Shots, the prenatal, the delivery, and the aftercare. And I want coverage for the others too."

"That's all Medicare and Medicaid. I can get the Shots a deal through the teaching hospital in the city. You'll have to travel. Is that it?"

"That's it," I said.

"Give me a few days," she said. She got up from her chair, came around the desk, shook my hand, then ushered me to the door, and when we got there she raised a finger and shook it at me.

"You damn well better know what you're doing, young man, and what you're getting yourself into." Then she smiled, shook her head, and laughed lightly as I walked away.

That evening I went to the Holiday Inn and told Georgia that I believed the deal was done. She grabbed me and hugged me, then went off to speak with the others, coming back in a half hour, shaking her head in the affirmative. Then we got them all together, as Janella Lemonjuice had in that empty room.

"Now, there's gonna have to be some rules," I began by saying, but couldn't keep the pleasure out of my voice.

"Georgia says I'll have my own room?" Emmory said.

"That's right," I said.

"Is there a pool?" asked little Laticia.

"Afraid not," I said. "But there's a great big hose and I have a few sprinklers for running through."

"That'll do," she said, and we all laughed.

"When the hell we gonna get on with this?" asked Carl Once.

"In two days," I said. "As soon as I get the charcoal cooker up and running again, so you can make us your special ribs."

"I got that," he said.

"And he can play the jew's-harp too," said Emmory Brown.

They moved in on a Saturday late in July, one on which a breeze had come down from the north to cool the air, the first comfortable day we'd had in months. The Jallas had two cars, and with those and my truck bed full of children among pots and pans we managed to get everything there in two trips. There wasn't really much. They'd been traveling light.

Both the children and the adults marveled at the big old house and none wasted any time going in and exploring it, checking out the room assignments I'd hung on a chart on the pantry door. Nobody complained about anything, though that might surely come later, I thought, and by evening everyone was settled in and the women were working on a pot of chili and salad makings in the kitchen. I had picnic tables out, and we ate on the broad veranda, watching the sun go down over the foothills in the distance.

"I *know* you got somethin' doin' with my daughter," Emmory Brown spoke confidentially at my elbow. "Just wanna say, whatever's goin' on, it's okay with me."

Let's see. Surprising to all, it was Carl Once who picked up the first job, half-time weekdays as a greeter at the big Walmart store, and because his wife Amble was all too willing to take on the care of the children daytimes, Bertha Beal was able to go out for interviews. She was hired as a receptionist at a new medical group practice in town. Beauty went in with her early on, roaming around town while the interviews were underway, and she landed herself a little part-time work at the ice cream shop, Saturday and Sunday afternoons once school started. She was convinced she was hired because of her poise and good looks.

Once we were settled in, I took Paul along on various small jobs, teaching him a little about electricity, and after they were all set up in school, Georgia herself got the itch and found a position at the local library. She knew little about that science, but she was a quick study and in only a few weeks was sitting in for the librarian herself on days off.

Our comings and goings brought transportation problems. The place was a long walk from the bus stop, which proved no difficulty for the children with their strong young legs, though it did for me each morning before work when I walked them there. But there was no town bus coming to the stop, so I had to buy an old junker for the working folks, so they could get into town and back home again. Bertha was the only one with a current driver's license, so she took control of that. The money didn't exactly roll in, but soon there was enough of it, and in two months it was my great pleasure to call Janella Lemonjuice, tell her about the birth of Opel's little Barbara, and that she could now stop the welfare payments.

"You've got to be kidding!" she said. "Oh my. Oh boy oh boy!"

Then she reported good news from her end. She'd had the water tested again and it had been found to be clean. It seemed some underground movements had diverted the leaching. It was now headed for the city. "Some geological business," she said. "I don't understand it, but I know it's there to be understood."

Soon Opal Shots was back from the hospital with her new baby, and we were all together again on the weekend, but for Beauty, who loved her little white ice cream uniform and was quite pleased to be away from all the foolishness. "That girl," Georgia would say.

I had a couple of old shotguns and I showed Paul how to shoot tin cans, and now that the pump was chugging again I hooked up the hose and sprinklers for running through, then got a big rubber pool through Carl's Walmart discount, and the kids refreshed themselves all the way into October out in the front yard. I took them around a good part of the property. We built little sitting places and cut paths with the mower. And we spent a little time each day working at the house, painting and building wooden platform beds for the new mattresses and bookcases for the walls. And when it got late in the evening and the children and old folks were sleeping, I took Georgia into my bed, our bed now, and we enjoyed ourselves, talking and doing those other things.

The years went by, and after six of them Paul was nineteen and joined the Navy and Beauty was off to the local junior college, as pleased as punch. She came home every night, visited for a decent period, then skulked up to her top floor room with the KEEP OUT sign on the door and played strange music softly enough to avoid trouble. And the little kids, of course, were no longer little, not even Jason and Barbara, who were seven and six. One might have thought death would have visited, and of course it did, but not in those six years or for a long time after, though it did raise its threatening head on a winter afternoon in the form of Dennis Davis, Georgia's estranged husband.

He came up the road leading to the house, the rear end

of the new Camry fishtailing in the fresh fallen snow as he gunned it aggressively. Carl, Emmory and I were sitting on the veranda, warm in our Walmart coats and enjoying the crisp December air. It was getting close to Christmas, and we'd seen to lights and the hanging of pine boughs along the eaves and a nice big wreath on the door. We could smell smoke coming from the chimney. Everyone was home that day, the kids in the house wrapping their presents and the women baking cookies, brown betty, and whatever else they had in mind. The three of us were sipping at warm eggnog. It was a perfect holiday Saturday, until he made his presence known.

He got out of the car and stood beside it, hands on hips and looking up at us. He was a heavy man, strong looking in his fine wool suit, and his mouth was twisted into a smile of the kind that promised a snarl. I heard movement in the house behind us when he slammed the car door.

"Well, well," he said. "Three peas in a pod. Good to see ya, Emmory. Didn't think I'd find ya, huh? And you, you honkey motherfucker, I've come for my wife and children, which you have stolen. Better get 'em out here. I might just beat your white ass otherwise."

"I'm comin' out now," I heard Georgia in the doorway, and when I turned my head to look, all four women were there, Amble and Bertha holding the old shotguns.

"Shit," Dennis Davis spat. "What you gonna do with that, ugly old woman?"

"Now just a goddamn minute." Carl was struggling to his feet when Amble lifted her weapon and shot the car. The explosion was deafening, and snow blew in the air. She got the headlight and the right front fender, blasting it into twisted metal ribbons.

"You done shot my car!" Davis yelled out.

"And the next one is up your fat ass," Amble said in a cold, level voice.

"And if that don't do it, it's right between the eyes," said Bertha.

"Georgia!" Davis said. "Come on now, this ain't right!"

"It's right enough for you," she said. "Now get on out'a here and don't come back."

He fussed around for a while, arguing, looking at his damaged new car, throwing evil looks at me from time to time. I thought it was my place to do or say something, but the women had things well in hand and I kept my peace. Finally, Davis gave up, mustered what dignity remained to him, and drove slowly away, the fender flapping in the winter air. When he was gone, and the women had gone back into the house, I fancied to clean their weapons, Emmory turned to me.

"Never did like the peckerhead anyway."

"I got it that Amble didn't care much for him either," Carl said.

"You got *that* right," I said.

We worried about his returning for the next couple of weeks and kept the shotguns loaded and up on high shelves where the children couldn't get to them, but he never did come back, nor did he lay any claim to his wife and children. After a while, when there was a little extra money, Georgia went to the social service and found a recommended lawyer, and before long the divorce was final and she had legal custody of the children. I asked her to be my wife then, but she said "No, Matthew. I can't do that, and besides, aren't we already married?"

A few years later, on a Friday near the end of April, Beauty brought a young man home to meet us. He was a senior at the city college to which she had transferred after doing quite well at the JC in town. She was a senior too, and both of them talked with us all about their futures over the weekend. He was a science major and had applied to pharmacy school and thought he would get in, a good-looking boy with short hair, nice clean khakis and a couple of cotton sweaters. He changed into a different one each night for dinner. Beauty was uncertain about what she might do. Her grades were good and she had been accepted to various graduate schools for the study of literature, the better ones a long distance away, and though she'd always acted as if she really wanted out of the place, away from all these boring people, in that weekend she listened to what we had to say, taking the advice and questions in with a due diligence. She was grown up now and could see that things had gotten serious.

"I just don't know," she'd said at Saturday lunch. "Can't seem to make up my mind."

"Why not try a job for a while?" said Amble Once. "There's no real rush, is there? You could figure it out over time. Make a better decision that way."

"And if it's here, we could still see each other," said John Balles. That was her boyfriend's name. He'd come from a broken family with no money and had worked his own way up.

"That's right," Ahmed said. He was eighteen now and kept in touch with his brother Paul, who was off making a career of it in the Navy.

"And you still have a good room here," said Laticia, who at sixteen had grown up to look very much like her older sister.

No decision was reached that weekend, but both Georgia and I had our hopes. We'd all had a good time meeting and visiting with this John Balles, and I could see he'd had a good time too and was loath to leave come Sunday evening. We'd played a few board games, had taken walks through the acreage and had eaten well, all together at the picnic tables back out on the veranda now that the weather was getting warm.

"You know," he said at one point, "This seems to be the life. This family life."

"You may have one yet," said Emmory Brown. "Who knows?"

"You got that right," said Carl Once.

We watched and waved at him from the veranda as he drove slowly away.

In the Meadow

A RUNDOWN RUSTIC cottage on a low hill. Evidence of repair in the sagging roof and siding. It's quiet inside. Nobody's there. But if one were and had come to stand on the sloping porch, that person would see a modest weedy yard, a well-tended vegetable garden off to the side, and beyond the garden the edge of a meadow that moved away in the vision, rolling down a few hundred yards, to end at steep cliffs and the often turbulent sea beyond.

The meadow forms a rough circle, its curved edges dressed in gnarled scrub oak, a few leaves fallen in late summer as fall approaches, and this meadow they surround is a shallow bowl. The sea is calm. A path starts at the yard's edge, then wends its way for a few moments, finally disappearing into grass, weeds and clover.

The meadow is mowed on occasion, when the grasses among the clover grow long and unsightly, for this meadow, sloping down from the weathered and dilapidated cottage that had once been a farmer's home, is kept up only for quiet talk and meditation. It had not been mowed in a while.

A sunny day. High, billowy clouds. A light breeze holds a few birds flying lazily and low. They are mourning doves. And in the middle of the meadow, lawn chairs in which two women are sitting, side by side, facing the sea, iced tea in tall glasses in their hands, a pitcher on a wrought iron table. They are speaking of loss. Her name is Liz. She is seventy-six years old.

"It was my shining light."

Her hair has receded just a little, exposing her lovely brow. A prominent nose. Heavy lids, below which her large blue eyes are dreamy and slightly out of focus.

"I cannot stop thinking about it. About moving through the aisles, checking the stock, chatting with customers." She lifts her glass to her lips, veins visible on the back of her hand.

As a young woman she worked on this farm, her father's only companion once her mother had died. He was a silent taskmaster, and when he too died she inherited this cottage that was her home, then quit it and headed off to a distant inland town to find work and adventure. She was twenty-seven, tall and lean, as she is still. Emma, her companion, who sits beside her in the other chair, is not that. She is shapely at seventy-seven, a little overweight and shorter, her dark hair streaked with gray, tied up in a bun. She has the face of an old Madonna without a child, cheeks bruised by the sun, small pixie ears. And her neck is a squat tower, without blemish. When she turns her head to examine the mood, sun blinks in her focused brown eyes.

When Liz arrived in the town, flush with the few dollars her father had left her, she set up home in a small apartment, then went out to explore. The town was quite large, but in no more than a week she had become familiar with it, the businesses and municipal buildings, the coffee shops, and the few bars she did not enter, though she looked in at the half-dark windows.

And the town was very clean. All the windows in the shops along Main Street had been thoroughly washed, and one might look through them without noticing that they were there. The sidewalks had been brushed and hosed, and beyond the pine trees that marched along the verge in proper order, the street was newly paved, a bright white line down the center.

She was comfortable in this place. For though the people were friendly, they left her alone, and Liz required aloneness. Yes, her father had been there, in that cottage, but she'd had only a vague awareness of his presence. He had been no more than a whispering shade.

"I remember the trees and the houses and the clear windows. They're vivid in my mind. They saved me from loneliness." A pesky dandelion licks at her exposed calf. She breaks the flower off and rubs it on her prominent chin.

Down at the end of Main Street, beside a bicycle shop, was the warehouse-like structure that was Mahler's, a huge used furniture and clothing shop, with a counter at which various sundries were sold. Clothing hung from hooks in layers on the walls, waving their ghostly presences when the door opened and a breeze danced in. And at the rear of the store, positioned so that customers would have to pass by beckoning chairs and couches, was a candy counter, and beside it a soda fountain where you could get sundaes and malteds and root beer floats. In the front windows were signs announcing sales and one taped-up near the door read "Help Wanted," and so Liz entered and filled out an application and was called the next day and offered the job. Salesgirl was the designation. She worked there for thirty-five years.

In profile, Liz has a somewhat aristocratic look. Chin slightly raised, lips tight together. Only her haunted eyes betray her origin – a farmer's daughter with little experience in life.

"A union?" Emma asks, looking across at her.

"Good Lord, no! We had no idea about such things. And age discrimination? Forget it."

She started out in clothing. Then, in a while, was moved to furniture, and after a few years was put in charge of that department, three girls under her.

"I loved the store, the staff, even the supervisor, Molly, rest her soul, who was gentle and kind even in her last days. I can't stop thinking about the place and my job; they run around in my brain. I was a good worker, always prompt, and a good seller as well. We had to keep track, and I was always at or near the top."

In her twentieth year, Mahler himself called her into his office. Molly had died, and he determined that Liz might take her place. He was getting old, he said, and his offer included complete control of the daily running of the store. She'd have the sales staff, a handyman who doubled as a security guard, and an accountant to take care of the finances. It was a big responsibility. She accepted without hesitation, held a meeting, Mahler at her elbow, and explained that things would remain the same, the same vacation times and assured promotions for those who did a good job. Everyone trusted in her abilities and her kindness, and she moved into her new position with the enthusiastic support of the workers under her command. Soon enough, Mahler could be seen only occasionally, and since, under her efficient tutelage, the store seemed to be running on its own, Liz took command of the soda fountain, which provided sightlines that allowed her to keep tabs on the candy counter, the furniture and the clothing, as well as the sundries. At first she thought her new position might be temporary, but it continued for many years.

"The beautiful children would leave their parents and rush up to the counter, and I would prepare ice cream cones and sundaes, and they would laugh and grin at me as if I were a mother. How delectable they were! And I, unmarried and childless, would think of them as family, would feel them as such. I remember one little girl, Lisa was her name. She always wanted pistachio, a strange flavor for a child, and we would smile at each other knowingly, as if we were both adults and knew things the other children did not know. Good God; she would be thirty now, even older. She is gone from me, as is my job, and there seemed, for a long time, to be no tangible future."

The sun is behind them now, and they can view the sea without glare. Gentle waves, the soft sound of them breaking upon the rocks below. A fishing boat in the far distance. Clover, dandelions and weeds rise up at their feet.

"We better mow it soon," Emma says.

"What a world," says Liz.

Then Mahler died, leaving the store to his two sons, both of whom saw new possibilities. Quickly the store began to change, no more soda fountain or used furniture, no more clothing. The new was brought in. Designer sofas, coffee tables, and chairs. And the sales staff was slowly weeded out, slim young men taking their places. Still Liz lingered, almost as a figurehead. She had nothing to do. She roamed around, bewildered, and one day, in her thirty-fifty year, the sons called her in. She was given a severance package, a box of candy as a gift, and was let go.

"Well," she said. "It's over. But it's not over in my mind."

Liz and Emma had been friends since childhood. Emma was the daughter of a fisherman and his wife, and when she bade farewell to her friend, as Liz headed off to town, she was twenty-eight and had been married to her fisherman husband for ten years.

Bereft of her dear friend, she set out to repair her marriage. It had been awkward from the start. Her husband was difficult, dramatic in his arrogance and demands. You're a housewife, he told her. Act like it. But she didn't feel that way. She had interests. She painted small landscapes, and she read books and listened to classical music. He wanted his dinner, hot, when he came home from the sea. He wanted her to listen to his boring tales. He left for the pub after dinner. He helped with nothing around the house. He was ten years older than she. He disliked her few friends and wouldn't allow them in the house when he was there. She tried gardening. He didn't like her choice of vegetables, and he never looked at the flowers she brought into the house to warm it up. He didn't want children. She grew dull in his presence, and when, in her attempt to repair things, she offered him a gift of dinner at a restaurant for his birthday, a certificate inside a carefully chosen card, he cast it aside. He didn't want restaurant food. He wanted her to cook the fish he had caught in his labors.

"Once he said to me, 'Let me give you some advice,' his words insistent and loud. I don't remember the advice, but I remember the tone of those first words."

A flock of gray doves sails low out of the sun on their creaking wings, then come into clear sight and settle down in the meadow a few feet away. They disappear in the tall weeds, but their soft moans are heard clearly by these two women, the one tall and dignified, the years having cast their map in lines and geometric figures in her beautiful face, the other slouching slightly, her lips slack in memory as she tells her story.

Shortly after her husband died, Emma moved in with Liz. They shared the upkeep of the cottage and the cooking and cleaning. They laughed and joked with one another. They listened to music, and they played cards. And they read books, often well into the dark night. They felt alive, as if they were the children they once were. And yet they knew the ages they were in and were comfortable there.

"His touch was often foreign. It was as if touch were a language, and he spoke in a foreign tongue, bewildering to me who was so young. He didn't want sex. He wanted, in his internal weakness, to conquer me, who was already conquered under his physical rage.

"And yet, there is sadness still, I guess, even though it has been ten years. But no, there's more to it. From the very beginning we were moving apart, so that his ending ended everything, what love there might have been, life's habits and their occasional congruence or lack of it, the daily grind."

"Life's a bugger," Liz says. "Yet here we are together, in our meadow with our doves and our grasses and the sea, and I think what we've lost may not be loss at all, but gain."

Night. The empty chairs are still there, but the pitcher is gone. Insects roam, invisible in the darkened grasses. Warm lights in the cottage windows. Beautiful music.

Hooter Girl Twins

"I'M A VOLUNTEER sign language teacher for the deaf Indian children."

"I'm deciding between geriatrics and Minnesota youth hockey."

"I have, like, two minors, in pre-law."

"My goal is eventually to separate conjoined twins."

"We'd like to have sex, for money."

"Those," Murray said. "The ones with the big tits."

"They all have big tits."

"Bring 'em round to the office, after the interviews."

"Gosh!"

"We're so pleased"

"you picked us"

"over all the others."

"Yeah, yeah," Murray said. "Do you always talk like that?"

"Well, not always"

"but on occasion."

"Okay. But before we get started," Murray leered, "what's the deal with this sex business? This is a family place, you know, sometimes."

"Sex?"

"What do you mean"

"sex?"

"What you said out there. Is that a goal or something?"

"Oh my God!"

"We didn't say sex."

"We said six!"

"Six dollars an hour"

"for each of us."

"We're minimum wage here. That's five-fifteen."

"An extra day too"

"at time and a half. Plus tips!"

He studied their breasts carefully. "Okay. I can do that. But the first week's probation."

In the first few weeks there were absolutely no families at all, but the tips were good. In the afternoon it was businessmen and those other men, construction workers and various service employees. Then in the evening and up until closing it was mostly college kids, a few old men, and the odd ones who came there for lack of a better place to go and had some money.

It was a sleepy suburb, south of Erie, and fairly conservative.

"*That's* a nice set of mammingas," said a chubby student from the JC. He was leering at Tanya, or was it Tina?

"Which one?" another chimed in.

"Both!" said his interlocutor. "All four!"

Hooting at Hooters, and hooters too.

Then on the fourth of July, a family did come in. A father and mother and two young boys, close to the same age, about twelve or maybe thirteen. Tanya had the table, and the first thing she noticed were the bruises on both boys, places on their upper arms, and on one of them a dark puffiness near the open collar of his going-out-to-lunch-on-the-fourth shirt.

The father unfurled his menu, smiling pleasantly. How

charming, his eyes seemed to say as he surveyed Tanya's cleavage. The required uniform, a tight black T with Hooters lettered on the rise, presented her breasts as on a platter, and the silicone enhanced the effect dramatically. He nodded to the boys, winking. Their eyes were as big as saucers. Something's wrong with this, Tanya thought. The mother seemed to shrink back into her chair. Wasn't there a bruise below her eye, under the makeup?

"We'll have this and that," the father said, "and for the lady a Caesar salad, junior size, she's on a diet."

He was thick through the arms and chest, what they call ruddy skin, balding, and his lips were pouty and feminine. The mother already seemed thin enough to Tanya. They returned again, a few weeks later, and it was Tina who had the table.

"What's it come to?"

"A little over nine."

They were doing six days, sometimes double shifts, just starting their seventh week. They had a nice little place, a second-floor apartment with a terrace overlooking an inlet. No car. Walking distance from Hooters.

"That averages fifteen hundred a week, at the low end."

"That's two-fifty to three a shift"

"between us. And in the year"

"it can be seventy-five to around eighty-five thousand. That"

"plus the thirty we've set aside"

"is plenty."

They were living on their week's salary quite well, dipping into the tip money only from time to time. The nice apartment, a rental car on occasion, whatever clothes they needed. Not much there: they were in their Hooter gear much of the time.

It was one in the morning, and they reclined beside each other on their twin beds.

"My tits are hurting."

"Mine too."

"It's just too much bobbing, rushing"

"around between tables"

"in those Ts. And it's hard as a rock in here."

"Mine too. It's the silicone"

"is what it is. That bitch."

"What did you think of that family"

"with the two boys? They were"

"weird, right?"

"And to bring them into a place like that, at their age?"

"Well, it just isn't right."

"Did you see the bruises?"

"On her too. Something below the eye."

"The eye? The one I saw was above it, her forehead."

"They don't move around. Must be"

"a new one."

"God, it reminds me of dear old mom"

"though she never hit us."

"Might just as well have."

"These tits."

They came again at the end of August, all spruced up for a night on the town, the first time it wasn't lunch, but a late Saturday night dinner. The place was jumping, and Murray had Tina working the bar, filling up pitchers of beer. It was the night of a big game, and all the TV sets were on. The World Series would be coming up soon. The World Serious

Murray called it. Tanya had the table and could hardly hear the father's order over the din of college boy chatter. She was sweating, her T-shirt wet and sucked up tight around her rack, breastage, knockers, head lights, boobs, torpedoes, whatever else they called them. And they hurt!

"I said, the fried clams!" the father's repeated sternly, looking from one breast to the other, as if he were angry with both of them. Somebody hit a home run or something, excited yelling, but the two boys were watching their father, nervously, Tanya thought. He had them dressed in suits and ties. Murray had a sneaky way of turning the temperature up on busy evenings, to get the T-shirts wet, and their collars were already stained, a film of moisture on their brows. The mother was staring straight ahead, at nothing. Tanya thought the boys were holding hands under the table. There was swelling in the lower lip of one of them.

"That's right, a salad! Burgers for the boys!" Sharp little gestures in his meaty hands, the boys flinching, just a little. The mother didn't move.

Jesus, Tanya thought, this is definitely and absolutely not right. He may have caught something in her eyes. She thought he winked at her but wasn't sure of that. He'd never once asked them what they wanted to eat. The food seemed like medicine or prison chow, and he the doctor or guard. Not right. She turned on her heel and went to fill the order.

Murray had them come to his office. "What is this?" he said, "a Saturday night?"

"But it's November," Tanya said. "They're back in school."

Murray lounged in his chair, looking at their breasts, one by one, as if counting them. "So what is that?" he said.

"They don't study. They fuck around. They come *here*."

"It's just this once," Tina said.

"Ah, yes. Others of your kind, huh? A convention no less."

"Twins, and we want"

"very much to go. We work hard"

"and you know that."

"Okay, okay. Why not. I guess you deserve it, a night off."
Murray raised a finger. "But *just* this once."

"Should we dress alike?"

"Why not? Others will"

"and mother would like that"

"the bitch."

"You're speaking of the dead."

"I know, I know. Sometimes"

"I can't get beyond it either. Feeling"

"like a child?"

"What they call battered these days. I remember *that*
very day"

"when she had us in those frilly dresses"

"for the pageant final? She was looking at our breasts."

"'We'll have to do something about *those*,' she said."

"We were twelve years old."

"No, eleven."

The convention was held at the Marriot. Five hundred sets
of twins, a thousand individuals from all over the country.
It was a little too celebratory, though there were a few lectures and seminars dealing with the downside. For the
most part it was music and dancing and the cocktail parties of various clubs within the larger one – Tall Twins

(over 6 foot two), Room 2108, 7 to 10; Dwarf Twins, Room 12, off the lobby, 9 to 11; The Gourmet Club (a demonstration with samples), Small Dining Room, 2 o'clock; Twins in Rubber, Room 1400, 10 into the night; this and more on the message board. There were inspirational talks, a few of which leaned suspiciously toward the commercial: T-shirts and mugs for sale, smarmy sayings printed in bold colors on them. The plenary presentation, given by the founder, a woman in her early nineties who had "lost" her sister three years before but still wept at the mention of her name, set the tone – something expressive, though a little vague, about the wonders of twinness on the long road of life.

They had Sunday off too, their regular day, and they splurged and took a room rather than commuting from the apartment. They walked out of a few lectures, crashed the Twins on Motorcycles party, though they didn't have the right clothes and left right away, then stayed up late into the night, dancing with a couple of good-looking brothers from Milwaukee. They wore identical black sheaths for that occasion, their breasts strapped down tight to keep them out of the way. That felt good, the support, and for a while there was no aching. They went to bed late, but rose early on Sunday morning, and when they went down for the communal breakfast, wearing cute little flowered dresses, they saw the boys.

They were sitting at a table off to the side, alone, and Tina went over to join them and save a seat while Tanya went to the buffet table to gather food. French toast and scrambled eggs, sausage links and a few strips of bacon, toast, home fries, orange juice and coffee, grapefruit halves, and a small bowl of granola, awash in milk, with strawberries stacked on the top for each of them. Ever since they had left home, their mother and her dietary vigilance, they'd gone for a big breakfast. Tanya needed two trays, and she carried them in the way she'd quickly learned to lug burgers for the college kids at Hooters.

"We didn't know"

"you were twins."

"Fraternal?" Tina said.

The boys were reticent and seemed nervous, much in the way they had been at Hooters, even though there was no father around this time. It was hard even to get their names; Bart and Brad, Tanya finally pulled out of them. They lived close to the inlet too, and Tina tried to use that coincidence to get them talking. They were dressed in identical outfits that were like costumes, brown leather lederhosen held up by broad green suspenders and crisp white shirts. They ate with great care, just corn flakes in skim milk, in order not to soil themselves. Their hair was slicked back with oil, clipped close above ears, parted carefully on the same side, as if with a razor. They weren't close to being the same, not in this gathering, anyone could tell; though they did look like their mother, the same pinched expression, guarded, moist eyes.

"So it *is* fraternal," Tanya said.

"No," Brad said, struggling to get out the negative, as if it might show aggression of some kind, which was not allowed. He lowered his eyes. "Actually, we're identical."

"Our father always wanted twins," Bart said.

"Does that explain it?"

"I mean the difference"

"is pretty obvious. How old are you?"

"I'm eleven," Brad said.

"Twelve," said Bart.

It took a while, but they finally loosened up enough to talk, stopped glancing at the door, continually worried about his untimely appearance, though he'd instructed them to be out front at three sharp, and when directions were given there was never an alteration.

"He said we had to get the idea right, that we were twins now."

"That's why we're here," Brad said.

"We're not supposed to talk to anyone." Bart lowered his eyes, sheepishly.

Then a phone sounded a muffled lyric and the boys jumped in their seats. *Body and Soul*, Tina thought. Bart was fishing in his lederhosen pocket, and when he got the cell free, Tanya saw the chain attached to its base, a short length ending in a small lock at his belt loop. He had to dip his head down a little in order to speak.

"Yes, father," then a pause, then "No, no one," then "Yes, father, three o'clock," then "Yes, father, we understand."

"Do we have to go now?" Brad said, as Bart pressed the disconnect.

"Soon," his brother answered, then, in a way that Tanya read as effort and a good bit of bravery, "but not just yet." He smiled and his face lit up.

We have them now, Tanya thought, the poor little boys.

They lived in a big house back in the woods overlooking the inlet, a long drive in on a dirt road. Each had their own room, even their mother, and their father's office and workroom took up the whole basement, which had been renovated for that purpose. They didn't go out alone, were home schooled, and their mother only went out alone for shopping, and that was carefully timed. She had a cell-phone too, connected up like Bart's so she wouldn't misplace it. This was the first time the boys had been free of their father, out of sight for a long period, but not out of mind. The phone rang again.

"Yes, father," then a pause, then, "breakfast. Yes, corn flakes. Yes, they have skim milk. Yes," then a longer pause, then "what you told us. Yes, we'll be on time."

"What exactly does your father do?"

"for a living, I mean."

"Does he work out of the house?"

"In his basement," Brad said. "Yes."

"He's a doctor," Bart said. "Well, he *was* a doctor."

"How can that be?" Tina said.

"We had to leave Wisconsin," Brad said.

"Two years ago," said Bart. "That's when we came here and he stopped going out to work."

"You're from Wisconsin!" Tanya said.

"So are we!" said Tina.

The boys smiled, a tentative lifting of their lips.

"Isn't that something."

"We're from the same place!"

"Eau Claire," Bart said. "He had a practice there, plastic surgery."

"We're only a little east of that!" said Tina.

"Just down the road, in Wausau."

"But what does he do now?" Tina said. "I mean, at home?"

"He cuts off people's arms," Brad said, his eyes lowering to his white shirt again.

"And legs," Bart said. "A couple of hands too, from time to time."

"And then there's the labia repairs and the anal bleaching."

The twins looked at each other.

"Jesus!"

"And what about you two?" said Tina.

"You mean the bruises?"

"And this fat lip." Brad touched it with his fingertips.

"Our mother," Bart said. "He usually starts with her, because she's not perfect, you know?"

"Then he's onto us after a while," said Brad.

Body and Soul tinkled again on the cellphone.

That night Tina wept for the loss of her mother and for her father too, dead by his own hand now, and for the image of the house itself, vacant even of the scents of human presence and empty of all but its furnishings, squatting on the farm outside of Wausau. Tanya heard the sobbing, rose up in the dark and crawled into the bed beside her, to hold and console her.

"She was such a crazy bitch," Tina moaned. "But we should have been there"

"at the coffin at least, when they lowered her."

"Jesus, what a complete waste."

"But she drove us away, and that's been good for us."

"But Daddy, how could he *do* it?"

"For the loss of her," whispered Tanya.

A few cuts here and there, their noses and lips, and a little something around the eyes. Well, we'll have to do something about *that*, after the onset of menstruation, smiling at their breasts. She'd taken them in for anal bleaching, side by side on tables presenting themselves that way, at sixteen, though God knows no one else was to get a look at that. Just a little start-up sex in high school, boys staring at the mounds of silicone, a few venturing even to touch them through fabric, just French kissing and a little benign rubbing. They remained inviolate still at twenty-one.

When they were eleven, she'd sent them to school dressed as pickaninnies for Halloween, their faces blackened with burnt cork, blond hair in twenty thin braids each, little black plastic butterflies at the tips. It had taken a day to prepare them, hair growing tight at the roots, impossible to sleep the night before. They kept telling her it's the wrong *day*! but she wouldn't hear them. They were the only ones in costume and appeared as fools.

The pageants had begun by then, and they had been bad at the prelims, their posture, weak smiles, awkward in dancing down the runway, something. She'd grinned into their blackened faces. Off you go, she'd said. And at seventeen, they did go, leaving it all behind, at least in body. They were as tough as nails by then, competitors with a wall of trophies. But inside they were soft cheese close to turning rancid, though their breasts were as hard as their artificial faces, beautiful and fake. They had no idea at all of how to feel, except vaguely desperate, and that was no fake.

What news there was came in mail, sent to general delivery at various places. They worked in restaurants and factories, on the move, wrote cards to their father. Then their father wrote to announce their mother's death, then one more postcard, then nothing.

"How much now do you figure?" Tina snuggled up, her face still wet from weeping.

"About thirty-five thousand, almost halfway," Tanya whispered into her neck.

"Tell me about it again, would you? Come on," Tina sniffled. And Tanya told her.

By the end of March they had saved seventy thousand dollars. Some Hooter girls had left, and others had taken their places as the Christmas season came, and with it colder weather. Then came the new year, and at the end of January the JC semester began, with the new influx of transfer students, both in tight black Hooter Ts and as customers with hooters on their minds. The family didn't appear again, though the boys never left their minds, their faces and bruises, thin legs below the lederhosen when they'd left the breakfast table near noon, already worried, it seemed, about cleaning up and changing in time to be in place out front at three o'clock.

"Good Lord," Tina had said as the two watched them walk away.

"This is unacceptable," said Tanya.

It continued to rankle, but they were busy and quite successful at Hooters, and they had nothing but the names of the boys, Bart and Brad, and only a rough idea about their location. There was nothing to be done, though Tanya finally came up with something quite obvious that neither had thought of. "There's at least that," she'd said. "We'll have to make a deal with Murray." He had called them in, for a "conference," all smiles, at the beginning of their next shift.

"I want from now on you should work the same sector."

He sat behind his desk, smiling and fiddling with his pencil, clearly pleased with himself and with them too.

"You're doing just a wonderful job, and I think we can bring in even more kids and such if we fool with them a little."

The idea was to work the same tables, one bringing the menus, the other the food, one maybe the drinks, the other the check. They could both be in sight some of the time, but never right next to each other.

"You mean they can't"

"tell us apart?"

"This is *exactly* what I mean." He couldn't tell them apart, most of the time, himself. "They will like the confusion, tell their friends, more will come in. And that's the *gonsa gashicta* in a nutshell. Murray laughed and winked, then was startled at the response.

"*Chochem!*" Tina said.

"*A shaynem dank dir im pupik!*" said Tanya.

They had picked up a little Yiddish at an industrial laundry outside of Omaha, where they'd worked loading massive dryers, wearing head scarves, for a year. Then they proposed the deal. Tanya needed a few evenings at the library, just a couple, and Tina would cover for her.

He wasn't entirely happy with that, but he bit his tongue. He thought he might have a goldmine here, and he wasn't about to lose it.

"Okay, okay, blondies. It's a deal. Now get outa here." He laughed and fiddled with his pencil.

"Thanks, Murray," said Tanya, as they headed for the door.

"*Biz hundert asoi ve tsvantsik,*" said Tina.

It was a Saturday night and very busy, no important sports event on the TV, but a good many college boys guzzling pitchers of beer, joking and laughing and checking out the hooters. Murray had turned up the heat again, and in only a few minutes all the girls were sweating, their shirts wet and clinging in the desired fashion.

Then Tina saw the family at a corner table. It was hers and she grabbed the menus and headed over there, noticing the contraption immediately, some sort of sling, made of satin or another similar fabric. It held Brad's left arm and was tied up at his neck so that nothing but folds of black cloth were visible.

The father reached out for all the menus, then, without opening them, spoke loudly above the din. He was looking directly between Tina's damp breasts, his narrow face like a metal wedge that might thrust between them to split open her chest at the sternum.

"The boys will have burgers, diet cokes, no fries. And the little woman here ..."

"What *is* that?" Tina stopped him, unable to stop herself.

"What?" the man said, looking away from her breasts, then around the room, then where she was looking, at Brad and his silken sling.

"Now just a minute," he said finally, his voice falling to a deeper register, almost theatrically. "What business is that of yours exactly?" He was looking into her face now.

The boys gazed up at her expectantly, as did the wife. It was as if she *did* have business here and could state it and solve everything.

"It isn't," she said, feeling herself a failure as the three slumped almost imperceptibly. "I just, well, wondered. Has something happened?"

The father put on a smarmy smile, his thin, livery lips pursed as if ready for a kiss. The mother glanced at him, then looked away into vacancy, and the boys glanced at her.

"If you must know," he said. "It had to be taken off. An unfortunate accident. These things happen."

She thought she heard Brad whisper, "it's gone" but didn't look over to be sure.

"Now," the man said, faking complete control, "the little woman will have a salad, junior size. Also a diet coke. And I," he opened a menu dramatically, as if it were some sacred text, and took his time studying it. Tina looked over at the woman who was looking ahead at nothing. Then she looked at the boys. The plea in their faces and eyes was unmistakable, and she felt it deep in her prominent young breasts. She nodded to each of them, not smiling, but in a way she hoped they'd read as conviction and a promise of coming conspiracy. In what seemed and was a long while, the father finished his investigations of the offerings, then placed his order curtly, and Tina left them at table and went to fill it.

"Colorful little fish, red, green, and even blue, in a tall jar. Gum drops. Then another jar, stiff twists of licorice, red and black. The glass"

"is clean as a whistle, right?"

"Of course. And there are little terraces stepping down, upon which, in dark paper flutes, caramel creams, pra-lines, chocolate truffles, coffee beans, all in their open white boxes, and chocolate-covered cherries too."

"What's inside?"

"Well, there are glass cases, the counter, also glass, and below it more glass cases. Fudge and turtles, non-pariels and dark and milk chocolate cashew and walnut bark, and of course almond crunch and peanut brittle."

"And the tin ceiling"

"reflects the light, fluorescent, onto the silver cash register, an old number, and looking from it to the right you can see out into the street, people passing, kids looking and a good many coming in, always smiling"

"when they catch the sweet smells emanating from the kitchen"

"where the magician works."

"Jelly beans, caramel corn, gummy bears, jaw breakers, sour balls and lemon drops, maple cuts, toffee, taffy and wal-nettos. These come in from the best places, on contract, but almost all the chocolate confections are worked up by him."

"A teacher?"

"He has been known for that, Ancient Hans-Jurg, all the way from Switzerland to Wausau thirty years ago."

"Say about the location."

"On one of the best streets in town. A hair salon with a French name to the right and Carolina's Exquisite Silver and Gold Jewelry to the left. But that wouldn't be enough, so there's the big department store, right across the street, fine women's and men's clothing, household goods, kitchen supplies, and beside it a children's shop, the finest knits, imported toys, and outer wear."

"But the real corker is"

"beside that. The Magical Play Land. Birthday, Holiday and Other Parties. Catering on the Premises. Games, Rides, Entertainment: all that on the big sign, hung up over the entranceway, tastefully inviting. And with the door open"

"they can smell the chocolate brewing."

"It would indeed seem to be perfect," Tanya said.

"How much more do you figure?" said Tina.

"Well under two months? Twelve to fifteen after taxes, I think. That should do it."

"How about the other two? Could you tell me about those again?"

"Of course. Okay." And she continued.

There couldn't have been that many in Eau Claire, and she had a rough idea of the dates and that there had been some trouble. She checked the Medical Registry online, got a few names and phoned the hospitals and clinics. That took a while, a whole evening without results, but early on the next evening she found a willing nurse and got what she was sure was the right information, his name, and that he lost his license as result of a malpractice suit, a botched breast job. Isn't that something, she thought. Then she got a phone number, no Dr before the name, but his name, and an address near the inlet right there in Erie.

The other was much easier, and by the time the library closed at ten she had gathered her notes into a folder and was ready to catch the last bus home.

"It's BIID."

"What's that?" Tina said.

They were sitting beside each other on Tanya's twin bed. Tina had prepared cocoa and cookies, and they sipped and munched away into the night, going over the findings.

"Was it a rough one?" Tanya said.

"No. A little sore in these tits is all. The animals were quite subdued. Final exams in the next few weeks, I'm guessing."

It was halfway into May now, the semester almost over.

"It will be over soon," Tanya said, "and"

"Hooters will be over too. But let's get to it."

Body Integrity Identity Disorder. No more than a few thousand worldwide. It had also been called Apotemnophilia (love of amputation) and Amputee Identity Disorder.

"These people actually want a limb cut off. Somebody wrote, 'in the false belief that part of your body is ugly or abnormal.'"

"And *that* sounds a little like what mother might have thought. Our breasts, I mean."

"Doesn't it. It seems very weird at first, but thinking about nose jobs, eyebrows, liposuction, implants, all the rest of it. Well"

"there doesn't seem to be that much difference."

"But then, of course, there is. At least when it comes to

legality and ethics. It doesn't seem to get done much in this country, if at all. The ones I read about went to Mexico, or across the sea – Switzerland I think, other places."

"So you think he's doing it here. As well as some other shit, like anal bleaching."

"Yeah, that's what I think. And that would be one thing, but"

"he cut Brad's arm off. And he's been beating the shit out of all of them. Remember the wife? Good God!"

They'd have to do something about this. A phone call? Maybe. But that might not do it. And if they went in, with their big tits, "some bimbo twins" the police might think, that might not do it either. And they had to talk to Murray, give a month's notice. They couldn't leave him hanging. Maybe that was the way, through Murray, a respectable businessman.

"We'll give it till next Tuesday, when things are slow."

"Sounds right," Tina said. She took the cocoa cups and the tray of cookie crumbs to the bedroom dresser, then turned off the light and crawled into her own bed.

"Think about chocolate," said Tanya.

"No question about it!" Tina laughed. "I'll see you in the morning."

"No – no, no, no, no!" Murray said. "How can you do this to me? I've been a father like! I cannot live without you! I'll die! I'll get fired!"

"*Halt din zoken!*" said Tina.

"My socks? My socks? What about my business?"

He settled down after a while, seeing the resolve in their faces. He was no fool, but he had grown to love them. Okay, he thought. Let it go. There will be no others like them. But let it go.

"And, Murray, there's something else," Tanya said.

"Oy, oy, oy." But he leant back in his chair and toyed with his pencil and listened as the twins told their horrifying story, and the next day he had them in again, having called the police twice and received a few calls in return.

"They didn't know a thing," he said. He had told them to sit down in chairs across from his desk, his little blondies. This would take a while.

When the police entered the house they found the mother and father dead, and the two boys huddled together behind a suction machine, off in a basement corner. There was a whole set-up down there, lights and a table, anesthesia, glass cabinets full of instruments and sterile packs, and a few specialized machines of a kind used in cosmetic surgery. And there were records too, dates, procedures and names. He had cut off a number of limbs, though he had no medical license anymore and such elective surgery was questionable at best, at least in the US. But there were desperate people who couldn't afford a trip outside the country. And he had kept up with other cosmetic surgeries as well, doing them more cheaply than legitimate doctors – noses, liposuction, breast implants, even those anal bleachings which might have been done by nurses in a clinic, even cosmeticians. He'd been very busy, and it was somewhat surprising that he had gone on so long without being discovered.

"This was for sure a madman," Murray said. "He had the boy with two arms strapped down to the table, and he was gonna cut his arm off, the other one, so they would be as twins, symmetrical you know? But then it seems the wife had had enough of this, one of the boys told them. She had all she could take or wanted, over a long time I guess, and it was, how do you say ...?"

"*Tokhis oyfin tish,*" said Tina.

"That's it! Put up or shut up. She just came at him from behind at an angle. Gave him a good clop in the head with a hammer, right there at the table. Killed the bastard outright dead. Then she fell down dead herself right there. It was a heart attack, from the effort?"

"Murray. How in the world did you learn all this?" said Tanya.

"Directly straight from the horse's mouth is how. My friend Meyer. Is a policeman."

"And the boys?" Tina said.

"To foster care. First in the hospital for looking at. After a while the shelter. Then placed with foster parents, I suppose."

"Jesus God," Tina said.

"You can say that again," said Murray. "Even I can."

Tanya tried often in the first few weeks, but she couldn't reach them. It was always, Are you a relative?, somewhat expectantly, then a quick closing down when they found out she wasn't.

"Do you think there *are* relatives?" Tina said.

"Not from the sound of it. They seem to be wishing there were." She didn't even know where they were being housed.

"Out of the hospital," Murray said. "In the foster care facility. Downtown." He'd spoken to Meyer, getting as interested as the twins were now. "Here is the number. You can say Detective Sacks said to call."

"*Biz hundert un tsvantsik,*" said Tina.

"*A sheyem dank,* Murray," Tanya chimed in.

"Yeah, yeah. Get outa here. Back to the floor."

Tanya tried that evening, and after a brief wait Bart

came to the phone. They were all right, he said, though Brad's arm was giving him a little trouble. Aching. A doctor had been looking at it. No, there were no relatives.

"They say we'll be here until they find a foster care home. I think it will take a long time."

If ever, Tanya thought. Battered little boys, one with a missing arm.

Brad was okay really, he said. It took a few weeks though. Our mother too, you know. They didn't miss her exactly. She had never actually been there. And they didn't miss him at all. Tanya heard a certain numbness in his voice. They'll be missing something before long. Well, why not, she thought.

"In that place ... is it okay? Do you get out of there?"

"Well, they take us out for the sun sometimes. For an hour or so. They keep an eye on us. Just walking around near the building, getting the sun? You know, they asked us a lot of questions. At the inquest."

"I'll bet," Tanya said. "How did that go."

"It was okay. But it was a while ago. Brad didn't like it much."

"What about the foster home deal."

"What do you mean?"

"Well, do you think you can handle that okay?"

"I don't know," Bart said. "We've always lived at home. We never even went to school. And Brad is a little frightened about that, and the people who might take us. But it would be better than being here."

"Okay," Tanya said. "Now listen up. This will probably take a little while. Then I'll call again. I can't say exactly. Maybe a week or two, maybe a little more."

"Okay," Bart said. "We'll be here. Waiting."

Murray held a little party for them, just wait-staff, cooks and busboys, after hours, near the middle of June. It was beer, champagne and dessert, whatever they wanted, and some light chamber music played softly through the system. They'd be leaving in two weeks, and he had come through yet again for them. His wife was there, a nice-looking woman with prominent breasts, and his friend Meyer was there too, with a date, a matronly figure with close-cropped blond hair, who just happened to be the director of the foster care facility downtown.

"This could be worked out?" Murray said, having introduced the twins. "These are fine, steady workers. Moral young ladies. I don't know what I'll do without them."

And it *did* work out, with the help of Meyer and Murray's wife, and Murray himself, and a good deal of intense conversation. They could come in and sign the papers in a few days, then it will take a week or so, the director said. She was serious, bright, and reasonable, a tall woman with porcelain-looking skin and bright green eyes that winked involuntarily from time to time, and she stood very close to Meyer, drawing a bead on him throughout the discussion.

Just as they finished, they heard a tinkling, and when they found the source they saw it was Murray tapping his champagne flute with a fingernail. He brought them to order and silence, then said a few words.

"What will I do now?" he said. "I have nothing left. Well, I *do* have my beautiful wife here, that's true. And I have also my fine Hooter Girls in their black T-shirts here. I have too my cooks, very good ones, and these conscientious busboys also. But a part of my heart? That I don't have or won't soon. Who could I here be talking about? It's my blondies! *Oy ve es mir!* Going, going! But you see here a philosophical man, and there are better days ahead for them. So I raise my glass now to bless them. *A gezunt ahf dein kops.* Goodbye, blondies! Be well! And maybe then you could send poor Murray just a little postcard from time to time."

They left Hooters with hugs and kisses and a few tears. Murray stood at the door waving into the night as his blondies headed for the bus stop. No others will be like that, he thought, then went back inside to turn up the air-conditioner.

Early the next morning, July first, Tanya called Mrs Kotski directly and made the deal, a hundred thousand for the shop and the goodwill. Mrs Kotski would live upstairs, rent free. For thirty years, the contract read. "Ha-ha! Good luck! I'm already eighty!" She and Hans-Jurg would stay on for six months to teach them candy. He was ready to retire too, but he, like Mrs Kotski, had known the twins since they were girls, those cute little blondies. The place was worth much more than a hundred, triple that at least, but she had no children of her own and no husband anymore, and she remembered them in the pageants and sneaking in with their father when that witch of a mother wasn't watching. "Do you still have those great big boobies?" she asked.

"Not for long," Tanya said.

Their father had left them twenty-five, and they had forty from the sixty acres of farmland they'd sold off. Then there was the hundred they'd managed to put aside in those years from seventeen to twenty-one, when they'd been traveling from place to place, working hard at various job. Add that to the tip and salary money from Hooters.

"How much exactly?" Tina asked.

"A hundred and fifty, now that we've committed that hundred to Mrs Kotski for the shop."

"The reduction?" Tina said.

"What we figured. Ten each."

"Goodbye, big titties!" Tina laughed.

"I've already called the dealership," said Tanya. "That will leave us about forty-five"

"to live on while we're learning to make candy!"

"I believe we've done it," Tanya said. "Do you worry at all about the house?"

"You mean the ghosts?" Tina said. "A bit, I guess."

"But we can clean it up properly, sweep them away."

"You bet!" Tina said. "Home again!"

The CLK55 AMG Cabriolet, all eighty-three thousand plus of it, was waiting, a conservative deep black, with drops of water from the delivery clean-up still on its gleaming wheels.

"Wipe those thoroughly," the salesman said to his over-all-clad attendant. The top was down, the seats a creamy tan leather. "Your Mercedes Benz," he said. "Beautiful, isn't it? V8 power. Ladies, please follow me."

They went through the showroom to his office, other salesmen in dark suits following their breasts. It's okay, thought Tina. Gone soon. And in the office they signed the papers. The check had cleared appropriately, and he handed over the keys and the fat owner's manual in its leather case with MB gold-stamped on the cover. Then he brought out the small box of candy, the bottle of champagne and the flowers. "Gifts from Mercedes Benz," he said, almost demurely. "You've joined our family." He led them out and opened the doors for them, and Tanya climbed in and found the trunk latch and pulled it, the lid opening slowly with no discernible sound. He placed the gifts carefully beside the suitcases on the pristine carpeting. Tina watched him, nodding and smiling. Then she too got in the car and settled herself into luxury.

It was 10.00am when they arrived at the foster care facility, and the boys were waiting, sitting beside each other on metal chairs, their little suitcases beside them, in the narrow hallway facing the office. There were only a few papers to be signed, but Tanya read each one carefully, which was her way, while Tina kept her eyes on Bart and Brad, smiling and giving them little finger waves from time to time. Then, around eleven-thirty, they were finished.

"Wow!" Brad said, when he saw the car.

"At your service," Tina said, lifting the passenger seat so they could climb into the back.

The director stood on the pavement, leaning over slightly, looking at each in turn. "Well, happy Fourth of July," she said. "Independence Day! Have a good trip!"

They made it as far as Buffalo, New York, that first day, then stayed over at a small motel on the outskirts. They were in no hurry and left late, after a good breakfast, the next morning. It was a trip of fifteen hundred miles or so, but would be longer since they had mapped out a scenic route that would take them through Buffalo, a bit of Canada below Toronto, then north, crossing the upper peninsula of Michigan and down into Wisconsin on their way to Wausau.

They spoke of the candy store and the house. Each boy would have his own room on the second floor.

"You can see out over the fields and woods from there," Tanya said. "And you can go out there too. Hunting around and picking wild berries. They should be ripe by now."

"We could have built a fort there if we were younger," Bart said, poking Brad's stump with his elbow. He winced, and his brother touched his leg in concern. Tina had turned and was looking back over the seat.

"We'll do something about that too," she said. "We've talked, and in a little while we'll have enough saved for a gizmo."

"A prosthesis," Tanya said, her eyes on the road. They were cruising below Hamilton, Canada, riding along the north shore of Lake Erie, the water gleaming in the sun.

"This is some car," Bart said. "It's beautiful."

"We're comfy as an armed camp in here," Brad said, raising his stump, which stuck out just a little below the short sleeve of his bright yellow shirt. Tina giggled, and Bart laughed out loud at the dry joke.

"Armed to the teeth!" said Tanya, her colorful scarf drifting up in the breeze.

"You could put the arm on him."

"A strong-arm tactic."

"Well-armed," said Brad.

"Clean it with Arm and Hammer!" said Tina.

"Here we are in the Arm-y."

"All arms on deck!"

"Arms and the Man."

"What's that?" said Bart.

"A play, I think," said Tina.

"An armature," said Tanya.

"Weapons from the arm-ory!"

"An armada."

"Arm we going, arm in arm, to the Armenian Church?"

"On Armistice Day."

"Pass me the armadillo."

"I put it in the armoire."

Top down. Breeze in their hair. All the way to Wausau.

Calavera

THERE ARE STORIES handed down through generations, not because children desire and are in need of them, but because their parents now understand them and can remember sitting at the knees of their own parents, listening to the telling. I sat at the knees of my mother, my child, hearing this one, and I remember how old she seemed to me then, though I had no conception of the passage of time. Her face was waxen there above me, her eyes closed remembering her own mother telling the story, and I must have feared that she was drifting away from me. And so I listened hard and didn't fidget, trusting I could hold her close for a while in that way. So, my daughter, I tell you this story not so much as I remember it, but as I remember my mother telling it, most probably knowing I would not really understand it until I too became a mother, one who had a need for keeping her daughter close for a little while yet.

Once upon a time there were two children, a boy and a girl, who were farm children. They passed through a shadowy wood on their way home, and at a turn of the trail in the wood they came upon a fallen oak tree and a *calavera* sitting on the trunk among branches, and they were not hesitant because they were children and had no fear of death.

This *calavera* wore the uniform of his last engagement in the dances of the dead, the vestments of a bishop who had sold the votes of his diocese for money. His grinning skullface stared out from the folds of his robes, his head cocked arrogantly to the side in remembered gesture. But there was a certain look of longing in his teeth and hollow eyes that the children noticed immediately as they climbed among the branches to sit beside him.

Calaveras are skeletons, my dear, the dead come alive again long after their moldering, and their dances, which are often stories of the foolishness in life left behind, have become fixed images in the works of many artists, in papier-mâché figures, and even in marzipan candy shaped into bones and skulls in Mexico on the Day of the Dead, a holiday that reminds us of our mortality.

And in these stories all *calaveras* have their parts, from the politician vomiting words out over the crowd, to the culpable businessman at his elbow and the henchman at the platform's edge. And each in the crowd, too, is an actor, in gesture of agreement or of disgust, varieties of pantomime, and the raising of weapons in the bony hands of the military at the periphery.

And yet, on rare occasion, in the image of a foot soldier, a carpenter, a provocative virgin to the side of a gathering of other virgins, one finds the empty skullgaze, the figure in ambiguous gesture beyond the story, head tilted in longing toward the might-have-been. These are the traveling *calaveras*, and whether they are few or many is not certain, for one may see the same one seen before without knowing it because they all look the same, being skeletons, and because of the traveling, that search for a proper circumstance in which the dance can be mindlessly entered, which is never found, because the skeleton is the free essence beyond longing or nostalgia; and these are the aberrant *calaveras* who can't believe their luck in being alive again, even as bones, and long for their living selves, dragging the memory of the flesh and desire with them. Be not afraid, my child. This is only a story. Remember the children?

They had climbed into the fallen oak tree to sit beside him, that *calavera* dressed in the vestments of a bishop, and the girl asked him, "Are you lost?" He said he was lost, but he was grinning, and they were not sure of the meaning of his answer. They could see his bare clavicles where his garment opened at the neck, and they thought he must be cold wearing only his bones under his clothing at the start of winter. The boy reached up to raise the hood of his cloak, and it fell down to cover his face, guarding against any clear view of it. They helped him to climb free of the tree's branches, and then they walked beside him, holding the bones of his fingers as they led him home.

It was a farmer's home, one large room with a big wooden table and a stove and sink and a larder and a stone fireplace. There was a double bed in a corner and pallets on the floor, and their mother fell back at the sight of the bishop in the doorway, flustered and honored, and she led the *calavera* to the table and put food and drink before him that he could not eat. He said he just needed a little rest, and she placed a chair near a window, and the *calavera* sat in it, the children gathered on the floor at his feet. And once he'd answered the few questions the mother put to him, she went about her business of cleaning and cooking, and he sat still in the chair in his spectral garments, watching her.

Then, at day's end, the farmer came home from his labors. He held the children up in his arms and kissed his wife and bowed to the bishop. Then candles were lit, and the family took up the routine activities of their evening. All was action and gestures of interchange, and the *calavera* thought of the possibilities in the dance of life he was witnessing and thought nothing of the next leg of his journey, the search for that future circumstance in which he might find his proper place.

The mother was at the stove, baking. The farmer had lifted a block of wood and was whittling the face of a man out of it, shavings cast in the fire, and the children sat on the floor a few feet from the bishop's hem, fitting paper clothing on small anonymous figures. All faces were lit in the waves of candlelight, and the *calavera* watched them dissolve and reconstruct as heads turned on their axes and words drifted in lazy half sentences throughout the room. And in a moment of silence he saw the mother's face pause in its animation, her hands sunk deeply in dough. She was looking at the night-darkened window and her gaze was vacant where it met the glass, and the *calavera* was stunned to see that same look of longing in life that he was aware of in his own face in death, and he recognized it was an avenue of possibility she was looking down.

It was as if between her and the window were her life's actions and the meaningful assumption of them, but at the glass itself was nothing, just her desire for a place beyond where the terms of her longing ended. And when he saw the same vacant look in the farmer's face as he glanced down to the floor in his whittling, he found he was seeing into the human condition with a new understanding.

He sat in his robes in the chair watching these manifestations as he mulled them over in his mind. He thought then of life as a central artery, running parallel to the spine, and each vein and capillary, extending out along bone to the exuberant extremities, as those possibilities of alternative bloody avenues down which one might glance but never go. He thought of his own life, before he was a *calavera*, and its necessarily stunted quality, though it had been a life of satisfaction and fullness, and he had walked its broad and easy causeway free of any care.

He'd been a journalist, this *calavera*, privy to the hidden corruptions of government, present at the forefront of shipwreck and devastating fire. On his bicycle he'd ridden to the brink of individual illness and family happiness and difficulty, often into circumstances of possibility where he might have stepped from the saddle into another life. Each of these lives had been ripe for engagement, but he had simply written their stories and moved on, life's longing recorder. Now his bones shook under his bishop's garment as he silently articulated his proposal.

All men and women, my daughter, long for the might-have-been, those avenues of life they didn't take, and in the recognition that each one was a possibility, held in the memory as vision grown hazy at terminals beyond all bright beginnings, longing becomes empty nostalgia as the veins dry and collapse along the bones and the broad gestures of the body wither at the outer reaches. Devoid of the animation of living, all come narrowed and regretful to their deaths, since of the many possible lives, only one was lived.

The *calavera* saw it all in the look of the farmer's wife and in the farmer, and though the children glanced up from their play and down those first narrow byways only with bright eyes and curiosity, he knew their time too would come.

And he knew now that the living he'd longed for again as a *calavera* held its own profound longing, and that when he reached a new circumstance the force of his look would be doubled in the intensity of its longing, drawing the eyes of the viewers to a bloody familiarity, and would overwhelm the dry extravagance of the dancing bones.

There was no sound, but the children turned to him as he fell down, the dark robes of the bishop collapsing to a pile of dusty fabric on the chair's wooden seat. It was bone dust, and it puffed through the weave, then settled into a haze, obscuring the chair's legs. And the farmer was rising, his wife turning, and the children's faces were invisible behind their bodies. But the face of the farmer was intense, as was that of his wife. Their jaws creaked open, the blocks of their teeth visible to the pink gums. All paused as they reached the chair, as if gathered around the last event in an old story. A wind came in at the window. It blew the door open and blew the fine dust of the dissolved bones of the *calavera* out into a final burial in the night.

And that is the end of the story, my daughter. An odd and frightening tale, there's no doubt. But do not be afraid. For though in my sickness I've grown as waxen as that *calavera*, I'm not going anywhere soon. I'm not leaving you. Stay close for a while more. This is the best story I can tell you. Please remember it until you understand it, then tell it to your children.

What's New?

I SAW MY face in a pig's mouth at a yard sale, a mirror-mask originally purchased by someone who had our taste and might have known a few things about mortality. Pigs get slaughtered, and in my mysteries someone always winds up on the autopsy table. Open mouths and other cavities, and what you see, inevitably, is yourself there.

Angelo laughed through his coughing when I spoke of this, as much at the mask looking up from the cluttered table as my portentous telling. It was a sunny July morning, yet he was coming into the darkness of the man whose belongings were on display there. The leavings of a life to be read and dispersed, possibly throughout the world, I thought but didn't say.

We live a few hundred yards away, only a stroll, but for Angelo a struggle these days. "Bon voyage," he says whenever we leave the house, his body prepared to measure each distance as if a last experience. We bought the mask, memento mori of this man we'd seen tending his flowers, who had greeted us in our passing. "What's new?" Angelo said, gazing into the pig's mouth. We'd hung him in our collection of small mirrors above the mantle.

In the church, every Sunday now, I see Angelo folded over at the kneeler and cannot be angry at his return to religion. I watch from the doorway until he's settled in the congregation, then I go out and sit in the churchyard. There's a willow there and a bench, and I drink coffee from a thermos and write notes until the music ends and the service is over. "Of course, you couldn't know," Angelo said, as he arranged figures in the crèche more than two months before Christmas. They're still there, the pine bough forming the manger's roof having dropped every needle on the Haywood Wakefield cabinet, though it's late July.

Chief Inspector Wakefield needed smelling salts, watching Doctor Josephson close up the baby girl with safety pins. Cause of death seemed insignificant at that moment. Wakefield turned away from the metal table.

Lesions are erupting on parts of Angelo's body, red lips reminiscent of the baby's small vagina, which I don't describe. I know the private parts of all my characters, but they don't enter into the writing. The nose, thinning hair, dramatic eye coloring, that's enough. The books deal in mysterious events, and people walk through them as shadow figures, coloring book outlines left for readers to fill in.

"You haven't changed a bit," Angelo said, looking up from the proofs. We were sitting in deckchairs in the sand at Coast Guard Beach. It was evening, and the tide was low. Downwind a gull was pecking at the flesh of a dead skate. He was squinting into the sinking sun. Handsome as ever, I thought.

"I must admit, I'm getting sick of the whole enterprise. I need a new detective, maybe someone younger, or a woman."

"What's new?" he said.

We had returned from Boston late in the afternoon, having visited Angelo's mother at the nursing home. We'd brought her a small mirror, an oval set in the chest of the crucified Christ. She'd looked into it. "How is the world treating you?" And we weren't sure if this was our greeting or a question asked of herself or even of the Savior. The music of late morning's rosary played softly on her small

portable radio, voices acting out piety. She dropped Christ
on the coverlet complacently. "Mother?" Angelo said. She
looked up and spoke. "Gee, but it's nice to see you again,"
as if addressing casual acquaintances, which I was to her.
We had hidden our relationship like schoolboys from this
aged woman. Angelo's father was long dead. "Why make
waves?" he'd said, and I'd answered, "I understand." We
sat in medicinal scents for an hour or more.

We don't sleep now in the same bed, but at the beginning of August we went to Pine Grove Cemetery lugging
lawn chairs and a picnic lunch, then reclined beside each
other in the grass over our plot. It's king size, and I'll reside
on the left. Pinot Grigio and lobster rolls, shadows from
overhanging tree limbs spotting our arms and faces, maybe
the warble of a bird or two were this fiction.

"Do you really think it's the last Wakefield?" His voice
is a little labored now. I don't often describe voices, but I'd
say there's some gravel in it. His question seemed serious
in the way he'd asked it.

"I haven't changed," I said. "But how did that romance
come through to you? He'd have to get back with his wife
or start something new with this other woman. And probably I'm boring you, this side issue in the reading."

"I haven't gotten there yet," he said.

"What's new?" I laughed.

"I can't manage to lift it."

"Just a damn minute here."

"But it's my leg!"

"Try leaning to the side a bit."

"There's a weeping wound."

"I know, I know."

"Will Wakefield wind up with that other woman?"

"Not now! Can you turn a little more?"

"Maybe. I'll give it a try."

"I think that's got it now. Are you comfortable?"

"Yes, okay. Can you pull up the blanket?"

"Right. That's it. Anything else?"

"I could use a drink. Something warm to drink?"

"Tea?"

"That sounds good."

"With lemon and a spoon of honey?"

"That would be great. And could you bring the rosary?"

My wife was religious too. So long ago that I have no particulars anymore. It was our only bone of contention, those Christ bones and the glorification of torture. Foolish arguments, her stern martyr's look when I shook my head against her seriousness, even in her pregnancy. She went to church on Saturdays, for rosary, while I stayed at home drawing myths of my own making, picture books for children. Now Angelo runs his beads and I grow jealous of the comfort they give him.

"Goodness!" Fat Jack said, his arms opening expansively in the archway. "It seems forever. Is it a year? But seeing you is grand!"

It was Ben's Fourth of July brunch, cold salmon, potatoes, and green peas, always held in August. About twenty men in shirt sleeves and light jackets, all over fifty, hands on their hips or gesturing in jovial conversation. Ben bustled among us, carrying platters and wine bottles. Paul was there and was fading in the way Angelo was, and the two had taken up company in the window seat and were talking things over. A crucifix hung from a chain around Paul's neck. Maybe they're praying, I thought, their heads close together.

"We haven't met since then," Jack said. "Wasn't it Paul's concert last summer?"

"The Debussy," I said. "But Angelo played too, his horn." I was a little offended.

"Of course, of course! I remember now. Is he still able?"

"No," I said, "his breath."

Someone had put on a CD, Paul's harpsichord Bach. Angelo looked up into the music.

"I'm sorry," Jack said. "Pardon my asking what's new."

We pass by privet in which gateways have been cut, brick paths at the end of which stand white doors and brass knockers, pass gardens sporting carefully mulched beds of cosmos, sweet pea and petunias, then a split rail heavy with rambling rugosa roses. Next there's Ben's house, then a ripe trumpet vine rising until its spread falls out like a fountain, then the sinister woman's curtains, the yard sale yard, now untended, then honeysuckle, beach plum, autumn olive, and sentinel pines. The two of us on the trail home, his pants billowing at the thighs, falling in folds at the cuffs. He hangs on my arm, cane poking in the grass in our slow progress. Just two old fags. I wear a cap, Angelo a battered cowboy hat against the failing sun. We stroll past elevated beds, arrogant day lilies, blue planters spilling with bright shooting stars.

"Very nice," Angelo croaks. "But how old is Wakefield? How many years has he been married?"

We are wedded to something that is not of our design, and lack of control has us on the ropes from time to time. Angelo weeps quietly in his incontinence. I smear Vick's on my upper lip before cleaning up after, his night clothes and the soiled bed, stained shower tiles, sometimes a chair seat, and try to think of other things.

When we were younger, we went whole hog for life's vicissitudes. I was an artist, and even the broken leg couldn't stop me. It was back to the drawing board, then the collectibles bought and sold for profit at weekend fairs, then the mystery novels, the first one coming from observations at such venues. Angelo took up his childhood horn again, late in life for a musician. He was twenty-four and a medical technician fresh from the Navy, working in the emergency room where they brought my wife and me. I remember his hand on my shoulder as she drifted away forever. I sat in a wheelchair at the foot of her bed, my leg freshly casted. Shortly after the days of the accident and its aftermath, I moved to Boston and Angelo quit and came along with me. I was thirty-six at the time. The girl had been born by way of cesarean, then died as my wife had, never a babe in arms.

Now, at seventy-five, it grows difficult to be a hand-maiden. Even metaphor in the control of thought in action can fail in the face of such extremity. That others of our company fall away too in this age helps little. I say "face," since that's where I often see it. Paul's face, his nose grow-ing more prominent as flesh recedes. Angelo's face, the two speaking in whispers, together again at Ben's end-of-season party.

"No one here but old animals," Fat Jack says, when I speak of the sinister woman who lives near the corner of our street. I'd been thinking of taking her into a mystery, that there would be a real mystery behind the cliché of the one she presented, peeking at us from between curtains as we stroll by. An old woman, I thought, about my age, a busybody. What was in the room behind her; was it her life?

"Well," Jack says, "but she watches the old animals. Perhaps she's a wallflower living with her ancient mother. Maybe an FBI operative. She could be a woman of means, fallen on hard times. Or maybe some convoluted events in her past life, in Florida? Beirut? Cairo? Is that open enough? I mean as possibilities for you to fill in?"

"Could be," I said.

Looking over his shoulder, I wasn't paying attention. A plate of crab cakes, asparagus and new potatoes wobbled on Angelo's knee. He sat beside Paul once again in the window seat. They were talking, and I fancied I could see all the years we'd spent together in his profile, changed only slightly since our beginning, and if anything, in his weight loss, moving back toward that beginning when he was only a thin young man. I didn't want our youth again. It was just that he looked that way, and I wondered that we had gotten on so smoothly for so many years. I still love you so, I thought, trying to get the words over to him through the air somehow. Then I thought about talk of our beginning, there at the foot of my dead wife's bed. "I knew it right away," Angelo had often said, never as memory of past jubilation, but as profound recognition in the face of death and change. I'd answer in a way that would bring romance back into it, because it was so painful, and I still felt darkly guilty. "And you were sweet to offer your hand," I'd say. "There on my shoulder. Do you remember?"

Chief Inspector Wakefield had enough information now and decided to have another go at the prime suspect. He took DI Jennifer Workman with him, though he had avoided involving her earlier because of their affair. She was much younger than he, only twenty-four, and he wasn't sure at all how things might turn out between them. She drove, and sitting beside her he felt guilt gnawing at the betrayal of his wife.

When they reached the steps of the old brownstone, Workman pressed against him. He looked into her jade-green eyes, light sparking in the hard pupils. She nodded, and he glanced to where she was looking, the slightly parted curtains, someone peeking out at them. An old busybody, he thought.

The apartment was on the third floor, and on the way up he told Workman he'd do the questioning, she could take notes. But if there was something she thought important she could feel free.

"Do you have cuffs?" he asked.

She reached under the light jacket, to where they jiggled at the small of her back. It was September now. Fall was on the way, but it was still warm.

The apartment was seedy and quite dark, and the suspect sat in an easy chair in front of the mantel, above which hung a large crucifix in shadow.

"My wife's," he said, seeing Wakefield look there, as if to avoid any confusion. "She was religious."

His pants bagged at the thighs and ankles and seemed too large for his thin body. He had called out softly when they'd knocked, and the door had been open. Wakefield sat in a hard chair across from him, and Workman took her position, standing beside the door.

Other things in the room spoke of his wife's presence. Framed photographs, a rosary draped on a plaster icon of the Virgin Mary, a sewing basket beside the couch, meager leavings of a gone life.

The suspect was not old, possibly late thirties, but his thin hair had receded and the skin covering his aquiline nose was parchment-like. Guilt takes a toll, Wakefield thought, then began the questioning.

"The deposition has you at work, on the other side of the city. Is that right?"

"Yes. It was new construction," he said. "I was finishing tile work on the sixth floor. I'm a tiler. All day long."

His voice croaked a little, coming forth with effort, and Wakefield thought this wouldn't take long at all. Thin curtains parted in a breeze at the open window. A stripe of light cut across the suspect's knees.

"Valuable appliances," Wakefield said. "It's a large building."

"Eighteen stories, I think."

"And did you know the guards were in place, and the security system?"

"Yes," he said. "I knew that."

"We have you leaving at midday, on camera," Wakefield said.

"But that was gone over before," the suspect insisted. "It was only a figure in work clothes, a view of his shoulders, a cap, the back of his head."

"No," Wakefield said. "High up in the corner at the rear exit, your face quite clear in a mirror."

The breeze died and the curtains closed, and the suspect fell apart completely then, almost too quickly.

"Oh, Angela!" he moaned, face in his hands now, his body shaking, "I didn't mean to do it! I have killed my wife!"

Wakefield heard Workman moving behind him and held up his hand to stop her.

"And the baby?" he said softly.

The suspect was weeping now, his face wet with tears when he looked up.

"I *had* to," he said. "I had to."

The idea was monstrous, and Wakefield was assaulted by that image of the infant on the autopsy table, the safety pins. He started to ask for an explanation, then thought better of it. That would come later, under extended interrogation. But he was urged to speak, not knowing what to say. Then he heard Workman moving behind him, the click of her cuffs, and felt her hand on his shoulder.

"Shouldn't we be leaving now?" she whispered, her mouth close to his ear. Then she was moving past him, light and quick on her fine young legs, and he watched as she helped the suspect to his feet and cuffed him.

They made their way down the narrow stairway to the ground floor. The case was closed now, at least their part of it was. It remained for others to negotiate the penalty.

When they reached the foyer, a door to the side creaked open and Wakefield saw the face of the woman who had peeked out at them earlier. She was much younger than he had imagined, perhaps twenty-four, Workman's age. She glanced down at the suspect's wrists, curious, he thought. Then she looked up into his eyes. Her smile was tentative.

"*Adieu*," she said.

Charley Needs

CHARLEY NEEDS A new comb. This one is clotted with remnants of old, rancid hair. Charley needs new underwear. When he steps out on his deck at sunset, the river is a placid, red pleasure. Charley needs that. He needs his houseboat, peace of mind, friends. Charley needs to be loved.

Yesterday, at the convenience store, Charley needed strong coffee on his way to work. At the bank, sitting daylong behind his desk, Charley needed a drink and a break.

Outwardly, Charley needs nothing. Fine clothes, inheritance, a good job. Charley needs to get going. He needs to write something down, the story of his life so far, in no more than ten pages. He needed a tricycle, then a bike, a few drinks, his father's car for the prom. He needed a date. When he got to page ten, the past had crumbled away behind him and he needed to stop or continue. He could hear the slow motor of a party boat on the river. He needed to go out there, to see them. Charley needs company. He needs a few ants in his pants.

Life is a bore. Charley needs to escape it. He needs to know what he's escaping from and into. Charley's memory is shot and he needs to recover it. He needs to know what got him here, to this place where he needs some justification for his arrival. He needs to get his head on straight. In that house where he lived with his parents, both of whom found solace in a bottle until they both died on a balmy spring afternoon in a drunk-driving accident and he was thirty-five, Charley needed only the accouterments of their life together, the porcelain kitchen table, two locked liquor cabinets – Charley needed to fend for himself, which he did, drinking before school and after, and often before bed – a couple of kitchen appliances, framed still lifes to gaze at, the scents in his mother's clothing and lingerie draped carelessly on the bed when she was absent, her gestures and scents when she was present, the river seen through the kitchen window, child's toys gathered as evidence of a past, their dog sprawled on the rug, chin resting on big paws, the sacramental certificates on which all futures were spelled.

Charley needs to lose a few pounds. He needs to get off his boat on balmy spring evenings, to go places, to see and engage in things. He thinks he needs a woman. At the bank, he needs to act as the president, which he is, to speak to tellers and investors in a professional manner. Charley needs a vacation.

Sitting at an outdoor table at a café on the right bank in Paris, Charley needed a glass of wine. People passed slowly on the sidewalk, this balmy spring afternoon, in quiet conversation. Charley thought he needed to be one of them. And then an attractive woman his age, around forty-five he thought, stopped on the sidewalk to dig in her purse, frustrated. She needs a pencil or pen, Charley thought. He needed to hand it to her. She seemed needy when she handed it back to him. Charley needed to wipe his brow.

Charley had gout in his big toe. He needed to exercise, to take pills and tone up before he met her after Paris on his houseboat for drinks before dinner. He needed to impress her, needed to know some things about her position as a dress designer and to tell her what he knew at sunset out on his boat deck. He needed a balmy evening.

In her beautiful linen outfit, what he needed most was to touch her, but he knew it was too soon, as it was even after dinner – steak au poivre, green beans, a Cabernet, and her choice of crème brûlée – and when she left him standing at the door, he needed to stay there, wondering.

Charley needed this woman, or he needed something, and he needed a present, an appropriate thing, not too expensive or personal. Candy, flowers, he needed to know, and he needed to know how to present this gift, how to behave when he did so.

Charley needed to know what was in his heart, what it meant not to approach her as if he were a teenager, back there at the prom again, where he had been rebuffed. He needed to know how it had been with his mother, how he had mourned her, what had been the nature of their relationship. He needed an antacid. He needed company and liquor. In the years since his parents had died, he needed his dog, which was also dead. He thought he might need a parrot in a cage.

Charley drinks copious amounts of alcohol. He needs to do so. Often, on balmy mornings, before he sets of for the bank, he needs a few shots of Irish whiskey. He needs to get to the bank on time, but on such mornings he sometimes finds he's a little awkward and slow on his feet, listing to the right and left.

The tellers and the two vice-presidents, four women and two slightly eccentric men, need to watch him, to see that Charley does not, after those occasional nips from a bottle he pulls from his desk drawer, fall asleep upon his scatter of papers.

Charley needs to wake up. He needs to alter his behavior, to straighten it out as he straightens out his tie most mornings. He needs a shot of Kentucky's best. What do all those people out there need? he often thinks, needing to consider his place in the world. He needs to see her again.

They met occasionally, not often enough as far as Charley was concerned. He needed more. They had hot dogs sold by venders who stood in shade under awnings extended out from their carts. They sat on benches in the park on balmy afternoons. He said a few things. She seemed to listen.

She needed only a glass of Pinot Grigio. He needed a couple of Beefeater martinis. He thought he needed only her face across the table, which was on a terrace under an awning looking out on the soft, steady rain. A fine French restaurant on the north side of the city, which was a country city in which people greeted strangers on the street. Fairy lights hung in their rich colors from under the awning. Piano music drifted out from inside, standards from the Great American Songbook that circled the years in which Charley grew from a boy into a dubious man: *Angel Eyes, Too Young to Go Steady, I'm Through with Love.* Charley wanted to reach across the table, his arm almost brushing the veal, and take her hand.

She told him about her work in the fashion industry, not the cutting and shaping, the draping, not even fabrics, but the people, artists and models, designers and photographers. They were brilliantly creative, and their products were often works of art. To be in that community, in their company, made work a distinct pleasure, made life a pleasure.

Charley needed this pleasure. His gout-ridden toe was aching. He had little to say, but when he spoke, which was seldom, he couldn't read her expressions, that curve of lip, those lagging gestures. She was listening, and she was not listening. The food was delicious, especially the artichokes, their tender centers. Dessert, served with a small bottle of

Vin Santo which he'd ordered along with a brandy to follow, was apple pudding. After the meal, the plates and silver cleared, he thought he should speak, say something
meaningful, but she beat him to it. She was tired out. It
had been a very busy day.

"You work on the weekend?" He managed to choke out
the words.

She told him, "Oh, yes. No rest for the wicked." He was
not tired. He imagined himself on the brink of something
new.

They walked to her place, side by side, Charley limping
a little. The rain had ended, and the wet streets reflected
ghostly images of the branches up above. The air was a bit
moist, but balmy. Neither of them spoke, until she did. She
was standing on the second step going up to the porch, and
this made her a little taller than Charley needed where he
stood on the walkway below. She raised her hand, then
told him he didn't need to come up. Then she turned and
finished her climb to the door, which she closed firmly
after entering.

Charley needs ... something, standing there, empty, his
toe aching.

Charley needed her, in her beauty, her clothing, her odd
smile in conversation, and he found that his palms were
itching as they often had in the presence of his mother.

She didn't need Charley.

Charley buys a bottle on his way home.

The Brain

Because of an awkward splashing, brought on by an urgency that had recently come to plague him, Roger found it necessary to sit down while urinating, and in time he found this posture quite pleasing, those brief moments of contemplation.

The toilet was in the far corner of the basement, and he rushed away from the worktable where he had been dealing with the old lamp he had only recently acquired, holding himself until he reached the throne.

He'd purchased the lamp at a secondhand shop in the town center. It was an elegant thing, a tall, hollow pewter cylinder above which a gathering of glass tulips, each fitted with a small white light, sprayed out in ascending circles, topped with a pewter finial shaped like a tulip bud. He had carefully placed the lamp on its side when the toilet called, and then, back at the table again, he adjusted the swing arm lamp and, removing the felt covering at the base, peered into the hollow tube, seeing that someone had replaced wires in a crude and thoughtless way.

The old wires had been clipped only five inches from their source, new wires clumsily taped to them. A real fire hazard, he thought. He'd have to rewire the whole thing, something he looked forward to with pleasure.

For over a year Roger had been on permanent disability. No more work at the shoe factory, where he had come to notice a gradual change in production. Military boots had become the order of the day, lows and highs with visible steel toes and small devices imbedded in their heels. And in his free time, which was almost all of the time now, he'd taken to shopping, mostly in secondhand and consignment shops, but also for clothing, groceries, and whatever else caught his fancy. He bought things, mostly electrical for fiddling, but he had also come to enjoy browsing, moving in and out of shops in the town center and at the large mall that had grown up on the edge of the highway. And books. He'd never been much of a reader before his accident, but in the last year he'd begun what he thought might end up as a not insignificant little library. History and art books, how-to electrical tomes, and even a few novels, mostly of romance, but some of foreign intrigue that argued for political change. He'd come across a book called *The Feminine Mystique*. It was there on the new bookcase he'd built in the living room. He seemed to remember the book somehow, though he had not as yet read it.

He had reached up into the bowels of the lamp, aiming to pull the frayed tape away, when the lights went out, the basement thrust into darkness.

A breaker, he thought. He knew the basement well, and without pausing to get his bearings, he headed for the small enclosure beside the stairs where the breaker box was located. He had a small light, together with a few pencils and pens, tucked into a plastic container that was, in turn, tucked into his shirt pocket, and he shined the narrow beam into the box, seeing that nothing had tripped. Puzzled, he stood there for a moment, considering. Then he turned and shined the little light on the main switch. It had not been thrown.

He stood very still, there in the darkness, listening, feeling silly, and suddenly the lights came back on. He could hear nothing, but he noticed a faint scent that seemed unfamiliar. Could it be sweat? A thing distantly burning? He shook it off. Something with that damned electric company again. This had happened before, and he'd called numerous times, only to be put on hold, then disconnected. He shook his head, adjusted his wig, and went back to his electrical work.

He had awakened in a fog of misunderstanding. His vision was hazy, and he could not hear with clarity. He thought he was in bed, coming back from a troubling dream. But then he felt the tube in his nose, saw the vague bag of solution hanging from the IV pole. Figures surrounded him; nurses, he suddenly realized. I'm in the hospital. What happened?

"An accident." A whispered voice. He must have spoken his last thought. "In the factory." Then he remembered bits of it: the toe-lasting machine, hot glue. He'd known the uppers on the boots were too thick. Was he burning? He didn't feel any burns. He had a headache. "We can't give you anything for the pain just yet." That soft, soothing voice again. "The doctor will be here soon." Then he drifted back into sleep.

He awakened to the sight of a small, chubby man with a mustache leaning over him.

"I'm the doctor," the man said. "Can you hear me?"

"Some," Roger said. "Enough maybe."

"Well," the doctor said. "At least there's that."

"At least?" Roger said, or thought he said.

"Yes," the doctor replied. "And I have news, and it's upsetting and rather urgent."

Roger didn't understand. "I can't see too well. I have a bad headache."

"To be expected," the doctor said. "But we can fix all that. We do have to hurry though."

"With what?" Roger asked.

"The transplant."

"What do you mean?" Roger said. "I don't understand."

"Well," the doctor said. "Let me explain."

He had been wearing a helmet, as required, when the toe-lasting machine failed, and hot glue had washed over the leather, then found the portal and flooded into his left ear.

"What it did was a little like cooking. I mean it cooked a good portion of your brain. And it is still in there, drying, and doing its dirty work, sealing, rendering further matter quite useless. We need to operate, and we need to do it quickly. Now I know you have insurance, but it won't cover the transplant, unless ..."

"What transplant?"

"Your brain, man! We have to replace your brain!"

"You can't do that."

"Indeed, we can. But there are options. Decisions. Forms to be filled out."

"And if I don't agree to this?"

"Then I'm afraid you're finished. Soon to be dead."

"What are the options?" Roger said.

"There are two. In our tissue bank we have a dozen or so male brains. These are somewhat costly and difficult to install. And I doubt that insurance would cover the operation. The brains themselves are expensive, as is the operation."

"How expensive?" Roger asked.

"Sixty-five thousand dollars each, plus around twenty for the procedure."

"My God! That's a fortune! I can't afford that. What did you mean by each?"

"Each male brain."

"But I'd only need one, wouldn't I?"

"Well, of course. Just one."

"You said two. What's the other option?"

"Well, there *are* the female brains. A few, about four, are available as we speak. And in this case the operation would be covered by virtue of a grant. We're studying them. The fit can be awkward. Different skull configurations, after all."

"How much?"

"Fifteen thousand. A flat rate. No hidden costs."

"Why?" Roger asked.

"Why what?"

"Why are the female brains so much cheaper than the male ones?"

"Well," the doctor answered, "they've been used."

"Used? Like a used car?"

"Sure. A metaphor. Something like that. Though maybe 'broken in' would be more accurate. And there is no warranty. You'd be taking your chances."

And so he took his chances, and the brain, that of a thirty-five-year-old woman, was installed. The fit was a tight one, and even after some necessary adjustments, Roger's eyes were slightly to the side of their sockets, giving him a rakishly provocative glance. So too had there been difficulties with the new brain's neural pathways, his getting used to them. It was almost as if he were two perceivers now, or at least had come to understand the world around him differently than he had before. Was there awareness somewhere in his body in addition to that in his new brain, something at the base of his spine, himself in his motor responses, something seated elsewhere?

Was he a woman now? The doctor had scoffed at that idea as he'd handed over the Geniux, a brain pill championed by Dr Oz. "This might help with concentration. It's like Viagra for the brain."

At first all this was quite unsettling, but in only a brief time he had grown accustomed to a kind of double vision. He began to feel integrated, though his hair had not grown back, and once up and around he had selected a wig that held waves and curls and a brush of hair that drifted over his left ear. Roger was fifty-five years old, but he felt much younger once the surgery and his recuperation were behind him.

Now he continued work on the new lamp, and while doing so he thought back on his visit to the secondhand shop where he had purchased it.

He was shocked as always, though less so since the operation, when he stepped beyond the front door of his house. The street was gone, as were the familiar houses that had faced his across from it. There was rubble still, both straight ahead and to the right, acres of it, and the only familiarity resided in the beginning of the forest that abutted his lawn to the left. Men had come to visit him, dressed in suits that seemed vaguely military. They had made offers, not very good ones, though he knew his neighbors had cashed in for much less. He might have sold had the suits come up with something substantial. They hadn't though.

He was at the very edge of the construction site, and it was clear that they could build what they wanted without his land getting in the way. At least for a while. He'd tried to learn what the project was all about. He'd gone to city hall to look at the plans, but none were available for viewing. The clerk had been sheepish, and when he went back and tried again, there was a different clerk, a stern woman dressed like the men who had visited him, who dismissed him and his enquiry immediately. "This is a government project," she'd said. "Nothing is available to be viewed by the populace." Her language was formal and strict, a little arcane, and he left with nothing at all.

He made his way across the empty acreage, coming to places where the ground had been leveled and cleared, where there was new curbing and cuts through brush in preparation for roads, and finally stepped onto pavement where the edge of the town began. It was late afternoon, and cloudy, and lights had been turned on in the various shops he passed by. On the door of each house and each shop, a small, sturdy metal box had been affixed, a series of buttons on each of them. Codes to be punched in. But by whom? New streetlights stood, every thirty or so yards along the curbing, and each sported an elaborate surveillance camera beside its hooded canopy. He heard a vague clicking as they turned to track his progress. He thought he heard the chop of a helicopter in the quickly darkening sky.

When he stepped into the dimly lit store, he saw that there were only a few shoppers milling around. The owner, who seemed somewhat tense, was standing stiffly behind the counter. Roger was focused on the section that held the lamps, but suddenly felt a little faint and gripped the edge of the counter to right himself. Beside his focused, pragmatic concentration, there was a more generalized awareness now. He could feel it behind his forehead and knew it in his eyes as they began to dilate, even though nothing in the room's dim lighting had changed. It's you, he thought. It's me. His focus broadened, opening out as his head lifted, and then ...

She was taking in the entire space, its feel and its gestalt. There was something ominous, an atmosphere she thought she would come to understand, but not yet. She scanned the room slowly, the bookshelves, the counters of electrical gear, the few people present, the nature of the dim lighting. Most of the books were light reading: mysteries, self-help, a number of large coffee table tomes. But there was something, a thin spine, Sun Tzu's *The Art of War*. What was it doing here? Why were the shoppers not looking to buy anything? They were just watching, gazing out the broad streetside windows, studying those passing by. They seemed to be waiting for something.

Roger had focused on the book she had drawn his attention to, but she had passed beyond it and was now staring at the man who had emerged from the bathroom behind the counter and was speaking intently to the store owner as his machine ground out a key. He was a tall, thick man, dressed in an outfit reminiscent of military garb. His jaw seemed slack, his thin-lipped mouth half open in dumb show, as he listened to the owner who then handed him the key.

Roger felt the skin on his face tighten, his eyes watering. He had recognized the shoes. My husband, she thought, the bastard, right here, right now. He can't see me, but I can see him. Soon, she thought. Roger lifted the lamp and moved to the counter. He nodded to the owner. Now he could smell the other, something rancid behind the scent of alcohol and cigarettes. He looked away from the owner, who was ringing up his purchase, gazed into the face of the other. Not one of the three smiled.

After a late dinner consisting of broiled lambchops dredged

in a little olive oil then rubbed lightly with Herbes de Provence and salt and pepper, this accompanied by sautéed asparagus spears and new potatoes baked in oil, garlic, and ginger sticks, Roger settled into his easy chair in the living room, a cup of fresh ground coffee and the morning's constructed crème brûlée in a custard dish on the table beside him, and read his paper.

Twice more the lights had gone out, then, in a brief while, had come back on. There seemed no reason to call. He knew he wouldn't get through. He spent these times in darkness, poised at the table, or sitting still with his paper in his lap.

He had taken up cooking since his transplant. Before that it had been TV dinners and various canned meats. Then he had discovered a complete Julia Child boxed set in one of his travels to a secondhand bookstore in the mall. He'd bought it, read it, and then embarked on what he thought of as a wonderful journey. I might become a cook, he'd thought, and so he had.

There was a good deal in the paper these days, much of it having to do with the new President and his accomplishments. He was a tall, handsome man, at least he liked to think of himself that way. But the campaign had taken its toll; his blond hair had thinned and turned gray, and a new softness had replaced muscle in his shoulders and hips. Even his behind now sagged in his finely tailored clothing, and his mouth was often pursed in an unattractive way, as it was in the photograph Roger was gazing at, one in which the President stood in front of a construction site, a large sign held up by some rough-looking men behind him. *America Has Been Made Great Again* the sign pronounced, somewhat awkwardly.

Very little had been made great, at least on the international front, as promised, in his first two years in office – the second year of his reign, Roger thought – but domestically much had been done, most of it having to do with security and surveillance: fear of the immigrant population, drug addicts, and domestic terrorists. Even in Roger's little town, the results of presidential edicts were in evidence. Cameras everywhere. Chips installed, often against individual wishes, in cars, shoes, phones, and even in houses and workplaces when just the vaguest suspicion was aroused.

And Roger knew this was only the beginning, for now the President had put forward his supreme court nominee, one to fill a vacancy in that august, though currently divided, body.

Alfred Bub Hawkins, known in his southern district as Big Bub, was a former mid-level official in the Ku Klux Klan. He had earned his law degree at a small Christian college, scoring tenth in a class of twelve, then had gone to work in his hometown, his practice consisting mostly of writing up contracts and notarizing documents, with a few divorce cases thrown in for good measure.

He was no great shakes. But he could write. He'd published a bevy of articles, all dealing with constitutional interpretation and its application regarding both central government powers and states' rights. His articles were deemed brilliant, at least by those in the president's coterie and the members of the senate that had been investigated and found culpable enough to be bent to his will. Yet it was rumored that it was Hawkins' wife who had written the articles for him.

Alma Hawkins was an uneducated housewife who liked to read. She had studied the Constitution and the Supreme Court opinions, both majority and dissenting, in great detail, until she had come close to memorizing them in the way some had memorized the Bible. She had also memorized the Bible and could quote it word for word, both the Old and New Testaments.

Roger had read the paper straight through. A few local arrests that seemed oddly unnecessary, some jargon about government construction projects, nothing at all of an international appeal. Still, he read on, his only interest piqued by the fashion section, new clothing, mostly for women, that seemed retrograde, very little for men there.

He'd finished his day's work on the new lamp, had carefully cleaned the small glass tulips that contained the miniature bulbs, a few of which had burned out and would need replacing. He'd have to shop for those, but that would come in a day or two. Now he was tired, though not exhausted, and decided he'd go up to bed and read a little before sleep. His bedroom was on the third floor, which was no more than an attic that he had refitted as a small study and bedroom. He liked the isolation, the coziness of the space, and felt oddly protected there, though why he needed protection was beyond him.

He had settled between the sheets in a seated posture, then reached for the chain on his bedside lamp. Nothing. A bulb, he thought, but when he felt for it, it was not there. How can this be? he thought. What the devil is going on? He rose from the bed and put on his robe, then moved through both the bedroom and his study, searching for any evidence that someone had been there. He could find nothing amiss. Tomorrow, he thought. I'll check the entire house. Then he went to the small storage closet where he kept his paper, pencils and pens and removed a new bulb from its sleeve. He returned to the bedroom then and screwed it in.

Back under the covers again, he reached for the book he was currently reading, *Our Bodies, Ourselves*, the chapter on violence against women. He managed to get through only a couple of pages before his lids were falling. Enough, he thought. Later. Then he pulled the lamp's chain, turned on his side, and in only a few moments was fast asleep.

Somewhere in the early morning hours, he had a dream that was not a dream but a gathering of memories that he had no recollection of when he awoke.

Early morning. Still dark. Could have been the salad, or the wine. Probably the salad. There are cracks in the ceiling. The cheap tulips he had bought, white, teardrop buds in the nightlight's soft gleam. The high pole with its miserable camera and flood. She could see it only vaguely through the open window, the curtains lifting in the soft, chemical breeze.

His smiling close attention to her needs. He had chattered across the table. Even candles. She can't move. She can move. But only her head. She's in the bed. Figures swaying in the room, furniture and shadows.

He had bent down over her, still smiling: "Are you happy now? I'll get what I want."

They had been married for six long years, and he had made the conscious choice, at the very beginning, to drift away from her, until she knew – his way of addressing her, a gradual hardening in his eyes, his distance in sex – that it was the money. Which was really very little, thirty thousand dollars from the sale of her deceased parents' house.

In the past year he had beaten her, pounding her in the ribs and kidneys, those thirty thousand dollars in his eyes. He was strong, and he would hold her by the wrist as he punched her. Through it all she remained stoic, at least she seemed so. She went to work at the coffee shop. She didn't socialize. She read books. And when she wasn't working, or reading, or cleaning, or fixing his meals, she spent her time hating him, wishing him dead.

He worked in construction, a small failing company of his own. Half a dozen men. Enough work to keep them alive, not much, though buildings were going up, and many were coming down to make room for the new. All this under a perpetual layer of smog and construction dust that blackened the town and its environs, causing the populace to move about in medical masks, their hair under their caps greasy and their faces and eyelids blackened. And he was looking for the big job, something to get him back on his feet again, and he'd told her he'd found something and was aiming to get it. And he'd told her that he loved her, repeatedly, after he'd beaten her. That smile. The obvious lie.

That evening, after the dinner and candles and wine, he'd left her. Put her into the bed. There was a meeting of his crew, he'd said. Discussion of the new jail that would replace the high school basement as the temporary venue for incarceration of those who were seen to defy, in any way at all, the new order. He had a small part in it, curbing and a sidewalk. She knew there would be drinking, possibly drugs, and women.

Fragments and regrets. Her eyes were alive. Her head seemed to be dying. She was tired. She needed sleep. She fell asleep. Ten empty minutes.

And when she awoke, she couldn't awake. She was awake, but only in her eyes. Fading cracks in the ceiling. Insubstantial shadows. I'm going away, she thought. Nightshade. She went away.

Roger awoke in earthquake. His bed was shaking, and when he sat up he saw that the whole room was rocking. He felt he was in a topsy-turvy fun house. His lamp teetered then fell from the table and bounced on the floor. He rose quickly, hearing a pounding down below, and slipped into his bathrobe, a lacy satin number that he had purchased in a small boutique at the mall. His wig, too quickly pulled on, had slipped down onto his forehead, and his slippers were on the wrong feet. The pounding continued, and he rushed down the stairs. It was the front door, shifting on its hinges. He opened it to find a small man in uniform and four large earth-moving monstrosities digging and banging their yellow scoops on the ground near his foundation. The man raised his arm and waved it above his head. The activity stopped, the machines belching and sighing into silence behind him. And in that silence the man spoke.

"What? What!" Roger said, his ears ringing.

"It's time we spoke," the man said, smirking, gazing at Roger's headgear and his strange attire, and they did, or rather the man spoke and Roger listened.

They wanted his house and they aimed to get it. The previous offer was no longer in place. Now it was twice that. The little man sat on the couch, his feet tap-tapping on the floor.

"Have you been having any problems with your electricity?" He asked this in an odd, conspiratorial fashion.

Roger didn't answer.

"I have the papers here. And the check." He produced them from the thin briefcase he clutched at his side.

It was a lot of money, and though Roger wished only to

drive the little prick out of his house, he swallowed his pride. He was surrounded by construction, noise and filth, and now the deal with the electricity.

"I have to think about it," he said.

"Yes, you do. But don't take too long."

"I won't. But now, how about leaving me alone."

The little man seemed about to speak, to bring forth further insinuations, but then he saw the look in Roger's eyes, nodded and left the house.

It was after dinner than evening, something light, a fillet of flounder, thinly breaded and coated with herbs, then pan-fried in butter, when Roger thought he heard something down in the basement. Actually, it was she who heard it first, then rocked their brain slightly to the side until Roger too caught it. I know who it is, she thought: his scent.

Roger rose from the table and went to the basement door, then climbed down the stairs.

The man was there, the one Roger had seen talking to the owner at the store. He seemed to be studying the walls. A heavy wooden beam ran across the basement ceiling, from outer wall to outer wall. It was supported by a couple of lally columns and hung low into the basement. Even Roger, who was only five-ten, had to duck slightly so as not to hit his head, and when the man turned, hearing Roger's approach, he had to bend down considerably. He did so, then came up smiling and extended his hand. Roger didn't take it.

"What exactly are you doing here? How did you get in?"

He was dressed in some sort of uniform, a breast patch, hard to read, identifying him as working for the government, Roger thought.

"Well, you see, I was sent in to check for any illegal devices. And the electrical." A sheepish smile followed this last statement, reaching for irony that wasn't there.

"It's nothing, just routine. I have a key." He held it out as a child might have, smiling as he showed his prize.

"But more to the point, I think I've got the contract to tear this place down. Not yet, of course. Not until the sale is completed. Will it be completed soon? I just wanted to have a look."

He was grinning then. Nothing snide, or conspiratorial. Just a grinning from and into a certain emptiness. Something wrong and primitively evil, Roger thought. It's him, she thought.

The man stared into his eyes as Roger moved closer, and when he was just inches from him, looking up, he saw her eyes where his had been.

"My God, I don't understand," he said, his voice squeaking. And that was the last thing he ever said.

Roger leaped up and rammed his forehead into the man's startled face, and as he fell, he hit him again, this time skull to skull. There was a sharp cracking, a rush of blood. He was dead then, sprawled out on the basement floor, and Roger smiled, or she smiled. And it was done.

They painted a section of the beam with his blood. Then they called the police, who came, a half dozen of them, almost immediately. Each wore a large breast patch that read *America's Great Again*.

He'd heard a sharp crack from the basement while he was eating dinner, then found the man, bloody and broken, on the basement floor. He must have hit his head against the low beam. The police seemed to know that he was there. They asked Roger if he intended to sell the place, and he replied in the affirmative. Each shook his hand. The ambulance came and they took the body away. There would be no further investigation.

Later that night, Roger placed two large pillows, end to end, in the bed beside him. Then, once the covers were pulled up over him, he lay on his side, snuggled up, spoon fashion, against them. One tucked in against his stomach and groin, the other, hugged close, rested against his cheek. He breathed in the smell of eucalyptus, the scent she had used most frequently throughout her too-short life. It was quiet now, no construction, no helicopters, no sirens.

"Did you mind very much killing him?"

"I didn't. You did."

"Well, I guess you're right. The instrument. But the intention."

"Did *you* mind it?"

"Yes and no. Mostly no."

"Well, at least *America's Great Again*."

"And will you really sell this place? Will you move away?"

"Yes. I've decided. Out of this town. Into the country."

"Where it's quiet."

"Yes."

"Can I come with you?"

"Well, of course. There is no alternative."

"Good."

"We'll dress well in bib overalls, a blue cotton work shirt, pearl buttons."

"And a straw hat, with a bright red ribbon around the crown."

"A little garden. Herbs and fine greens."

"I like to cook."

"And in the evenings, a good brandy. Books. A little TV."

"Then off to bed."

"I'm tired. It's been a busy day."

"But what about cakes and pies? Ice cream and custard?"

"All that as well. Anything we like."

"I can bake. I'm good at that."

"And I can help."

"No two have ever been this close."

"As one."

"But, boy, am I tired! A long busy day."

"Well then."

"Goodnight."

"Night. Sweet dreams."

The Old Hand

THIS HAND HAS traveled, into water in a basin, into swimming pools and into the sea, in salt where the father's ring slipped from one of its fingers and was lost forever, years ago. Outwardly, the hand could belong to a twenty-five year old; but inside, the structures of vessels and tendons, allowing the hand to reach out for a woman, there are years spent in holding, squeezing, and the stroking of many dog's heads and muzzles, and wishes for the fingering of various musical instruments.

When the hand moves, the mind seems to direct it, but this is not true, though it is true partially. The mind. But the history of endeavors is in the hand itself, eighty years of it. Holding instruments for eating and repair, for gesturing, for handling sandwiches and, delicately, women's apparel.

In fending off attacks with a closed fist, in the shoveling of snow through generations, in bowling and fishing, in the events of everything ever touched, and in scalding and blistering. The hand remembers in the five digits and the palm with its lines of nostalgia. The hand can see, and hear, even on the floor of this room, where it crawls along the sofa's edge, and one man stands at the window, the other in the plush chair. Even if they see it, they don't believe it.

At the window in a dark, rumpled suit.

"Did you take care of the old woman?"

"Yes."

"And the money?"

"It's right here, in the bag. The jewels too."

The hand moves carefully across the rug, like a crab. Fingers caress the soft leather.

"Did you see that?" the man at the window asks.

"What?" the other replies.

"Something moving across the rug."

"Look. The job is done. She's dead. Don't be imagining things."

The hand pauses beside the bag. Previous lost memories lurch up in its fingers, its sweaty palm. She is the one from his childhood, the one he loved.

"Did you wipe down the place? The bedroom?"

"Yes. Of course."

The man turns from the window and looks at the other. The hand sees the gun as his coat drifts open. The other one sees it too and rises from the chair.

They were children, and she was beautiful. Her name is embossed below the bag's handle. They swam together in the placid lake, teenagers, water flowing between splayed fingers. The hand remembers it all: her silken hair; the grease on the barbecued chicken; their parents' laughter and knowing smiles; her wet leg brushing against his in the warm lake, electrically; lying on the sand under the stars; her jade necklace against the white skin at her neck; once again, her silken hair. It is gone, and yet it is here again. The hand is eighty years old. Her body, now dead, is also eighty. If only a hand could weep.

"In the future," the man at the window says.

"What?" the other replies, his hand searching in his jacket pocket.

There is no future, the hand thinks. Only the past.

"In the future? No more murders. It makes for difficulties."

"Like these?" the murderer says.

"Like these," the man at the window answers, reaching for his weapon.

The hand scuttles across the floor, heading for the other's leg. He remembers her. He loves her.

A shot rings out as the man at the window fires. The other topples to the floor, the hand holding tight to his ankle, before the bullet hits.

"What!" the man at the window calls out, as the hand climbs up on the fallen man's clothing and reaches for his throat.

The man at the window grabs the bag and rushes to the door.

"What?" the fallen man squeaks out as the breath leaves him. The hand, given its years of knowledge and love, holds tight.

Nora's Research Club

I HAVE OFTEN wondered about the variety of sexual positions, and a while ago I set out to catalogue them. I stayed away from bondage, S&M, and other sick materials, wanting to concentrate on the healthy, those positions that play a part only in conjugal affairs. It took me a good long time to compile my list, one that was only articulated in words. Visual depictions would come later, I hoped, since I had no ability when it came to drawing. My list grew until it ended with one hundred and nine, some of which might bring excitement, others that promised no more that tedious preparation and tortuous body manipulations. Of the latter, Nora and I did the best we could. At our age, we were no longer athletic. Arthritis and various muscle conditions made such movements quite difficult, at times preventing them altogether. I'm eighty-two. Nora just turned eighty.

Each weekday evening, promptly at six-thirty – we're early to bed and early to rise – we attempted at least three. Such work, if I can call it that, taking us to nine at the latest. We recorded our sounds, and I took notes upon the completion of each one. There were problems, of course, awkward positioning, even boredom at times standing in the way of arousal, and we often experienced pain that made it difficult to arise from bed when we awoke in the morning.

Still, we soldiered on, and in the eighth week, shortly after our weekend respite, which we spent just lying around exhausted, reading, falling asleep in our chairs, our heads dropping in front of the TV, we came upon something most interesting, a rather fragile ritual that gave us such shocking pleasure that we could hardly keep ourselves from passing out. I will try to describe it here, which will be difficult as I work to remove the most concupiscent details.

It involved a goldfish and a wooden implement for scratching the back. There was a highchair and a small goblet of heated oil that was edible. Olive oil? I don't think so. Nora took care of such matters, and she gathered and provided whatever tools, liquids and balms were required with, I must say, a high degree of enthusiasm. She even whistled while she worked, a new lightness in her gait.

To continue. The goldfish was presented to Nora, where she sat in the high chair. It was a large goldfish indeed, and it was all I could do to hold onto its tail while it wiggled away. I stood between Nora's legs as I worked at this, and she gently applied the backscratcher.

Our union followed, of course, but before we positioned ourselves for that welcomed task, Nora found another place for the goldfish, offering it to me, a line tied to its broad tale for tugging. My God! I must say, it was magnificent. I shook like a wet dog! Nora delivered herself in a flood!

In the morning I woke up troubled. Had I missed something in the first seven? Was my list inaccurate? I was unsure as I went back and studied those first weeks, worried that we might have to start all over again, a daunting prospect to say the least.

Happily, I found nothing that I couldn't correct with a few strokes of the pen. Each alteration, which was an addition, had to do with narrow objects and a variety of other implements that might be added. I discussed this with Nora. Should we start all over again? She only smiled, then said, "No way! I want to head onward. And upward!"

We agreed, and agreed too that I must study the great variety of available accouterments and apply them, though sparingly, to the list and future enactments of it.

And so time went by, week by bloody week, and when we reached week seventeen, which was close to fifty positions, we decided to take a break and headed off to Paris for a month, where we discovered yet other considerations, ones that involved various foreign settings and objects, things like French furniture, window seats, rough marble counter tops, and appliances, considerations missed entirely on my list. Such exotic placements were only a fake of the foreign at home. Consider the bidet, for example.

We didn't take advantage of such things. This was vacation after all. We jotted down notes and spent the rest of the time attending plays and concerts and recuperating. We traipsed around that wonderful City of Light, Nora pushing my weary bones, getting me out on the streets every damned day. We enjoyed our month immensely and came back home refreshed and with no desire at all to begin again.

"We need others," Nora said, and she was right. So we started a club, she and I in joint presidency.

Nora is a woman of small physical stature, and this, given my height and girth, might account for our occasional difficulties as we made our careful way through the list. Five-foot-two and quite slim, she moved around the house like a quick elf, keeping our wares, as well as our finances, in good order. And while I, with my pot belly and soft muscles, lounged around and watched TV, it was she who fashioned a rough draft of activities and devised a list of possible club members. She had become an energized dynamo, an almost frightening one, and I in my lazy complaisance felt a little intimidated by her. Still, the loving shackles that bound us together were unbroken.

At first there were few recruits. She'd placed a subtle ad in the local supermarket throwaway, the one that could be snatched up from a wire container while shopping. Nothing. Then she printed up flyers and slipped them into the mailboxes of those in the neighborhood who seemed possible. She'd researched the demographics. We were looking for couples our own age, even a bit younger, staying away from youth, fearful that they might get carried away in their potency.

The first couple that came knocking at our door were Lois and Bruce, known as Big Bruce, a couple a bit older that we. Lois was eight-six, Big Bruce eighty-eight. They lived just a few doors down, and though we'd never socialized, we knew them well enough to chat when we saw them weeding their plethora of flowers and plants as we passed by on our occasional walks. Lois, who was about the same size as Nora, would smile and chatter, and Big Bruce would continue with the weeding, joining our brief colloquy with remarks thrown over his shoulder.

And now here they were, ready and willing, and in our initial conversation they suggested others in the neighborhood who might join our endeavor. The club was to be called *Nora's Research Club*, and though I was a bit offended that Nora had more or less stolen my idea and my list, she had after all done most of the legwork, and I couldn't in good conscience fault her.

With the help of Lois and Big Bruce, others were quickly recruited: George and Rochelle, both of whom were stay-at-home coupon clippers; Julian and Beatrice, retired railroad workers; Oliver, known as Fat Ollie among his friend, and his wife Harriet; and a few others of our generation, or at least close to it. The group of recruits grew until we were twelve couples in all. And though we were joint presidents, it was Nora who carried the ball, explaining the list and procedures to the gathering at our first meeting.

Initially, three positions were parceled out, together with my crude drawings, to each participant, and almost immediately Geraldine Spalding, who was a Sunday artist somewhat efficient with smarmy watercolors, volunteered to refine the drawings, making the positions more detailed and explicit. "Will there be any swapping?" her husband, flamboyant Jimmy, had asked, a twinkle in his eye. "Absolutely not!" Harriet had answered, "Or else I'm outta here!" There was a brief verbal tussle, then Geraldine said, "Now, now. He was just joking. Shut up, Jimmy." There were a few other comments, some protective of couple's autonomy, others expressive of some reluctance. Nora just let these concerns be vented, wisely I saw, for in a while all the participants seemed at ease.

Though I was reluctant, both because of the exposure and my lingering exhaustion, Nora was insistent, brooking no refusal. It was our job to demonstrate, she said, and so at our second meeting, there in our living room, we took on number sixteen, a position we had tackled before, early on, with some success.

Sixteen was a western number, one that simulated a bit of horseback riding, and Nora had burned a CD as accompaniment to our procedures. I wore a cowboy hat, boots and spurs, and a set of reins was draped over Nora's shoulders, which I flicked to the music of *On the Trail,* from Ferde Grofé's *Grand Canyon Suite*, clip-clop, clip-clop, as Nora called out "Yippee!" and I answered with "Ki-yay!"

We worked it for a while, and though I was ready to quit in a short time, Nora pressed on, calling out various barnyard phrases, pressing me on as well, and so when we disconnected I was quite worn out, but Nora remained vibrant, jumping up nimbly and asking for questions from the members.

There were a few, mostly from the women, some having to do with weight and pressure. How was it that such a slight woman could bear the onslaught of her rather fat partner? What was the nature of the comedy in the event? Who makes the decision as to an ending? Is the position difficult to master? All these were answered by Nora with great aplomb. I stuck my two cents in only briefly.

After a few false starts, things went smoothly. We met once a week, and in each session four of the couples demonstrated an assigned position taken from the list, some becoming more accomplished than others. Harriet and Jimmy were especially enthusiastic, even triumphant, when they took on position number sixty-two, one in which Harriet, surprisingly limber for an eight-one year old, did a handstand leaning against the wall beside our painting of sailboats on a rough sea, while Jimmy sought comically for his venue. They were met with enthusiastic applause.

In time, the word went out, and others joined the club, until we had thirty-six couples and had moved our enterprise to the VFW hall on one of their dark nights, each pair chipping in for the rent. Nora was geared up for the move, expecting possible difficulties with the authorities. She'd studied the Constitution, the First Amendment's freedom of assembly clause, and she had readied herself for any engagement, though nothing was forthcoming. We were allowed to do our thing, so to speak.

As the months went by and the couples worked their

way through the list, there were suggestions for additions to it that rose up from the floor at our meetings. Some seemed absurd, but there were many reasonable ones, and the list began to grow until my initial one hundred and nine became two hundred with no end in sight. Music was added, and films were made, the best of them shown at the beginning of our sessions in order to stimulate the night's activities.

At my insistence, Nora and I slowly withdrew, pressing for the election of a board and a chairperson, a secretary and treasurer, though there would be little work for the last of these, only the rent and keeping track of the dues, those required for various accouterments.

We continued to attend the now bi-weekly sessions, and though Nora wanted to keep on performing, I said there'd be no more of that. I was tired of it all, the growing list, the ongoing enthusiasm of the participants, the theatricality that had tainted the purity of my research. I began to drift away from the whole business, Nora, my reluctant partner, drifting away with me. She managed to keep her hand in, though not her body.

She became vibrant and excited about most everything as time went by, coyly moving me into one or another of the positions only now and then. She took up racquetball, and as I watched her move swiftly around the court like a teenager, I was reminded of how lucky I was to be married to such a superior woman. Most recently, she's been talking about franchise, how we might copyright our idea and then sell it. We could become like McDonald's she said, and we both laughed. Still and all. Just maybe.

Now it's time for reflection. Sex is personal, and while there might be great fun in being observed in the acts, even when they are legitimized as research, there is no avoiding the thrill of exhibitionism, which is, to my mind, perverse. Adventure, coupled with loving kindness, that's the ticket. Let us all enact the list of positions. But let's do it in the privacy of our homes, in places abroad, on the lawn, in cars, on countertops, chairs and furniture in every room in the house. Love is the answer. Sex is the enactment of love.

The Last Gasp

SHORTLY AFTER HIS wife died, her ashes scattered in the manure surrounding the stalks of her beloved rose bushes, he found the ones he thought were friends had abandoned him, and he saw the little girl, lingering on the sidewalk under the heavy green branches of the old Norway pine, in front of his house.

It was winter. There was a thin dusting of snow on the ground, and he saw the girl's footprints moving down the sidewalk, then disappearing where the street angled off to the right and the window frame and wall blocked his view. There was a framed photograph on the wall, her friends and a few of his co-workers at a cookout in the forest preserve before her illness, years ago. She had toyed with photography and was not in the picture, though she had taken it. Her friends had abandoned him too.

The little girl just stood there, looking at the house. She was not dressed appropriately, and she seemed to be shivering. A short cotton dress, tennis shoes, a sweater, but no coat. Her legs and arms were stick figures. She needed a haircut. This was the third time in the last week that she had stood there.

Turning away from the window, he thought that they might be coming after him. Or maybe he had been shunned because of his last screw-up, the Sski business. Whatever. He had nothing to fear but fear itself. He'd heard that somewhere. He crossed the room to the stereo and put on the Mantovani. Then he poured a stiff Irish whiskey, splashing a bit of the liquor onto his fingertips, and settled into his plush easy chair and thought about his life.

Robert had worked in a hospital and was an orderly there. Orderly: an attendant in a hospital responsible for the nonmedical care of patients and the maintenance of order and cleanliness. He'd looked it up on Google, the better to understand both the responsibilities and the limitations of his job. It was these limitations that he constantly breached, edging into the medical realm as often as opportunity presented itself.

I fear that the portrait I've painted so far depicts Robert as an unlikeable and somewhat ignorant fellow. Actually, he was a nice guy. Take the little girl, for example. Though Robert had not gone out to comfort her or bring her a blanket to wrap herself in against the cold, he had been very moved by her presence, seen from his window. His heart went out to her, so to speak.

Robert's wife, before that very brief illness had felled her, was a woman of means and backbone. She ruled the roost. She insisted, because work is good for a man, that Robert continue in his orderly job, and for him this was a good thing. It kept him away from the house and from her.

"You stupid bastard!" she would say, when he did something stupid and even when he didn't.

They'd met at a garden party, a fundraiser for one of her charities. He was there only because the hospital staff that were free at that time were urged, in no uncertain terms, to go. The hospital was the recipient of large amounts of ready money from his wife's charity. Clear enough? Their meeting was not without turmoil. He had spilled the contents of his scotch and soda, wetting her party dress and his own raiments, soaking, mostly, into his crotch.

She took him into her mansion house, the one that before long would become his and he would sell for a good deal of money and move into a more modest though elegant dwelling, the one he was now in. And they laughed and talked and winked and smiled as they dried away the dampness, he awkwardly wiping at her soaked dress, she boldly working at his crotch. He was good-looking and seemed quite malleable, and she liked that. They were both in their mid-forties.

And so they married, and the years, just a few of them, went by. He only got in her way at home and occasionally at get-togethers, where he broke a plate or two and once tripped and fell into a table of food, scattering a bowl of caviar and a tureen of vichyssoise that splashed onto the floor causing a guest to slip and fall, whacking his head on the knee of a heavy, seated woman who gasped in outrage at this unconscionable behavior. His wife was just about ready to get rid of him and his maddening awkwardness when she fell ill and, before she knew it, died.

About the Sski: saturated solution of potassium iodine, six drops in eight ounces of water, stirred and applied into the nostrils in order to break up mucus deposits.

He was bored. He'd made all the beds on the ward, had cleaned up the bedside lockers, glasses and wastebaskets, and had scrubbed out the bathroom. The nurse was very busy, and as he was wandering around, looking for something to do, she told him to take the tprs: temperature, pulse, and respiration. This pleased him greatly, and he took on the task, working through the dozen or so men on the ward with pleasure and almost a little efficiency, and when he was finished, feeling very much like a doctor, he noticed the sounds coming from the old man in the solarium, some coughing and wheezing and a bit of gurgling, so he went to the foot of the man's bed and lifted his chart and read the most recent notation. Sski it noted, six drops in each nostril, prn, and it did seem prn to him. He saw the bottle and the eyedropper on the cabinet, had not read the instructions, and proceeded to attempt the ministration undiluted.

The man, half-conscious, turned his head away, and Robert's first drop and the second landed on his cheek, sending a red trail down to his jaw. Not to be deterred, Robert climbed up on the bed and straddled the man, then held his head in place and administered the drops. The old man's head was shaking all over the place, but Robert got all the drops in there, and when he was finished, he looked into the man's face and started to smile. The man's eyes grew large and he jerked once, then gasped and died, and Robert leapt from the bed, tripped, and fell to the floor. He recovered awkwardly, then headed to the nurses' station to report the calamity, but halfway there he stopped, went back to the dead man's room, searched out the fallen eyedropper, returned it to the bottle and checked the room for any disturbances.

The nurse rushed to the man's room, asking how Robert had discovered the death. "Oh," he said, "the door was open. I was just passing by. He seemed a little too still to me." She looked sharply at him, not really buying it, but then and in the following days he stuck to his story. He didn't quit his job right away, knowing that might seem suspicious. He waited awhile, then presented the doctor with his resignation. Too much to do, now that his wife was dead. "Her affairs, you know." The doctor smiled at him, but there was a bit of suspicion in his eyes.

I met Robert at a tea dance, just weeks after his wife's death. He had plunked himself down on a folding chair just hard enough to break the thing. He wobbled for a moment, then crashed down to the floor. I was close by and moved to him and helped him to his feet. Then we spoke for a little while, him telling me about the mansion he was trying to sell, me taking in his good looks and stature. He was tall and lean, attractively muscled, and his hair was especially nice, blond and full, with just a hint of gray at the temples.

And so we went out a few times, and once he'd sold the house and moved into the place he now inhabited, I moved in with him. I had no job and no prospects, and Robert was cute. It was a good move for me. I tried to keep the house in order, cleaning up broken plates and glasses, repairing damaged furniture, and on the day in question, I entered the living room to find him sprawled in his easy chair, Mantovani playing, and a tall Jameson and water, tilted slightly, in his hand.

"The girl," he said.

"Again?" I said. "How long?"

"Hours, I guess."

Then I went to the window and saw her there.

"It's snowing," I said.

And Robert rose and came to the window and stood beside me, looking out. A heavy snow was falling now, large flakes, distinct from one another, patterning the girl's sweater. Her dress was soaked, and her hair was now a snow cap. I could see how the snow was slowly filling her footprints, obliterating the marked passage identifying where she had come from.

"Good God!" Robert said, then repaired to the blanket chest in the guest room and returned with a down comforter.

I watched from the window as he stepped carefully down the steps. He slipped once and almost fell, but righted himself, then continued to wobble down the stone walkway to where the girl stood under the old pine tree, now snow-dressed as if ready for the application of Christmas lights. Good old Robert. He wrapped her in the comforter, then leaned down and spoke to her.

I can only imagine what happened next. I stood at the window and watched as the two walked, slipping and sliding, back in the direction from which the girl had come. Then they disappeared where the street bent off to the right.

She had said they needed a witness.

"A witness to what?" he asked.

"My mother's recovery. She was very sick, and now, by the grace of That Holy Spirit, she's better."

"What Holy Spirit?"

"That which the prophet CanMan demonstrated. His cans were runes or cards. *That* Holy Spirit has no other name."

That's a recitation, like in school, Robert thought.

"But why me?" he said.

"I don't know," she said. "The family sent me there."

Robert tripped going up the steps to the old house, and small as she was, and wrapped awkwardly in his comforter, she was able to grab his arm in a tight grip until he could recover. Then she opened the door and led him in.

The house was warm, and a rich scent greeted him as he entered the foyer, a mix of burning wood and perhaps incense. He knew nothing about such things. He had expected some icons, paintings, but there was no religion, only winter coats on hooks, a little dresser, but no mirror above it.

She led him into the living room with its high ceilings and broad, ornate molding. Two tall curtained windows facing the street let light in, and a log fire chuckled away in the large hearth that was placed prominently in what Robert thought was the north wall of the room, its marble mantle set with giant candlesticks and a gathering of curious knickknacks, small clay figures resembling mice or other rodents.

This is where her family waited, her father, two brothers, an old aunt, and her mother in a hospital bed far to the side of the couch on which sat the aunt and the two brothers, introduced as Barry and Philip. Her father, Constantine, was pacing, his hands alive, his face lifted to the ceiling. The girl's name was Val for Valery, the aunt was Aunt Edna.

"You've come at last!" the father said. "Would you like a toddy, some nibbles?" His arms flew up around him. He gestured toward various places in the room. He was tall and somewhat stooped and gaunt, yet under that thick mop of gray hair that fell down to his shoulders, his face held the glow of a much younger man.

"Why, yes," Robert said, referring to the offer of food and drink. He'd had no lunch, and he was hungry.

"Philip, get them!" the father called out, and Philip rose and headed out of the room, pissed off it seemed at being ordered around in this way. He was gangly and awkward, and Robert was drawn to him when he tripped on the old tattered rug as he was leaving the room. There you go, Philip, Robert said to himself.

"Who the dickens are *you*?" Aunt Edna said from her perch at the couch's end. "Have you come for the rent?" She was thin, small, and tough looking, and her wizened face resembled a coconut shell inset with cruel eyes and a thin-lipped slash for a mouth. Only her prominent hooked nose seemed human. Long, blue-painted fingernails, and she had tied up her thick bluish hair and placed a knot in it that rose up like a brain tumor, right in the middle of her head. A nod to some current fashion? Robert wondered. She seemed to puff up as she interrogated him.

"Now, Auntie," the father said. "We'll have no more of that!"

"Says you," Aunt Edna rejoined.

The other brother, Barry, seemed the favored son. He was of average height, buffed up, yet lean and handsome in a very conventional way. Philip's good looks were delicate, even mysterious, and his awkwardness promised a sweet vulnerability. He was interesting.

"This is your wife?" Robert said, his head turning to indicate the pale women in the bed.

"That she is! That she is!" the father said. "Look at her! She's recovered!"

She looks like hell, Robert thought.

"This is Belladonna! Bello! Donna! or *Bellissimo!* as we like to call her. Here! Come meet her!"

Robert went to the bedside, leaned over and greeted her wan, wasted face with a warm hello. She attempted to answer but was prevented by a thin stream of green vomit squirting from her mouth.

"Ah, the pea soup!" Constantine said. "No matter! No matter!" And he lifted a cloth from the metal hospital locker beside her bed and wiped the fluid away.

"I'm okay," the mother finally managed to say, in a weak gurgle.

"Okay! You see? Recovery!" Constantine lifted his hands and eyes to the ceiling, gazing up at something Robert couldn't see.

The mother was tucked in tight, her head resting on a heavy pillow, and Robert thought she might be approaching death or coming back slowly from that promised travail. He thought of the old man and the Sski, then swallowed that unpleasant memory when Philip returned to the room carrying a mug and a few crackers and nuts, some of which fell and plunked before he managed to settle the mug and the paper plate on the coffee table.

"No alcohol," Barry said from his place on the couch next to Aunt Edna. "We don't do alcohol."

Too bad, Robert thought, as he lifted the mug and took a big swallow. The taste was vile, and it was all he could do to get it down.

"Pretty good, huh?" Aunt Edna said, an evil twinkle in her eye.

"Yes, yes!" the father said. "Top-notch grog!"

The little girl had said nothing once they arrived. She stood off to the side, near her mother's bed, her eyes alight with an inner glow, looking between Robert and her mother, back and forth, as if she expected something. She had folded the comforter and placed it on a recliner that was aimed at the large television set affixed to the wall above the couch.

"Down to business! Down to business!" the father said, and Robert wondered just what this business might be.

"Boo hockey," Aunt Edna said.

"Now, now!" the father said. "This is about That Wholesome Spirit!"

"Not Wholesome. It's *Holy*. That *Holy* Spirit," Barry said from the couch, sporting a satisfied smile.

Aunt Edna quietly farted.

"Right you are, my son! Right you are!" Constantine nodded his bushy head, grinning, a bit of spittle dangling from the corner of his mouth.

Philip rose and moved to a place in the room where he could see Robert, no structure or other person intervening. He slouched back against the mantle, presenting his good side. The fire in the hearth caught a certain log and flared up, and Philip, feeling the sudden blast of heat on his buttocks and legs, leaped away from the mantle, caught his foot on the leg of a nearby table, and fell gracefully to the floor. Then he climbed slowly to his feet, dusted himself off and started all over again, looking for another place to stand.

"So you see, mister," it was Barry, speaking somberly from the couch. "The light of our dear spirit has returned to take up residency in my mother's body. She has been very ill, but now she is in recovery."

Doesn't look like it to me, Robert thought.

"Let us pray!" the father said, and the two brothers moved to form a loose circle containing Robert and their father. Aunt Edna and the little girl stayed where they were.

"Dear spirit of old-fashioned love and obeisance, he or she that loves way down even to any rodents" – he glanced at the mousy figures on the mantle – "and who has provided us with the required witness, hear our prayer which will soon be coming ...

"And here it is, O Thou, That Holy Spirit, high up above the clouds ..."

"Above the clouds," the brothers chanted.

"... and your prophet, the CanMan, also known as Kosta, which is short for my name, Constantine, that I am humbled to carry along with me and all of us, accept our joy at the recovery of Bello, your daughter, whom you have cured. So many months, well, weeks actually, have we labored over this sickness that we did not have but were infected by in Bello's presence. Tinctures, herbs, and all sorts of medical business. She couldn't eat, Father. She couldn't hold her bodily functions in check, though in delirium she spoke incessantly, uttering all sorts of profanity. Nothing attacking you, Father, just mountains of gutter utterances that shocked us all."

"Not me," Aunt Edna spoke up, then farted again, this time in one explosive burst.

"Nevertheless. In all this have you stood behind us, or in front of us, putting your invisible hands on our hands, guiding us toward cure. And now, finally, we have a witness, he who arrived a short time ago, guided here by the sweet young daughter Val, which is short for Valery."

He gestured emphatically, waving his arms in Val's direction, then Robert's, beckoning both to join the circle, which they felt compelled to do, and did, Robert edging himself between the two brothers. He banged shoulders with Phillip, and both of them staggered slightly. Val was across from him, beside her father.

"And now that the witness is here ..."

"The witness is here," the brothers intoned.

"... let us move to the bedside of your daughter, my wife, the mother of these three children, the niece by marriage on my side of the aunt."

"What?" Aunt Edna said, adjusting her thin behind on the couch.

And so, as a group they moved to surround the hospital bed in which Belladonna, Bello, Donna, or *Bellissimo!*, whatever the heck, Robert thought, rested. Then, at Constantine's unspoken yet gestured direction, they all leaned forward and gazed into the bed wherein the mother lay, almost as if in state, Robert thought, though observed as no official, but mother and wife. Then Robert felt woozy and had to grip Philip's thin arm to stay erect, tears fell from his eyes for no apparent reason, and the room seemed to darken as he worked to isolate images of it in his head.

Was it the grog? Robert thought. But I had only one taste of the nasty stuff. Then he looked down at the figure of the mother that lay before him. Her face was aglow with health. She had cast the blanket that covered her aside, exposing herself in street clothes, form-fitting black slacks, a gray cashmere sweater, patent leather low-heeled shoes.

"Dressed for arising!" Constantine said.

"Is this the witness?" the mother asked, her voice as clear as a bell.

"I am," Robert said, without thinking before he spoke.

"The witness," the brothers said in unison, and Philip put his arm around Robert's shoulder.

"Rise up now!" Constantine called out, a little too loudly, and the mother shrank back into the mattress for a moment. Then the side rail was lowered, and she threw her shapely legs over the side, slipped down until her feet touched the floor, then stepped away from the bed and the gathering.

"I'm thirsty. I'm going to make tea," she said over her shoulder as she crossed and left the room.

Robert had witnessed a miracle. He was sure of that, though he was still a little wobbly as the father and the two sons guided him to the couch where they all sat, pushing Aunt Edna to the side.

"Let us pray, again!" Constantine said.

"Quit pushing!" Aunt Edna exclaimed.

And they did pray. And Robert, not knowing the words, bowed his head and joined into the spirit of the thing. That Holy Spirit, he thought, and before long found the religion that he must have been seeking all along as much as he had been seeking the company of men without knowing it. He didn't know the name, the scriptures, or the hierarchy, but he knew of the miracle, the evidence of which entered the room carrying a cup of tea and a plate of chocolate chip cookies, then plopped down in a chair close to the fire.

And the praying continued, and in a while Robert picked up on repeated phrases and began to pray with them. His head cleared as all of them spoke, somberly now, of the one and only, That Holy Spirit, not some other, that one. Philip leaned in against him. He could smell the Hugo Boss perfume on his neck. Soon he was at peace.

Ah, well, what can I say? I stood at the window again. The snow was heavy now, and the big pine was leaning under the white weight. Then I saw Robert coming, stumbling, kicking snow into the air as he struggled to move swiftly down the sidewalk. He seemed to be yelling, throwing his arms up and about, and when he reached the house he stopped and began a joyful dance, unaware of the snow and the cold, even the shovelful of it that fell from a pine branch, soaking into his head and shoulders.

I went to the front door then and opened it. The freezing air hit me hard in the face.

"Robert!" I called out. "What's up?"

"I've been saved!" he screamed, still dancing, throwing his arms around in the falling snow. "That Holy Spirit! I've found him!"

And found yourself? I wondered.

The arrangement was that I'd look after the house. I'd live there, and he'd handle all the expenses. There was a trial, of course, well after Robert went to the police station and confessed to the Sski fiasco and what appeared to be the murder. He got himself a good lawyer, one his wife had used at various times before she died. Still, there was his confession, and the medical issue about some sort of malpractice or other.

The hospital was on the hook, and his dead wife's reputation, especially as a hospital donor, was on the hook. They wanted him to take the fall, and he wanted that as well, something about forgiveness for his sins, though there was only the one in question.

Involuntary manslaughter. Five years, possible out in three for good behavior.

I went to the living room bar and built a scotch and soda. Philip was curled up awkwardly on the couch, his hand grasping the leather cushion in order to keep himself from falling to the floor, and I fixed one for him as well. Then I put on some quiet jazz, Miles Davis, *In a Silent Way*.

There was no snow anymore, spring was approaching, and before bed we spoke about Robert, wondering what his life was like in prison.

Sex

I'VE ALWAYS HAD trouble with my name. It's not that I don't like it, nor do I spend much time considering it, but when I find occasion to speak it, in introduction, announcement, or even simple identification, the letters forming the two words feel foreign in my mouth and are not familiarly articulated, so that those who might write it down often misspell it, placing an e where an o belongs, an s instead of a z.

The reason for this awkward glossolalia, though unclear, has led me to other considerations, such as those dealing with aliases and pen-names, and most recently gender reassignments. What happens, for example when Karl Hulse becomes Carla Hulse or, more extremely, when Caroline become Gunther?

If the identification is made early in life, then it might be that the male appellation that hides the true female one, Freddy and Barbra, becomes foreign in the mouth, but if Barbra is only hinted at vaguely as a future possibility, then it too might be spoken, privately I assume, in a language awkwardly foreign. But names are only the tip of the iceberg, so to speak.

In a recent discussion with a friend, who insisted that sexual reassignment surgery should not be covered by either the government through Medicare and Medicaid or by insurance companies, I pointed out that plastic surgery, when elective, was at this point not covered, and that it might be useful to compare the two.

With few exceptions, such as breast augmentation, elective plastic surgery is for the most part diminishment. Face, neck, and other body parts are carved away. Care, brought about by years of living, is carved away, and wrinkles, sagging cheeks and eye bags are made to disappear, so that the figure is returned to an earlier time in a kind of cleansing by retrogression, a time in which internal sexuality is seen once again on the surface, or if sexual vibrancy had been lost, it was now back again, and one could enter the world as the one who once had it or had at least wished for it. This returning, which is a choice, does not come cheaply, neither psychologically nor financially, and choice, when it comes to the latter, is not covered by insurance.

Is gender reassignment surgery a choice? My interlocutor must be proposing that it is, and thus it should not be covered. And yet, for the subject of such surgery – Karl to Carla, Caroline to Gunther – such reassignment is a necessity, a movement from the inauthentic to the appropriate. The subject of plastic surgery returns to an earlier self, the reassigned to the authentic one, so that Carla and Gunther can participate in the world as who they are and not flounder there as fakes of real persons; and so, for the good of society, gender reassignment surgery should be covered by insurance, and elective plastic surgery, an ego-driven choice, presenting to the world a fake youthfulness, should not.

My argument is for the most part, of course, a shaky political one that has to do with liberation, and sexual liberation has been a concern of mine for many years, ever since I discovered I was Consuela in the body of Javier and accomplished, at no small expense, the change. I was only nineteen at the time, and while in recovery I began a study of various sexual anomalies. I read Krafft-Ebing, Lenz and Kinsey, looked into Magnus Kirschfeld, and even examined

various forms of pornography and molestation. Then I
entered college, receiving a degree in experimental psy-
chology and one in social work. I'm thirty-six at the present writing and have for five years now been a board-certi-
fied sexual therapist practicing under the name of Doctor
Consuela Lopez. My doctorate was acquired through the
mail, and though I am a woman of Latin origin, most of my
patients are gringos.

Here, then, I present three of my case histories. I've
selected these because thinking of them still gives me professional pleasure. I have, of course, changed the patients'
names, and have included my own comments, to give flavor to the narratives, in brackets.

Edward Colcheck was a thirty-five-year-old accountant, a
large man who obviously spent a good deal of time behind
his desk. He was soft in body and sported a significant
paunch, and he seemed to be somewhat out of breath when
he arrived. I ushered him into the easy chair across from
my desk, where he sank into the leather cushions, and I
studied his face in order to ascertain a hint of his character. He seemed at ease, though I suspected that, at any
moment, he might turn belligerent.

"So why have you come here?"

"Well, there's really nothing wrong. It's just that my
wife thought it might be a good idea."

"And?" [I was drawing him out.]

"It's the sex, I guess. I like to do it under the bed."

"Doesn't it get crowded down there?" [*Ay, Caramba!* I
thought.]

"It's only me and my wife!" [Here was that belligerence.]

"No, no! I meant the space. Isn't it a little tight?"

"I would call it cozy."

"I can see that, cozy. But what about your wife? She sent you here, after all." [I was prodding him.]

"I came of my own free will." [His tone was cold, almost accusatory.]

"I'm asking about your wife."

"Well, she does it, you know. But she really doesn't like it. She's bigger than me, and she hits her head on occasion."

"On the floor?"

"No. On the slats. It's a platform bed."

"So, she is on top?" [I could see a hint of embarrassment in his eyes. He feared the coming sex talk.]

"Yes, that's true. I feel protected that way, covered."

"Do you undress under there?"

"No, no! We put our clothes on top of the bed. The lights are off."

"So, you really don't see each other."

"No, but we feel each other."

"Are you sure? Given the tightness, maybe you're feeling yourself."

[He hesitated, having no answer for that.]

"I want you to try something," I said. "I want you to plug in a nightlight. Then only get under the bed up to your necks, both of you. Make sure she can see your face and you can see hers."

"I don't have such a light."

"Buy one."

He returned a week later.

"Well?"

"It was okay, her face and all. But she caught her nightgown on one of the slats and ripped it. It was her favorite."

"But you said you put your clothing on top of the bed!" [I spoke in a surprised way.]

"Nightgowns! I never said we were, you know, like, naked!" [He was getting angry.]

"It could have been your wife's back! She could have cut it on the slats."

"That couldn't happen."

"Okay, but what if it did?"

"I don't understand the problem."

[It was time to lay things out.]

"Sex has various facets. It involves touching, of course. But it also involves seeing, and even talking. One must display the loved one's body, and your wife must display yours. You must look into her eyes. You must talk to her. You must fight against your own pleasure, concentrate on hers. These and many other practices are necessary, both for pleasure and for satisfaction, and possibly even for love. Go home. Rip away your nightgowns. Keep the lights on. Give it a try, both for your sake and for hers."

[He left the session with uncertainty in his eyes.]

The following week.

"Well?"

"Good Lord! It was really something!" [He was jubilant, as he plopped down into the chair and crossed his legs. He was grinning.]

"You both enjoyed it?"

"Yeah, sure. Oh boy, did we!"

"You looked at each other, and you talked?"

"Yeah, yeah. We did everything!"

"And no embarrassment?"

"Hell, no! We loved the romping and talking! We loved our bodies and the things they could do!"

"And where exactly did you do it?"

"In our daughter's playroom. On top of her stuffed animals, surrounded by all her dolls!"

[*Caramba!* I thought once again.]

Retired Rear Admiral John "Cush" Flake was a sixty-two-year-old white male born into great wealth. He was a tall, thin man, ramrod straight, who entered the office and looked around as if he owned the place. Before I could direct him to the chair, he strode over to it and sat down, then he removed a pipe from his suit jacket, fussed with it for a few moments, then struck a match and puffed away.

"The smoking lamp is not lit, Cush." [I used the Navy jargon and addressed him informally in order to take control of the session, and he slowly removed the pipe from his mouth and covered the bowl with his hand. A few wisps floated up between his fingers.]

"Sorry." [He glared at me, though uncertainly.]

"Time to get down to business. Your intake suggests some sort of language problem?"

"Well, yes, and I'm absolutely sure I don't understand it."

"Can you say what it is?"

"Baby talk." [His voice had moved from stridency to a whisper.]

"What about it?

"I can't seem to stop doing it." [Frustration now in his words.]

"Can you give me some examples?"

"I don't wanna do it." [He seemed to be pouting, which was odd given his military bearing.]

"Look here," I said. "This is sex therapy. That's why you've come here. Let's have it!"

"Well, you know, my wife is dead. And mostly I have sexual relations with prostitutes."

"Yeah, so?"

"I say things, you know. To them, I mean."

"Attention, Admiral!" [He stiffened slightly.] "Let's have it, sailor!"

"Well, it's just things. 'Do you like my little pe-pe?' 'Can I touch your cu-cu?'" [His voice was now that of a small child.] "Just thingies to say."

"This is nonsense," I said. [I wanted to shock him.] "What about your wife? How was that?"

"What do you mean?"

"My God, man! The sex! How was that?"

"Well, there wasn't too much, I guess. Maybe you could say she was cold? Something like that, I mean. Maybe it was me. I don't know."

"You must get a grip, Cush. Seems you're afraid of the body, the way a child might be. You must begin to call it as it is."

"What do you mean, the names? Things like penis and vagina?"

"The words, but not those words, will set you free!"

"What do you mean?" [He was honestly confused.]

"You must call it as it is. 'Do you like my big cock? I like to feel your sweet pussy.' These are not dirty words. They're the appropriate ones. Talk is good. You've already got that. But your words are pushing sex away rather than engaging in it. The prostitutes will let you say anything. They don't care. But if you get the talk straight, you may find other women. Not prostitutes, but ones you can engage with, and they can engage with you in a relationship."

"Okay," he said. "I'll try."

[He cancelled the next three sessions.]

Our second meeting, a month later.

"I've missed you, Cush. What's happening?"

"Sumbitch," he said. "I've been getting more ass than you can imagine! There's pussy everywhere. I get a hard-on just thinking about them!"

"Wow, wow! Not in public!" [*Santa Madre de Dios!* I was beginning to realize I'd gone too far, had unleashed a monster.]

"Hell, yes, in public! They all like it, all those beauties! They want cock! Every one of them! And I've got it. Right here!" [He quickly uncrossed his legs and grabbed his crotch. He was grinning. His tie was waving as he gyrated in the chair, and saliva was running from the corner of his mouth. Delusional, I thought. Quite out of his head.]

"Stop that, Cushie! Right this minute!" [I'd picked up my ruler and was slapping it into my palm, glaring at him in the way of a stern third-grade teacher. I'd pushed the button.]

"I sorry," he said. "I a bad, bad boy. I so sorry." [He had slouched down in the chair, released his crotch, and was cringing. Regression to that baby talk, I thought. Then the door opened and the boys in the white coats came in and took him away.]

Madre mia!

Barbra Bogardus was a seventy-five-year-old mother and grandmother. She was slim and athletic and had been married to her husband Jimmy for more than fifty years, the two living together in the farmhouse she had inherited from her father years ago. Dressed modestly in a loose dress that looked to have been fashioned from those flower sacks of old, she stepped gracefully across the floor and settled into the chair across from my desk. In the paperwork she had presented as a "nymphomaniac". Her term. Clinically, that designation is no longer in use.

"I like your hair."

"Oh, thank you!" [My ego overtook my professionalism momentarily, and for a few seconds it was unclear who was to speak next. Then she did.]

"I'm really here because of my husband."

"What about him?" [Her hair was quite nice too, as was her carefully applied makeup.]

"Well, he's tired. He's getting old. He's almost eighty."

"And?" [She was slow in getting to it.]

"There's only the two of us, you know."

"Do you get out and around?" [I was playing her game.]

"Occasionally. Shopping. Things like that."

"And is it women and men, or just one of the two?"

"Oh, no! It's only men."

"Straying?" [As if a tease, but she could see I was serious.]

"No, never! It's only him." [Adamantly.]

"How often?"

"All the time! Everywhere!" [She was giving in, letting it out.]

"In the bedroom?"

"Sometimes. But on the floor, the kitchen counter, the bathroom, out in the yard, in the car (we have a comfortable old Buick), up against the wall, dancing naked in the living room and on the couches and chairs in there, just anywhere."

"Under the bed?" [I recalled another case.]

"Of course not! That's silly! How would we move?" [She seemed close to hysteria.]

"And your husband?"

"That's the point! He's getting tired. Maybe sick of it all. I can't tell. I get very excited, you know." [As she was now, though she had slumped down in the chair and was shaking slightly, almost as a child might, this beautiful, dignified woman. *Ayyy pobrecito!* I was feeling her frustration and pain and had to force my professionalism.]

"*Te gusta?* Sorry. I mean, do you enjoy it?" [I knew the answer.]

"No, no! Not a bit! I hate it!"

"And that, of course, is the problem. Go home. Think about that. What it is that you enjoy. Our time is up. Come back in two weeks."

Two weeks later.

"Good afternoon." [She seemed sure of herself as she moved to the chair and sat down, the box she was carrying resting on her lap. Maybe I had struck the right chord.]

"Hello, hello!" [She was perched at the edge of the seat and was smiling.]

"Relieved?"

"Oh, my, yes!"

"And the sex?"

"Well, my husband is really relieved. Just now and then. And mostly on the bed."

"And do you like it?"

"Somewhat. Now that I've found the real pleasure."

"Which is?"

"This." [She tapped on the box with a finger. I knew what it was. I could smell it.]

"What kind of stuff?" [We were playing the same teasing game as before.]

"Everything! All the time! It's about all I do!"

"Okay. Let's have it, Barbra."

"Here I come!" [She rose to her feet, the box in her hands, and sauntered, hips swinging in a very provocative way, the few feet to my desk. It seemed to take a long time. Her tongue licked her lips in a lascivious manner, as she stared straight into my eyes, and when she reached the desk she handed the box over as if it were herself surrendering.]

"Open it." [She grinned, and I did. And there they were, a baker's dozen, each lovely cupcake frosted in a unique way, and each holding a letter, the thirteen spelling out C-o-n-s-u-e-l-a-L-o-p-e-z. I lifted the C and took a bite. She shivered.]

"My, oh my. This is delicious!"

"I thought you might like it. This is what I do now, all the time." [She slowly pushed her long hair away from her face, and I think she winked.]

"Baking?"

"Oh, yeah! Cakes, pies, muffins, brownies and scones, chocolate chippers, sticky buns, and on and on. You name it! And, of course, cupcakes!" [She was drooling.]

"And you like it?"

"God, yes! I love it! It's so sexy!"

"There you go! It's good to like the things you're doing." [I rose then from my chair and reached across the desk and took her sweaty hand in mine. Our time was up, and I watched her as she sashayed across the room and left me there, smiling.]

So. Three case histories that demonstrate how rich and interesting sex therapy can be. I love my job. And my patients too.

Tonight I'll go out to dinner with Don. He's a banker, but I don't hold that against him. We'll eat, then go to his house for dessert and brandy. Then we'll talk into the morning's first hours. We might fall asleep, and I might spend the night. There will be no sex.

It's strange, I guess. When I was sixteen, wanting to be the Consuela that was hiding inside my Javier, I was obsessed with sex. It didn't matter: trees, mattresses, the bathroom of course, tabletops, in the closet with my mother's fur coat, holding my sister's underwear up to my nose. *Ay, no me gusta!*

Don is my best friend, though as Javier I would have been all over him. It's the sex itself. After the hormones, the operation, the medicine, and the pain as I recovered, slowly becoming Consuela, I began to understand the woman I had become, both in spirit and body. I was a woman whose pleasures are taken in books, music, gardening, and peacefulness. I felt isolated, and I liked that. Sex meant nothing to me, insignificant when placed beside music. Or books. Or the many wonders of the world, learned and observed.

And so I am celibate, beyond the usual connotation suggesting denial. I'm simply not interested, and I feel liberated from sex, that known to me through Javier and his grubby passions. There is life after his death, and I set out to take it, in studies, in art and literature, solitude, and in the strange and wonderful worlds presented to me by my patients.

And so it is. *Adios!*

The Liar

FOR MOST OF his life he had prided himself on his honesty. In college, at his various workplaces, in his family (just the two of them, he and his wife). And even at thirteen, when he had beaten up another boy and stolen his bike and had denied the whole thing, protesting his complete innocence often, and loudly, he had learned the lesson: lying has consequences.

He had been caught out, of course, and had been stripped then chained to the damp wall of what seemed a dungeon that was situated below the cells in the village jail. The Chief (they called him the Sheriff in the village) was a rustic pig farmer who had squeaked through the competition when his opponent, the father of the boy whose bike had been stolen, died. He had a warm relationship with his pigs.

The Chief beat him, tried hard to bugger him, but the boy's tough, young, virginal glutes had flexed and repelled the onslaught. Starvation, dehydration, pig shit, even a crude form of waterboarding. Three long weeks. His mother had died of a heart attack just a few days into his incarceration, and his dog had run away. She was a beautiful German Shepherd, her eyes the deep blue of his mother's, now dead, and he had held her, and he had loved her.

Then his grieving father, while out on a slow walk in farmland, while weeping for his wife and son, had come upon the Chief mounting one of his pigs. He was exposed, and the boy was rescued and was sure he'd never lie again, not once.

He lied, of course, as all of us do. He lied about his wife's new dress, calling it beautiful when he didn't think it was. He lied about the pastor's sermon, the taste of Aunt Betty's cake, the presented politics of others, both at work and at home and out in the world.

He was late for a very important date, a meeting dealing with the necessity of letting some workers at the firm go, a budgetary matter. He had reached for the snooze button and had shut the radio alarm off by mistake. Good thing the traffic was light, or he would have been even later. All seats around the long table were taken, but for his, an absence that seemed monstrous, and heads turned as he entered.

Premeditation? Well he *had* reached under a fender to grease his hand. They all were silent.

"A flat tire," he said. "I'm so sorry." Then he showed them his palm. The lie didn't work. He was one of those fired on the very next day.

This was different, but for the bike fiasco years ago, when he was young. In earlier cases he had lied so as not to hurt feelings, and this seemed acceptable. But this time it was thought out and spoken only for his own benefit. Was this the first time? Were there others, conveniently forgotten, that might have severely accused him were they remembered? It was useless, he knew, to look back, and he vowed to watch his step from now on. He had some inherited money, a good deal of it, and he was now sixty-five years old and looked ahead to the freedom of his forced retirement.

Then there was that garish affair. He and his wife had been invited to a charity auction held at a crude, wealthy man's house. What was on the auction block, among other things, was a painting from the man's collection. It was a beautiful religious piece, one of that great number of renderings of the Madonna and Child. But this one was different. It was a modern painting, the mother in street clothing, the child holding a stuffed rabbit, his little Adidas and drooping sox resting on the fabric covering his mother's knees. She wore a little hat.

"Would ya like ta see more?" It was the voice of the wealthy owner addressing the small gathering, six or seven people, who were admiring the painting. "Le'me take ya in the house to see my best."

His best was a mess. There were paintings of ducks and fish (unintended cartoons), of ladies dancing in crudely rendered landscapes, of boats on turbulent seas awash in the whipped cream crests of suspended waves. Godawful, he thought, as the owner paused before a still life and began his lecture.

Here was a painting of a bowl of grapes that looked like pale green marbles of shattered glass, or oblong sticky tears, certainly not delectable. Beside the grapes stood a silver Victorian table lamp with a clashing brown paper shade, and to the right of this were globs of various color, some sort of large urn or maybe a hat rack, that resembled lumps of fecal matter that had been ejected from a grazing cow. All this was perched on an antique chestnut table that looked more like cardboard than wood.

"This is my very best. The artist's name ya see, right there in the corner. I know him. He's a friend of mine. He gave me this painting for my birthday." He smiled and raised his hand to the painting's side. "So. What do ya think?"

Some raised their heads and nodded, others simply

smiled. It had been his birthday after all, a gift of celebration, and though the painting was awful, no one deemed it inappropriate, if only thorough gestures, to lie. But for him.

"It's a piece of crap," he said softly, while some in the group tried to shush him. And a little louder, "I really can't understand what you see in this mess." His statement invited no discussion. There was silence in the room, and he turned and gathered his wife and left. The truth had set him free, momentarily, but the dreams didn't.

He must have been thirty-five and single and well on his way to success when the dream, which seemed a reality from memory, and maybe it was, started. He was in a bar close to home, and he knew it was late afternoon because of the slant of sun coming through the draped windows.

There was a couple behind him at a table, and he was able to see them clearly in the mirror behind the bar. He could hear them, the man especially as his voice rose in anger, but only a few words formed themself for understanding. The woman was weeping; her long blond hair, that fell down in two thick waves, parting like a theater curtain, so he could see her wet cheeks. She was beautiful, almost a Madonna, in her creamy skin, those deep blue eyes, and her naturally full lips.

Her companion banged his fist on the table, then turned and left, and in the dream he also turned, on his stool, to face her. There was great clarity in the space between them. Tables and chairs, silver napkin holders, a salt and a pepper, even the dingy tiles on the floor, each had commandeered its space and was resting there, confident and a little smug. And she? She was irresistible in her figure and fine clothing, even as she held her hair across her face and wept into it. She was beyond him in her elegance, and he knew this, and yet he rose from his stool and glided across the floor to where she was seated.

She looked up at him, her face aglow with tears. Her eyes were questioning, a little fearful and suspicious. He smiled as he reached for her hand.

"It's okay. Don't worry, my dear. I'm a minister."

Then the dream came crashing down into the bedroom, shards flickering before his eyes as he awakened and opened them.

A time for lies. All his life the truth had been his challenge, and by conquering lies he had elevated it, feeling ethical and almost holy, qualities no others, in his sense of things, possessed. And yet the dreams continued, and in their aftermaths he was forced to re-evaluate his character and his past. The lies had become natural and were no longer delivered for personal gain, though gain there always was. Many times, maybe all of the time, the lies had to do with identity. "I'm a minister," of course, but usually it was more subtle than that. It could be something from the personal past, vague comments hinting at child abuse (to garner sympathy and even mystery), or what his grades had been like, often slightly elevated, in the schools he attended (to accrue a little admiration), or the small and illusive, like the smooth ordering of a mixed drink he had read about but never had.

People lie with every breath they take, at least the mature ones do. They lie to themselves about their mortality. They lie about their need for drugs, cigarettes, and liquor, about their mastery and their command of things. Most poor people don't lie, for they have no prospects to be lying about. Rich people lie about greed, even as the pleasures slip away, and they become bored, then lie about that. His grandmother never lied, at least he didn't think she did. Political discourse is full of lies. Most attacks are ad hominem, and facts and ideas have no place in both civil discourse and bigoted exclamation. Most animals don't lie, but the ones that do often get away with it. Karen Cole had lied to him, saying she had a previous engagement when he offered to accompany her to the prom. Richard Nixon and Donald Trump lied so often that before long their lies became their characters, which was the truth. The Grim Reaper doesn't lie.

And so he dreamed about his lies, recovering them, amazed that there had been so many and so frequently told. I am a liar, he thought, and have always been one, and as the days went by he became ill in that knowledge, which was itself a lie, one that brought on self-pity and the feeling that he was unique. He knew he was slipping away, feeling that his lies were feasting upon his organs. The doctors and nurses lied to him, even his wife, who smiled with tears in her eyes and told him she was sure he'd get better.

At the funeral home showing, where he rested in his casket, relatives passed by, looking at him where he lay. One of his aunts, Rebecca, whom he had loved, spoke to those beside her.

"My, my. What a nice job. He looks the way he did in life."

Which was, of course, a lie.

The Wall

AFTER MORE THAN a year of architectural and political dis-
agreement, the section of transparent wall rose up along
the border, yet ran for only a few miles separating America
from Mexico.

"It's only the beginning. You can believe that," the President tweeted from one of his many golf courses in the east.

Eighteen feet high, the wall was situated between moats
containing alligators in slimy waters in which gentle wave
action was provided by buried, watertight machinery acti-
vated at a distance. You could see right through it at certain times of the day, could spend awhile observing those
standing on the other side, looking at you and shifting
their bodies in order to view that variety of things behind
you. Then the sun might sink or rise, casting a glow on the
wall's surface, and you could see only your own face looking back at you from what, moments before, had been the
other side.

Alfred often walked along the wall in the later afternoon
and early evening, the transparent surface opaque, the sun
again, and nothing visible but the shadow of his own passing. He was born and raised in Bisbee, Arizona, just four
miles from the small border town of Naco. Poor as a
church mouse, he lived out a lonely existence in his parents' ramshackle dwelling, "up the divide," at the end of
Tombstone Canyon Road, the house tucked into the first
pines. His father was dead. His aged mother had returned

east to live with her sister, and now the house, three rooms outfitted with failing plumbing and occasional electricity, was his.

Alfred was sixty-two years old and existed on a few dollars of disability, garnered as the result of a hip-cracking fall on unrepaired pavement at the door of the pool hall on Main Street. Repair was the responsibility of the town, and so this bit of money came his way. He walked with a pronounced limp, and he had no job, unless the gathering of bottles and cans for deposits could be named as such.

He got to the wall, on his thumb, three afternoons a week, and in short order was riding the four miles in the cars of the same three people.

Jack Bean was a cowboy, plain and simple. He rode the range, a gas-powered one in a restaurant in town that specialized in huge steaks with all the fine fixin's. He spoke of the old days, and though he was ten years ahead of Alfred, the two got along on bits of common memory.

"Shit fire," Jack often prefaced his comments. "Once'it those durn javelinas a'most shat on my rollup walst I was sleepin'. Buggers were thet close! Was workin' the fence line up in them Mule Mountains." "Shit fire ..." and so on. His weekly trips to the border were for tacos and refried beans at a restaurant he thought better than the one he cooked in.

Second was Betsy Derulo, who ran the town's pool hall and liked the cheap whiskey found in the numerous bars in Naco. She was dry as a bone at work, but raised a little hell down south, dancing with Mexican ranch hands to the strains of mariachi music.

"Y'all enjoy that walkin' down there?" She came from N'Awlins originally, having married a mine worker who dumped her for a younger woman after only six months, stranding her in Bisbee, far from home. She was smart and had handled her situation with intelligence and vigor.

"Yes," Alfred said. "I like to a lot. It's quiet, mostly, and the sun on the wall casts lonesome shadows."

"Y'all lonesome?" Betsy asked.

"Maybe," Alfred answered, and they rode for a while in silence.

Finally, there was Mr George, a black man, one of only a few in town. He was a freelance accountant, exceptional with figures, and he enjoyed some late afternoons at the Turquoise Valley Golf Course in Naco, near the border on the American side. He was close in age to Alfred and played to a handicap of six.

"So, another day," he'd say on every trip. "A pleasant walk along the wall?"

"Yes, sir," Alfred would reply. "And for you? Some golf?"

"Can't say that I won't," Mr George would answer, glancing at him with a broad smile.

This afternoon it was Betsy.

"See y'all later, hotshot," she said to Alfred's back as he limped away.

The sun still bathed the wall on the American side, but across the border, where Secondino and Julian rested, shadows extended to cover the moat and the nervous gators. They had carried the duffle down a dusty trail for a least a half mile, and both were exhausted when they reached the wall and the shadows that hid their activities, which at the moment consisted only of deep breathing.

"*Que hora es?*" Julian coughed.

"Almost six-thirty, almost, *ese*," Secondino replied in the same breathless fashion.

They had just under an hour, a short time really, given the heft of the sixteen-foot ladder, the plywood platform, the riggings, a rope, a pulley and the grappling hook, all of which they'd hidden in a gully thirty yards away. Wayne Shorts would be there at seven-twenty, when darkness had just set in, but before the bright lights atop the wall came on.

That bumbling *idiota* emissary, Secondino thought. Why do they send this *cabrón*?

Wayne Shorts was the clumsy son of a powerful mine executive whose connections ran all the way to Los Angeles and back east to New York City. He had a blind spot for his son, and this is why he tutored him in the trade, though a bundle of concern murmured like the faint sound of crickets at the back of his brain. For a while he had used him for packaging, patiently showing him the ropes, and only now, on this warm June day, did he send him off for his first transfer.

Wayne had a terrible headache, too much booze and little sleep in the night before, and dressing he managed to get both feet into the same leg of his Levi trousers. "Son of a bitch," then stumbling, kicking at the pants, then falling to the floor, banging his head against the edge of his night table. Stunned, he lay there for a while, then freed himself from the Levi grip, grabbed onto the mattress, and pulled himself to his feet. Blood was in his eyes, yet he managed to make it to the kitchen, where he pressed the superficial cut with a sheet of paper towel.

At first, his truck wouldn't start, so he lifted the hood and gazed into the engine and its mechanics, understanding nothing, so he slammed the hood, kicked one of the tires, climbed behind the wheel, and tried again. There was a cough, then a roar as he jammed down on the gas pedal, then released it, and the engine settled down into an idle. His girlfriend, Wicked Molly, stuck her head out the door.

"Quiet, knucklehead! I'm tryin' to sleep!" though it was late in the afternoon.

Bleary-eyed, blood seeping at the edge of the bandage he'd awkwardly applied, he grinned at her, waving as he drove away. Slow, he thought, cars passing him on the two-lane road as he headed for the border. Still, he arrived too early. American Naco. He pulled off into the parking lot of a Mexican bar. Hair of the dog? No way, he thought, then settled back into the seat, blinked a few times, and fell asleep.

Meanwhile, Alfred limped along in deep thought, though observant, the wall rising in the slowly sinking sun on his right. The alligators were no longer restless, possibly sleeping, at least sunning themselves at day's end. The cactus was still in bloom, red and pink flowers bursting from green stems, riding off into the distance, once the last houses had ended, and he was walking along the narrow sandy trail in the desert, the wall somewhat ludicrous in this place. A few animals, a family of coyotes off in the far distance making their way to somewhere, a desert fox, and a thick gila monster sliding into his den. The peaceful, ominous desert, a place for thought and digging, not into the past, but what's up in the present that might define the future. Limping along, at times stumbling then righting himself, at least that, if not his life. There must be something to do, to change. Even at sixty-two, there were years ahead. But for this damned limp he was healthy. It certainly wasn't time he needed. He had plenty of that. It was something else. A woman, possibly? A hobby? He didn't know, but he knew the town was a dead end.

He had lived in Bisbee all of his life, and had traveled, on his thumb again, to Tombstone to look around and to St David for swimming, and once he had traveled to Tucson, ninety-six miles away, in the band bus. He played the oboe, of all things, but beat on the drums at the football games. He had no friends: who in the hell plays an oboe in a border town? One girlfriend. They held hands. He never kissed her. Then all the years went by. His dead father. His absent mother. He'd lived his whole life with his mother and father in this decaying house, and now, no longer a child, he'd been left alone, and for him loneliness was not sadness, or absence, or all the life-long objects – the sink, the table, the wooden spoon – accusing him in some way. Loneliness was who he was.

He shuffled along the path. The sun was almost gone.

"*Callar, hombre.*" Secondino was whispering, looking down from his perch on the ladder, the grappling hook in his right hand. Julian had been moving, making a tinkling as he brushed against a rivet. Then Secondino tossed up the padded hook with the rope and pulley attached, so that it might grab the top of the wall, which it did.

The time had almost come. Secondino was up on the ladder because of his height and ears. Julian hooked the platform onto the ascending rope and slowly pulled it up, so that Secondino might get a hold on it, then reach up and affix it to the wall. They called it *el trampolín*, and it was designed to clear the moat. Then Julian sent up the duffle, and Secondino slid it carefully along the narrow platform as far as he could reach.

"*Lo oigo.* I hear him," Secondino whispered down. "Hand me the stick." Julian got on the second rung of the ladder, slowly, then tucked the stick end into Secondino's palm.

Moving along without any furtiveness, almost casual. That's odd, Secondino thought, but he pushed up the stick to touch the duffle and waited in the near silence, listening carefully to the shuffling steps. Another odd thing, they seemed to be moving almost automatically, that there was no question of their pace, that it was inexorable, that there would be no stopping. Yet he kept the stick pressed into the bottom of the bag. The steps were approaching. One, two, three, he thought. The steps were almost there. One, two, three, and he poked the stick hard into the duffle. It teetered for a moment. That always happens. Then it fell out of sight on the wall's other side and hit with a thud and a groan.

"*Madre de Dio!*" Julian whispered. "Did you hear that?"

"Maybe he tries to catch it," said Secondino.

"I hope he is okay."

"Of course he is, *ese*. He is a *professional*."

"*Bueno*," Julian said without much conviction.

They packed up their gear and stowed it in the hiding place. Then they moved off into the desert before the wall's lights came on.

Alfred woke with a start, recognizing immediately where he was and knowing what had hit him. It was right there at his side, as if the two were in bed and had woken quickly.

He was picked up by Betsy for the ride back. It was dark now, and the bundle he lugged was shapeless and from a distance appeared harmless. He pushed it into the back seat of her Honda and climbed aboard.

"Y'all are for sure not looking too good."

"I can believe that."

"What's in the bag?"

"Just some bottles and cans I picked up along the way."

"They is awful quiet."

"Rags. I tucked them in there. Don't want to make a racket."

"Uh-huh."

They spoke little on the way back to Bisbee, and though it was quite dark on the road, Betsy managed to glimpse the bruise at Alfred's temple, and when she asked about it, he said it was nothing, he had tripped and fell, but he was okay now.

Tombstone Canyon Road was almost empty, and she drove up the divide to Alfred's place, keeping her lights on as he climbed out of the car and fetched his duffle. She watched him as he lugged it up onto his narrow porch, then opened the door and pushed it into the house. Then she turned the car around.

"Bottles and cans, my ass," she said aloud, as she drove away.

Three Airstream trailers sat in a row near the edge of the massive open-pit copper mine, one of the largest in North America. The first two were worn and dirty and might just as well have been located in a down-at-the-heels trailer park somewhere in a poverty-stricken area near Tuscaloosa, Alabama. The third in the row was pristine, its aluminum body shined to a fare-thee-well, and inside the floor was covered by a rich red five-by-eight hand-stitched carpet from Lebanon. Prints of miners engaged in various jobs, or just posing, hung from the curved metal walls. They had been attached so that each one was tilted slightly forward, and to the observer it appeared that at any moment the various miners might fall out of the frames and crash down to the floor. A large mahogany desk, with some files and various papers upon it in good order, occupied much of the area beyond the door, so that anyone wishing to get to the end of the trailer and the small bathroom had to turn to the side and edge between desk and wall. It was a very tight fit. At the end of the trailer there were two leather chairs and a love seat pushed in against each other, too big for this space that the owner might have dreamed to expand by overloading it, thus pushing the trailer's walls out and away. Wayne, sitting stiffly, occupied one of the chairs, his hands gripping tight to the arms.

"Son of a bitch!" Paul Shorts ejaculated into the air of the over-burdened space as he paced the few feet behind his desk, to and fro.

He was a small, plump man in a light green seersucker suit, ludicrously double breasted. His thin, dark hair was combed over to cover his receding crown. He needed a haircut, and spikes stuck up in tiny trees suggesting a sparse forest on his head. He wore a bow tie that matched his suit.

"I needed a goddamned haircut!"

He did indeed.

"And they called me out even before Gene got started. And you! Where in the hell were you?"

"Well, my truck ..."

"Yeah, yeah, we know about the truck, outside of that bar in Naco."

"On the American side though."

"What?! Who gives a shit about that? Where the hell were you? The drop off!"

Wayne squirmed in his chair. "Well, I was early, so I parked and waited until it was time. I never went in the bar. I had the engine running and the air on. It was very hot. Must have been some fumes leaking in, so I must have gone unconscious, and when I came back to myself it was too late. I'll have to get the truck checked out."

"Bullshit, bullshit, and more bullshit. You fell asleep! Give me something. I need something."

"Well, I went to the drop-off place. It was dark by then, but the lights were on, and I searched, but there was nothing."

"Okay. But did you see anyone? Do you know of anyone?"

"Well, there is this one guy. He walks along the wall a lot. I didn't see him though."

"A name."

"I don't know."

"Okay then, recognizing you've screwed up everything, you're gonna find out this guy's name, quickly, and you're gonna get it to me. This is a simple assignment, and I don't want to learn of a single fuck-up. And if I do, you'll be leaving the fold."

"What fold?"

"Your family, asshole! That's the fold! One mistake and you'll be no son of mine!"

He doesn't really mean it, Wayne thought.

In an unprecedented visit to a place where he was unaccompanied by his cadre of zealous, vacant-eyed supporters, the President stood before that small section of the wall, the whole of which he had promised would be completed more than a year ago and was now extended out to no more than a few miles. His Vice President stood beside him, well back, a foot or two, and the only others present were the twenty or so Mexicans who had gotten the word of this secret visit and a few members of the carefully vetted press. Between them and Potus was the gang of secret service guys, young men mostly, in suits that had heated up so that the skin under them was soaked with sweat. Their eyes, blinking in the moisture, darted around, looking for danger that wasn't there. The VP was grinning below his cap of gray, not a hair out of place. He had it trimmed every day. He was waiting for the President to speak, which he soon did.

He was leaning forward slightly, squinting to see through the transparency, as if to catch the eye of some Mexican drug dealer, but all he saw were the shadows of old women moving along, heading for stores or home. Dressed in his typical light-gray tailored suit, the mistaken color only exaggerating the bulk of his soft body, he gazed around as the sun brought down its midday slant and revealed the image of his own face in a mirror. His mouth formed a pucker, as if he might lean in and kiss himself. And his hair? Nothing to be said about that.

"Very, very beautiful. That I can tell you. Incredible. So good."

"Yes, sir, it is," said the VP.

There was the beginning of a laugh that turned into a cough coming from someone in the audience, behind the secret service guys.

"And this is just the beginning," the President said. "There will be more. Very, very soon. You can count on that. It will be perfect. One of my finest achievements. As I promised. I will be announcing it next Monday. Well, sometime next week. Count on it. And you, in the back there, Mexicans, but Americans, we love you, I love you, and America loves you!"

"Didn't you say we can count on that more than a year ago?" It was Wayne Shorts, who was coming along the path, searching for evidence and a name. The secret service guys pricked up their ears and watched him closely.

"*Cogeto un burro!*" Words spoken softly from the observant group.

"What was that?" the President said. "That isn't English."

"That was just an alligator croaking," said the VP as Wayne Shorts passed by, his bloodshot eyes blinking as he tried to examine every nook and cranny.

"Yes! Very, very smart. These alligators. So smart."

Once he was satisfied, the President called for a member of the press to step forward and take his picture, the VP beside him.

"Let me see it," he said, then asked for another, himself alone, palms raised like a supplicant, the index finger on his right hand pointing at the photographer and the clutch of secret service dandies behind him. He wasn't looking up toward God in his prayer-like posture, that would come later, when he addressed the Christians, but was grinning straight into the small lens, his other hand making the okay sign he had become famous for. There he stood, in front of the early beginnings of his few achievements.

"What am I going to do?" Alfred said.

The four of them sat in the ratty upholstered chairs almost in a circle, the duffle bag elevated on the coffee table for all to see. It was eight o'clock in the evening, the sun's last rays casting thin spears of light on their legs and arms in the growing shadows. Alfred had turned on the lights. Either the bulbs were low wattage or the power entering the house was weak, for each saw things, even those close to them, in a faint fog. There were prints on the walls, but the only things to be seen there were framed squares. It had been hot all day, and though a whisper of breeze stirred in the tattered curtains, it was still hot. Alfred had provided lemon in solar tea poured from the jug he'd placed in the sun in the early morning.

"Well, shit fire. Don't ya think we ought'a palaver a while?"

Jack still wore his cook's apron, his big white hat perched square on his head. His smile was only half visible in the dim light.

"Well, there it is, y'all. And we all know what's in there, not the damned drugs, that marijuana on top'a all that damned cocaine, but the Alfred dilemma. Is it better ta just give the duffle back, however that might be possible? Or are there alternatives? Durned if I know."

It was Betsy who had brought them all together here. They all knew each other. Jack spent considerable time at the pool hall, and Betsy spoke to him after steak at the restaurant. Mr George did the books for both places, and Alfred was, of course, the passenger. She had smelled marijuana on their ride from the border back up the divide to Alfred's place.

"Here's the way I see it." Mr George spoke, for their attention. "First of all, this," he pointed at the duffle, "is found material. Finders keepers, so to speak. That's not going to work, for even if you throw it away, they'll be after you, both because of the loss and the humiliation. Secondly, we could take it back to him. I know who he is. I do the books for him. Turned out there was fakery in them.

"Of course, he'll know then who we are and that we know who he is.

"Now, Alfred is stuck here and needs to get out of this

place. Get on with a life that has been dormant for many years. We all know this, and Alfred himself knows this. Right, Alfred?"

Alfred nodded.

"So we make a deal. Alfred gets the two hundred thousand that we'll ask for, the man gets the drugs. Two hundred is, of course, street value, the value it would be for Alfred if he went into the drug business on his own. The man will know, of course, that we know what he is doing. He'll be shocked to see me there, given my access to his books. But, no, we will not blackmail him. That would be our crime. We'll say not a word about any of this. I suspect he'll get the point. Oh, and of course I'll be tape recording our conversation, the device hidden under my suit coat. Are you ready for this, Alfred?"

"You bet I am." A weak bravado in his words.

"And you two?"

"I am. Absolutely," Jack spoke uncharacteristically, then added a "shit fire."

"Hell, how can y'all even ask?" Betsy said.

It was Jack who arranged the meeting. He knew Shorts from his frequent visits to the restaurant, where he often ate gigantic steaks and complimented Jack on his skill at the grill. Jack told him it was personal. He had to see him. He couldn't speak of the matter over the phone.

In the late afternoon of the following day, the four of them drove to the copper mine in Mr George's dark blue Cadillac, and though the seats were that kind of sumptuous leather that embraced the bottoms and backs of travelers in perfect comfort, not one of the passengers allowed themselves to sink in. All, with the exception of Mr George himself, were tense and had pushed up to their seat edges, intent on what might be coming.

"I'm ready," Betsy said, tapping the broad section of a customized cue stick against her leg. She had unscrewed the thing and carried only the first foot and a half in her grip. Jack sat beside her in the back seat. He wore his cook's apron, ready for work after the meeting, and held a heavy cast iron frying pan. Alfred was in the front beside Mr George. He was shivering, not because of the cooling air-conditioning, and Mr George reached over and massaged his neck.

"Shit fire, ready as ready can be."

"I hear you," Mr George said. "And Alfred here is ready too. Am I correct, Alfred?"

There was a brief pause, then Alfred spoke.

"Uh-huh," said uncertainly, though he was no longer shivering.

"Here we are," Mr George said as he pulled to a stop in the drive running along the edge of the pit. Then they opened the four doors and got out.

Jack lugged the duffle bag up to the Airstream, then handed it over to Alfred. It was his, after all. Then Betsy knocked firmly on the metal door with her stick, and when it was opened, all four pushed their way in, Alfred bringing up the rear, the large duffle bag held awkwardly in his arms. Paul Shorts stepped back in surprise.

"What in the goddamned hell is this?!"

He was dressed in a light pink leisure suit, no tie, and he sported an expensive pair of white wingtips. The four crowded around him, and Alfred dropped the duffle. It hit the metal floor behind the desk with a thud.

"And what the hell are *you* doing here?"

"Soon enough," Mr George said. "Let's all get comfortable."

"Comfortable my ass!" Shorts coughed out in the beginning of a rage, then banged his hand down on the desk, searching for a button, which he soon found. They could hear heavy feet on the steps outside, then the door was flung open and two large, burly men in roughware burst in.

"Get them the fuck out of here!" Shorts screamed. "Leave the duffle bag!" And the men approached, their hands in fists.

Betsy raised her cue stick, Jack his frying pan, but before the battle was joined, Mr George spoke.

"Stop!" he said. "Look at this!"

He had removed a silver dollar linked to a thin chain from his suit coat pocket, and he held it up, fingering the wire so that the dollar spun slowly, catching the light that the sun cast through the windows. Betsy and Jack had their backs to him, their weapons raised, and Alfred stood off to the side. Shorts had pushed his butt into the desk edge as if he might sink into it, and the two aggressors were watching the spinning coin.

"Look at it," Mr. George whispered. "Keep looking. Now do as I say."

He instructed them to back away, to move to the rear of the Airstream. They did so until they were pressed against the wall leading to the bedroom. Then he instructed them to slide down to the floor and to sit there and to sleep.

The four moved to the couch and chairs, and Shorts, bewildered as he stared at his sleeping muscle, finally turned and sat down at his desk facing them, trying to capture some of his lost dignity.

"What do you want?" he said, and Mr George laid out the terms, the two hundred thousand, street value, and silence on their part.

"How can I trust you?" Shorts said.

"Not to worry," Mr George responded. "We're taking the money, after all. A payoff, if you will."

"Okay, but no papers, the audits ..."

"I found him! I've got the name!" It was Wayne Shorts standing in the doorway, smiling.

"Get the fuck out of here!" his father screamed, and Wayne retreated.

They gathered in the cramped living room at Alfred's house. There were hugs, and Betsy planted a firm kiss on his lips. Jack wished him well. "Good luck, pard. You're gonna have fine times a'comin'." Mr George called him aside and spoke quietly to him, his hand on his shoulder, and Alfred nodded, looking up into his eyes. Then they shook hands, and it was over.

Two years later.

The grandchildren rolled on the lawn under the lakeside willow. Two little boys, they were dressed in shorts and baggy T-shirts. Anna Janeway, their mother, watched them. Her eyes glanced up from time to time to glimpse the old city far off across the lake. There were high, wispy clouds, yet a soft summer sun shone down upon it all: the house, a small old Victorian; the quaint little shed where the lawn tools were kept, its shingles glowing in the light; the six willows dotting the lawn as it moved down to the wooden dock at the lake's edge, a rowboat there; the energy in the three-year-old twins.

"Come here to your mommy, the two of you." Her voice was gentle.

After the unexpected death of her wealthy husband,

Linda Carpenter gave up the city and decided to spend her life here at the lake. She read a lot, enjoyed baking, and on this mid-afternoon she'd played a couple of Philip Glass études on the piano. The fluid, repetitious strains were quiet yet crystal clear out on the lawn. Now she was fixing the drinks, solar tea, with a good deal of mint floating in the jug.

How has this happened for me, this good fortune? I am no longer alone. This is what she thought as she fussed with the glasses and the tray, the sounds of the twins' squeaky laughter creeping into her ruminations. And my daughter, she thought.

The lake was glowing now, as the sun's slant entered at an angle, the tall buildings in the city beyond were golden spires, and the lawn shone bright green, the blond heads of the children bobbed up and down in their play. Their mother was watching them, grinning. Then she heard the screen door's squeak and saw her own mother coming down the steps carrying a tray.

She walked across the lawn in certain slow strides, her flowered dress, roses and sprays of lilac, slipping along her shapely white legs, and headed toward the recliner where the cane rested in the grass. She arrived there and handed the glass of cool mint tea to Alfred. He smiled warmly, as he raised his hand to receive it. Then he sipped for a while, and afterward placed the glass on the low metal table at the chair's edge. He looked over at the grandchildren, their mother, then his own Linda Carpenter handing a glass of tea to her daughter. His body sunk deeper into the chair's cushion and he closed his eyes against the sun. Then he leaned his head back and yawned.

Beautiful Dreamer

THOUGH ALMOST AWAKENED occasionally by life's busy throng or smoky tea scent drifting across my corrugated face, I have been in this dream of reality for many years. They call it coma. Voices are heard in the day, but I can't see them, the speakers. Their words are there only for moments as they speak of the brain, trauma, and utter soothing adjectives of possible recovery in time. Then the consonants in their language begin to fracture and fall down upon the blanket, and I am once again gone into dreaming of this past that seems to be mine.

The underside of a balcony five floors up. I'm on my back, in the grass, my vacant eyes led by the moonlight. Looking up. Perhaps a darkened hand there at the railing's edge, then a distorted face looking down. At me? I can't be sure. We were doing something, talking, moving around, the smell of cooking, something risky, sinister. Will it come back to me, here and now? It doesn't. A fog of mystery. In my head. That's all.

Sounds of the rude world, nurses come to me out of a moist chemical cloud. Tprs, bps, click of pans, an emesis basin, the sour scent of urine. I don't know where I am. Only the feel of clean linen as, after washing, they push me on my side, tuck in the sheet, then push me the other way. But for the dreaming, that is awareness, almost pleasure. No longer on the grass looking up, I remember. What? We were fishing on Justin's whaler, Rob, Justin and I. On a lake. It must be Michigan? And the two were, as usual, arguing. Something about futures, I think. And they too, at some point, were yelling and screaming at one another. These college friends of mine, out on the boat after a hard week in the market. Two days off, and this seemed almost like a college reunion, the three of us back at Chicago Circle. Justin was rich before his successes. His father's construction companies. And Rob and I, even after college, were his followers, or better yet, his somewhat bewildered juniors. Followed him into the brokerage firm where, in the past few years, we'd each made a bundle. My house in Oak Park, a Frank Lloyd Wright, full of his furniture, my Benz. Rob was in the city. His women. Night life. Not a care in the world. Justine, twice married.

Rob was standing in the prow, waving his pole and yelling back over his shoulder. Justin was at the port rail, removing weed from his hook. Then Rob screamed something, and Justin froze, weed hanging from his clenched fist and wiggling along his arm. Then he threw his pole down. It clattered on the wooden deck. I think I hear it. And headed for Rob ... I can't. No. It's going. The dreaming. Rob was ... It fades away. Like sleep.

The nurses are touching me, tubes are shifted. A needle burns. A gurgling. Then a man's fingers, gentle and sure. The sound of footsteps receding. I hear catheter, fecal collector, saline. Too soon. The hearing falls away into that smoke. Memory, as if jigsaw pieces float in a circle in the air, then slowly move toward the center and form the picture. Rob. Justin is coming toward him, fists clenched in a rage. Rob turns in the prow and looks back. His face is unreadable, even when Justin reaches him, grabs him by the shoulders, and pushes him over the side.

I think I went as quickly as I was able on the moving

deck, heading for the prow. I never reached it. Justin raised his arm like a gate, holding me back. I stood there and watched him. We both knew Rob couldn't swim. Justin was gazing down into the water, fascinated. He looked down there for a long time.

After Rob's death and our necessary presence at the funeral, Justin and I spoke little at work. Then, wouldn't you know it, he began to come on to me. He touched me at the water cooler. He pressed his arm against mine at daily conference. Then he proposed dinner. We went to a fine restaurant on the north side, and after eating and a good deal of drinking he invited me back to his place and we made love. But it wasn't really love. Yet I was there, spending time in his apartment and out on the town. Greek food, jazz, evening cruises in view of the city lights. Abstractions of such pleasures, indulged in to ward off painful understanding.

As time went by, I grew increasingly guilt-ridden, angry, and depressed. Justin killed Rob and I had watched him do it. And I had done nothing to stop it. I slept now with his murderer. I was a disgusting human being. I too should be dead. This clarity. The puzzle pieces are a tight fit. I'm there, very clearly now, in his apartment. I can see the furniture, the sink. How odd, I can see the undersides of my eyelids. They glow. I'm going somewhere. No. I'm coming somewhere. I'm thinking this, or am I seeing this? The door, the machines, my covered feet. I'm blinking and I still see it. No welcoming committee. So what. I just look around, awakened and dazed by all the light and figures.

Then they are all here, the doctors, the nurses, my parents. "My God, Amy, we've missed you!" It's a party, a sip of wine. They come and go. Friends. Fellow workers. A policeman. My eyes are as much on objects in the room as on these people, smiling and moving, bending over me. Their lips. Then I must rest, the doctor says, and everyone leaves me alone with only this room that is now mine but won't be for long. And by myself again. Awake. I remember the rest.

I'm cutting the carrots, chopping celery and lettuce, weeping as the stewpot churns. A glass of Cabernet. Justin is out on his balcony, watching nocturnal birds in the dusky sky.

I cannot stand it anymore. I am behind him at the railing. He turns, smiling, and I stick the knife into him. Once, twice, then bury the blade up to the hilt in his chest. He seems surprised. He looks down at it. He begins to fall. He's caught by the spikes and hangs there. I'm almost satisfied. I push him to the side, climb the rail, and fly. Then, in the damp grass, I'm looking up. His arm. His tortured, agonized face.

My wrist is cuffed to the bedrail. I'm searching for the dreaming, but it won't come. I'd like to go back there, to that beauty. How sad to be awake.

Smoke

I'VE BEEN SMOKING for almost forty years, maybe a little longer. My mother smoked most of her life and in her seventies was hypnotized and quit. Others I've known have succeeded through various forms of therapy. Once I went with my wife Mona to some guy who stuck staples into our ear lobes. People we met would look to the sides of our heads, leading us to explain why we were wearing these odd earring devices. We've quit smoking, Mona might say, and these have helped us. She was successful, but I was caught by a colleague with a cigarette dangling from my lips and had to think of another explanation for the staple, which was hard to do. After a while it was either this thing or a cigarette. I chose the latter.

Smoking is no longer a pleasure. It's an addiction, but the addiction itself is a pleasure, and I don't seem able to let it go. I did quit once, cold turkey, but that feels so far in the past that when I light up I can hardly remember it or the satisfaction it might have brought with it.

Once, Mona got on my case quite aggressively, and I said, okay, I'll quit. Then, of course, I started to sneak around. I hid a pack high up on a shelf in the utility room, and when it was time to leave for a swanky affair, I groped around in the dark and grabbed the pack, tucked it into my jacket pocket, and headed out. There was a side door leading to a garden at the elegant house, and when I stepped out and retrieved my smokes, I saw that what I held was a small container of rat poison.

Another time, sneaking again, I attempted the one-hand strike. I was in the garage, and the whole book caught fire, flames scorching the cuff of my new dress shirt. Thankfully there was no one around, but Mona found the shirt in the garbage and gave me that dangerous stare of hers. After that, I revealed the fact that I had continued with the "filthy habit". Mona was not pleased.

I tried cigars, but they stunk up the house, and my wife insisted that when I smoked them, I must stay at least one hundred yards from our property. I tried a pipe, and while I thought I looked quite distinguished smoking it, the required paraphernalia – the tamper, the reamer, the lighter, the bulky package – quickly became a bother, and I went back to the cancer sticks, though they too can be a pain in the behind. In the summer, in a short-sleeved shirt without a pocket and tight pants, how to carry the darn things and the matches or lighter as well? I longed for those high school days when I had been a pretend hood, rolling the pack up in my T-shirt sleeve.

There was a time when everyone smoked. I remember it well. In cars, in restaurants and bars, in airplanes, on the street, in meditation on the toilet, before lovemaking and after it, which reminds me of an old joke. The sex was so good that after it everyone in the neighborhood lit up.

People don't mooch anymore, you're the only one on the terrace at a party with a lit butt cupped in your palm, or you're out in the yard, tucked in among the trees, or you're sneaking a few puffs in the bathroom with the fan on high.

Smoking is no longer conventional or fun. No more gesturing with your cig to make a point. No more being cool as you light up. No more sticking a pair into your mouth, lighting both, looking like a fool, and handing one of them to the girl and later the grown women you have eyes for.

Smoking was communal, seductive, the smoke rising up to form a protective blanket, while those under it reveled in good fellowship. Smoking was the glue that held society together. Well, something like that.

There is, of course, the coughing, the dizziness, the upturned noses of friends, the smelly clothing, the film of crud on the glass covering the pictures on the wall, the burnt holes in the best shirts and jackets, cancer, the avoidance and the shunning, emphysema, the nervousness on long drives where the wife won't allow it, chest burns, problems with sex, the lingering possibility of death.

We decided to dress for dinner. We knew that Mona's parents would dress formally as well. It was Friday night at the lake, and though the Ronson Queen Anne cigarette lighter sat on the coffee table, there were no cigarettes there to be had, but rather a crystal dish holding Jordan almonds and beside it a bouquet of various blooms. The ancient maid had gathered them from the flower gardens that edged the property's broad lawn, which itself fronted the placid blue lake. A boat was docked there at the pier, a powerful vessel that often took us out on the water for skiing and fishing.

Mona was an only child, born into a wealthy family. Her father, a businessman, was the owner of a small pharmaceutical company, and he had gathered a crew of the very best scientists and through them had managed to produce drugs that became very successful. His most recent score was a drug that treated Irritable Nostril Itch Syndrome, or INIS, a condition that he had invented. It was named Nostrodrome, and once on the market thousands of people bought it, even though most were unaware of their syndrome until the drug was available. I didn't care much for her father, was unsure about her mother, but then they had brought their daughter considerable wealth, and I shared in it and couldn't really complain. They seldom used this lake house, and to all practical purposes it was ours.

I met Mona at the airport when she climbed up on the high seat to get a shine. I was smoking a pipe then, and I set it aside immediately as her dress hiked up to reveal her lovely thighs above the boots. They, the boots, were made of the finest leather, Marc Jacobs I thought, and they needed little shining. Still I found a way to linger over them, applying wax and a transparent coating that would deliver deepness to the leather, very much like the spit shine applied by those in the military to give a glow to their shoes.

We spoke of books we had both read, of desired foods, and the music that might set us to dancing. In a while, we'd made a date for dinner, sushi at one of the best places in town. The rest is our brief history. Married for twelve years, childless by choice, very much in love. Her parents objected, of course, but over time I'd become at least somewhat successful, having opened up twenty-five shoeshine parlors manned by the best shiners that I could find. The money was not great, but it was sufficient. I didn't need to come begging from my wife or her parents, though I thoroughly enjoyed the gifts that were forthcoming, most having to do with money provided.

Once we were married, Mona tried working for a while. She had a master's degree in art history, which was close to useless in the working world, and so she found a job as a salesgirl at some designer clothing shop. Quickly she became bored there and quit. Back home again, she took up the task she was born for, the creation of small sculptures made from various pieces of junk that she altered to fit her needs. Tin cans, bottle caps, bits of child's toys that had washed up at the lake's edge beside the dock, twigs and fallen branches from the yard, and much more.

She sawed and sanded, soldered and welded, hammered and bended, all this in her workshop shed in our back yard. Her products were beautiful. Materials that had once been life's rubble and detritus were now melded together, and in each small abstract structure they had become a romantic club, a sisterhood, maybe even a family. Continually smiling, full of energy and wit, Mona seemed centered and satisfied in our life together. Yet she was alert, always on the lookout for adventure, even here in these peaceful days at the lake house, anticipating the arrival of her parents. One of her elegant sculptures rested prominently on the mantle, and I gazed at it as I adjusted my clothing.

My tuxedo jacket was a light wool burgundy number set off with black lapels. The chest was wide open and filled by a white shirt, its ruffles hiding the buttons. My bow tie was traditional in shape, though yellow, as was the cummerbund that peeked out where my jacket was joined at the waist. I had gathered my long blond hair tight against my head and tied it off with a red ribbon, so that my ponytail fanned out to cover my shoulders. I went to the small bar at the end of the room and fixed myself a single malt with a splash of water from the carafe that stood nearby. Then I watched Mona as she made her entrance through the double doors that led into the living room, where we would sup.

Her dress was on-trend, long, light blue, and gossamer, studded with numerous beads and sequins that created an ombre effect, one color hue melding into another, as if clouds had filtered the sun, then returning to a brightness that mimicked the lake's sparkle, seen beyond the floor-to-ceiling windows as the day began to give in to dusk. She spun, smiling, to face me, her long cathedral train brushing the floor. Our golden retriever, Bart, was attacking it. Mona looked back and shook a finger at him, and he desisted. Then the bell rang.

"How are you doing, Melvin? Shining the boots of foot soldiers at the door? At least it's not frivolous women's work." He glanced toward the mantel where his daughter's sculpture rested. Mona stiffened beside me, and "*Pendejo*" slipped quietly from his wife's mouth.

This was Fred Hackberry's greeting. I was used to his opening ploys. He was a short, fat man, and Mona told me he often wore a kind of men's girdle to provide a little slimness. He'd chosen a powder-blue tuxedo of a kind and color favored by disco dancers of old. I wondered if the cuffs were bell. He always put on a look of sternness, figuring, I guess, that this was the way of all big business owners. A slight twitch of his thin mustache suggested the phoniness of his scowl. "How many women scientists in your lab, Fred? Or was it only men working on your crooked nostril scam?" I smiled at him.

"*Buenas tardes!*" was Gloria's defusing gambit. It kept her husband from responding.

Her serape was Eileen Fisher. She had taken up the study of Spanish, though French would have been more appropriate to her assumed station in society. But that was Gloria, always pushing slightly against the grain. Fred glanced at her, his eyes a little steely. She was short and plump, her hair laced with flowers piled high on her head, which she kept steady lest the whole complex structure collapse like an imploded building. I thought of Carmen Miranda, chica chica boom chic, even though she was no Mexican or Spaniard. Gloria wore a loose designer dress, pink, that looked like pajamas. Her nails were red as the sun.

The ancient maid brought in the dinner. She had been with the family for many years, and Mona had conferred with her, asking what her father liked best but was seldom allowed given society dinners and the Mexican fare that Gloria had recently insisted upon. It was fish and chips, to be followed by hot fudge sundaes, then coffee and a taste of sweet kahlúa.

"*Delicioso!*" Gloria exclaimed as she gobbled down cod. "*Muy! Muy!*"

"Right," Fred said, as he waved a French fry half-heartedly. He didn't want to talk about the meal. He wanted to figure out ways to hassle me, and he started in earnest after dessert with his pipe. I'd anticipated this. I'd been clean for close to six months, and I'd positioned a small fan on a table behind my chair to blow the dark heavy smoke away as he puffed and coughed.

"Six months, huh. Don't you miss it?"

"Come on now, Dad. Take it easy," Mona said.

"*No vuelvas a fumar nunca mas!*" said Gloria, jerking her head toward her husband in his veil of smoke. "*Fumar te matará!* Just look at him!"

"What did she say?" I asked Mona.

"Something about smoking."

Fred was choking and sputtering as the smoke he aimed in my direction was blown back into his face by the fan.

"Yeah, six months," I said, smiling as he convulsed. "Got any new drug for that?"

Mona's parents left early. Gloria had said *vámonos* and kissed Mona on the cheek as they took their leave. She tilted her head toward her husband and whispered something into Mona's ear, then patted her on the hair. It was only eight o'clock, and once the dishes were cleared away, and we were alone, I suggested dancing.

The music was Guy Lombardo, his big band, and Mona held her long train up near my shoulder as we waltzed between couches and easy chairs, our arms extended, pointing the way, not quite cheek to cheek. We could see lights across the water, the city in the distance alive and aglow, the lake like a vast window holding the city's sparkles. The full moon was high in the sky.

"I hate the way your father treats you," I said.

"I know who I am," she laughed.

"Should we make love?" I whispered into her ear as we spun past the dining table, Mona's train, loose now, whisking across the surface.

"Yes. Of course," she said. "But I have to bathe, then dress up properly."

That warmed me. "I'll take Bart out. Then I'll come back and get ready."

"Take your time," she said.

It was a warm night, a very light breeze, and I inhaled the sweet clean air, my lungs unobstructed by gunk. After Bart had done his business and I'd bagged and disposed of his offering, I settled into a lawn chair under the big sycamore, Bart in the grass beside me, and gazed out across the water to the illuminated city in the distance. Dark birds chirped and sang softly in the branches above my head, their voices both pleasing and somber.

It was a beautiful and peaceful time, a time for conviviality, though I was the only one there. A time for nostalgia, good fellowship and community. A time when the past comes back and old habits are indulged in once again. And I thought of Mona, watching her at work, that concentration in thought and action that I could only imagine. Then

I thought of a time when I was a shoeshine man, a time between customers, at night, when the airport was almost empty. My hand was in my jacket pocket, as it had been then. It took a moment. Then the match was struck, its light illuminated my face and that section of the lawn surrounding us, Bart and I, and I drew in the smoke, the graceful cigarette an old friend between my fingers. Mona was getting ready. I was happy.

Jury

Timothy Bates was born and raised on a small farm in the foothills of the Rocky Mountains just a few miles from Jury, which was no more than a village tucked in among low rocky hills and aspens, and when he was twenty-two and his parents were dead, he sold the farm for what he could get and moved into Jury, which had escaped the recent spate of bombings, though many of the towns and larger cities had not.

After many years of war, and changes in the town's administration and culture, various rules and regulations were instituted. Night blackouts, Duck, Cover and Hold On drills, and the registration of newcomers, were in place. Most significantly, every house and business were ordered to hold tight to family and belongings. But for carefully sorted old clothing, the owner of which must receive a chit for presentation when these were donated to the effort, nothing must be thrown out. This, of course, was an odd requirement, for if Jury found itself in the way of bombardment, houses and businesses hit would lose everything, family, documents, and other valued belongings. What, then, was the point? One might ask the mayor. He knows.

Jackie Burnwell was a forty-six-year-old mechanic, owner of the one auto repair shop in the town, and he ran for his seat on a platform suggesting that pragmatism was the answer. "A town is like a car, when it's broke the only answer is to fix it up, replace parts, tune it," he was fond of saying.

He seemed to have little chance of election, but when the incumbent failed to return from the city to which he had traveled for business, the seat was Jackie's. "Hold everything close," he said. "It's the only way!" And the townsfolk, though unsure of the reason, were confused and frightened and went along with the edict.

When bombs exploded in the countryside, Tim's farmhouse was spared, but his parents, at work in the fields, were not. It was either a landmine, rare in these parts, or a ball of fire thrust down from above. Surely they were not the proper target, but they disintegrated nonetheless. Mercifully, Tim was in the basement fussing with the coal stove and did not witness the event. It was in the aftermath that he sold the farm and moved to town. He had enough money to get along for a while, but he knew before long he'd have to find work. Shortly after his arrival, Sandy Tempkin showed up, having fled to Jury after the town she had lived in had been destroyed. It had been a thirty-mile hike and she was exhausted when she arrived. For a while, there were no more bombs.

Jury, under the tutelage of former mayors and the one replaced by Jackie Burnwell, had worked to become self-sufficient. Water was no problem. The town depended on wells, some of which had become polluted by war's toxins and had to be decommissioned. Still, new ones were drilled, and there was enough water to service the town as well as the private dwellings and businesses therein. Electricity was still available, wires on tall poles waving in the breeze all the way into the far distance, and Jackie, together with a few others more accomplished than he, had built a natural-gas-powered generator, just in case. Gas had been drilled for and discovered in the flatlands just beyond the town. There was plenty of food, since many private homes provided vegetables from small gardens, and beef, chickens and pigs were raised in communal pens where Jury met the mountains at the village edge. Jackie Burnwell controlled these pens. After all, he was the mayor. As to clothing, a clutch of women volunteers fashioned shirts, underwear, skirts and trousers in the style of the 1950s from the worn garments that had been donated by family members who had produced chits at the small "factory" that was no more than an old tilted barn that had once been used to store haybales. And many other accommodations were provided, such as whiskey stills, a park containing various playsets for small children, rifles and pistols for hunting, and the canning and sale of fruits and vegetables. Jury grew slowly as straggling refugees arrived, some of whom brought needed expertise with them, and the town managed to hold its own in the face of what some saw as impending doom, while others were vibrant in their view of Jury as standing up for the American Way, whatever that was, in the face of continuing wars.

The wars that indeed continued were thought to have their historical source in a time when the United States involved itself in an escalated confrontation with North Korea. The archives that would legitimize this claim were lost in the Washington bombings. The Capitol building was not hit, nor was the White House, in which the then President ensconced himself in order to experience the pleasure of his smugness and to contemplate a nuclear attack, which was avoided, history proclaims, when this madman was removed forcibly from office and was shepherded away to an asylum for the criminally insane in Cleveland, Ohio. Rumor was that he had soiled and wet himself as he was shackled to the seat of the van that had transported him. Thus, the weapons, crude devices at the time, had been conventional, and long-distance war had continued through the ages. In all this time, Jury had survived, an isolated community that continued to thrive in a distant past.

I own the bookshop on Jury's main street, right next to the ice cream parlor, where I spend a good deal of time. I like the malteds Jane Zane serves at the old-timey counter, where through the windows I can see people passing on the sidewalk. They call me Freddy, as in "Freddy, would you like a malted?" but I prefer Frederick. Frederick Rush is the name. He, I mean I, arrived in Jury close to twenty years ago. I was Professor of English at the university in the city, while the city was still there. Now the bookshop is my position. I lend a good number, for there is little to do in Jury in leisure time but read. No more TV or phone service, as the bombing has taken out cable and dish power. I have a good stock, close to a thousand volumes salvaged from my city house and office at the university, and I lend books at a reasonable price, usually for food and other necessities, and when they are returned, I lend them out again. This is a common enough procedure, since Jury operates for the most part on a barter system that, like a black market, circumvents the "hold everything close" rule. I'm sixty-four years old. Yesterday, sipping my malted, I observed events and heard talk from a booth a few yards away.

The two held hands across the table, their chocolate sundaes, topped by whipped cream, nuts, jimmies and a cherry, melting into soup between them.

"Gee, Sandy, this is really nice!" Tim said.

"Really, really nice!" Sandy responded.

They smiled at each other, blushing like teenaged lovers, though they were both in their early twenties.

"Do you wanna sleep over?" Tim asked. They often shared nights in his apartment. He slept on the couch and Sandy took the bed. She had her own small place and for the most part slept there. Her funds were running out, as were the monies Tim had garnered from the sale of the family farm. They spent time in the town park in the evenings, sitting on a bench, watching the moon. Sometimes they kissed.

"Stay over? Sure!" she said, squeezing his hand.

They were about to rise and go out, when Jackie Burnwell arrived, slid into the plastic seat next to Sandy, edging her toward the wall, grinned and began to talk, tapping his fingers nervously on the formica.

"It's a proposition," he said. "I gotta get somebody. And I can get you things and a few dollars of real money. It's a job." Then he laid out the terms.

It was pretty clear that families and businesses were fudging the "hold everything close" rule that Jackie had initiated, selling and bartering household goods, providing services, and Jackie needed someone to check on things.

"You'll go around in an extremely unthreatening way, observing people, just watching, checking garbage. And you might even go into houses and buildings as nothing more than an admiring passerby, seeing there's no extreme disarray."

"Can Sandy come with me?" Tim asked, and Sandy giggled.

"Of course! Of course! Why not. That's a very good idea, as a kind of cover."

"Harumph," Sandy said. "I'm no cover."

"Well, of course. It's just that, well, you're friends, right? Why not together?"

"How much?" Tim asked.

"How much what?"

"How much stuff and money?"

"Oh, that! Well, I can get you a big slab of bacon, a chicken, a few jars of preserved fruit and vegetables, and fifty dollars. All of it each week."

"That's not enough!" Sandy said beside him. "We've got rent!"

"Okay. Let's make it seventy-five."

"Each," Sandy said.

"What?"

"Seventy-five a week for each of us. That's a hundred and fifty, plus the pork, chickens and preserves."

Jackie leaned back in the booth, tapped again on the table before answering, which he finally did.

"Okay, okay. One-fifty it is."

Then Jackie left, and Tim and Sandy finished their soupy sundaes, got up, and paraded out of the ice cream parlor door, heads close together, arm in arm.

Money. There wasn't much of it, and Jackie Burnwell had cornered a good deal of what there was, worn bills that circulated then found their way into Jackie's pockets as he overcharged for work done at his garage. "It's the gas," he would say. "It's running out! It's like gold!" He seldom repaired the few cars that still managed to continue running, somewhat unnecessarily, in the small village. Most of his time, when he wasn't running around being mayor, was spent working on lawnmowers, chainsaws, and other small engines. He had no city council to get in his way, and no sheriff. He'd taken on the duties of the latter himself, handing out citations for various dubious infractions and pocketing the fines. In Jury, he was thought of as a harmless buffoon. That's why he'd been accepted as a candidate for the post of mayor. He was more than that, however; a sly and somewhat dissembling customer. The town was self-sufficient, and as long as Jackie didn't get in the way, what was thought of as his harmless peccadilloes were acceptable.

The next spate of bombings was heard at a near distance, and given a stiff breeze, the smoke generated by fires and explosions drifted in and covered Jury in a thick, acrid fog. This had happened before, and large fans had been installed, high up among boulders at the mountainside edge of this town that sat in a kind of shallow bowl in the foothills. In earlier times, such smoky pollution had lingered for days, keeping residents inside buildings and houses, futilely cleaning up ash and dust that crept in under doors and round the edges of windows. It was at least a hundred years ago that a still-revered mayor had seen to the fans' installations. They were as loud as sirens, but they were very efficient, and people watched as the smoke was pushed back over the flatlands, where it lingered at a distance, a dark blanket casting the earth into shadow.

"That's where my farm is, well, was," Tim said.

They were standing beside a boulder that rose to shoulder height, looking out into the smoky distance. She wore a wide-swinging poodle skirt (they were going dancing later), ankle length white sox encased in saddle shoes, and a starched white blouse, short-sleeved. Pink ribbons at the ends of thin braids, pink lipstick. He was dressed in khakis, tennies, and a red button-down shirt. The dance would be held at the old cement factory building, recorded music, and would be casual.

Earlier in the day they had begun their appointed rounds, and the experience had unsettled both of them. The mayor had instructed them to keep a low profile, but the people at the houses and businesses they approached had been guarded. It was as if they were there to take things, to in some way violate the "hold everything close" rule, and they were awkward as they held hands and leaned against each other like the two young lovers that they were. They had found nothing that seemed amiss, no obvious violations, and it was only when they gained entrance to the home of the two elderly sisters that they felt somewhat at ease.

Edna and Emma Bollinger were in their eighties, and the living room in which Tim and Sandy sat on a couch and sipped the tea that was offered was full to the brim with the product of the sisters' endeavors. They were both potters, their wheel in the kitchen, and the objects they created – strangely beautiful and at times slightly pornographic sculptures, many of which suggested war and its implements – were purely decorative. They sat on the mantle, on tables, tucked into chairs, on windowsills, and on all other surfaces that were available.

"Gee, they're really neat!" Sandy said at one point, and Tim squeezed her knee.

"Yes," he said. "Clearly these are art. But what can you do with them?"

"Well," Emma said. She was the younger of the two. "Nothing actually. We *would* sell them if that were possible. But as you know we must hold them close until, well, things change."

"Do ya think they will?" Sandy asked.

"Oh, yes, we're sure of it," Edna exclaimed, "and pretty soon too."

"But the rules!" Sandy said.

"Temporary," said Emma.

Tim changed the subject. "Are you still making them?"

In answer, the sisters rose from their crowded chairs and ushered them into the back bedroom. There, on tables and bureaus, were larger pieces, all depicting forms of weaponry, rifles and tanks, planes, canons and mortars, even hip-sliders and machine guns. Monumental figures, muscled and sure-eyed, attended many of them.

"These are amazing," Tim said. "But why war?"

"Well, it's all around us, isn't it?" Edna said, her flowered dress billowing slightly in the light breeze that entered the half-open window. "We were trying for some sort of celebration with these. Do you think we accomplished that?"

"I do," Sandy said.

"So do I," said Tim. "A way to face the bombing, to take it into your work, to control it."

"What?" Sandy said.

"Possibly," said Emma.

"Gee, they were nice old ladies," Sandy remarked as they were walking back to Main Street and their apartments, to change for the dance. It was early evening by then and the town was quiet, most folks tucked away in their houses, preparing dinner or reading. A dusky full moon sat in the sky above them. Tim had taken a few notes, something to present to Jackie Burnwell as proof of their work, but there was nothing of much substance in them. Though they had found a few things that might be thought of as violations, they'd discounted them. Their unspoken impressions held only the benign. Live and let live, Tim had thought, and when he spoke the words aloud, she had agreed.

"The smoke is ominous," Sandy said. "But heck, here we are, doing okay!"

"That's ominous. But right!" Tim said. "And soon we'll be dancing. But let's go to the park first, sit around and talk for a while."

"Sure," she said, looking up at him, smiling.

In the center of the town park was an old oak, the trunk of which was surrounded by a brick walkway and a comfortable bench. The two sat there, tight together. They weren't talking. The branches of the oak formed a lush canopy that guarded them. Vines clung to the oak's trunk. A narrow bed of tulips surrounded the bench that surrounded the tree. There were birds. Always there are birds. They sang in the tree's limbs, sparrows' light tunes couched in the moan of a few mourning doves. He touched her waist at the edge of her hip and turned her. He kissed her, a brief touch of tongue tips. He placed his hand on her stomach, his finger touching the bottom edge of her breast. Again, they kissed, just lips pressing against each other, and when they came up for air, she spoke.

"Oh, Tim!" she moaned.

"Yes," he said, taking her hand in his.

It was dark under their tree, and yet there was light. It was the full moon, its glow dancing among the branches, and on the dots and small rectangles that dressed the black field of her skirt. Even the stitched-in poodle was alight. And their faces, their arms, their finger-entwined hands. The bench was warm on this pleasantly cool night, and a stream gurgled in the near distance. The chaste lovers formed statues of lovers in their stillness, there, in the peace and quiet.

The scene was discovered by old man Nicolas Rogers, who spend much of his time foraging and panning for gold that was never there in the narrow river that carried snow melt down from the mountains and enclosed half the town in a quarter-moon shape.

The naked body hung low in a tree, in a place where the trunk had sent out two limbs to form the shape of a giant slingshot. It had been nailed there in a kind of tortured crucifixion, one arm, dislocated at the shoulder, twisted up into leafy branches, the other, crooked at the elbow, displayed its bloody palm at head level. It was as if the man was attempting a wave or salute but could accomplish neither since the nail held the hand in place. His only clothing was a kind of soft cotton loincloth, and though the figure's head hung down, chin pressed into chest above his fat belly, I could tell by the broad forehead and unruly blond hair that I was looking at Jackie Burnwell. There was a note, written in fine calligraphy, nailed into the trunk above his hand. I stepped closer and read it.

Here hangs the Hypocrite. The King Mayor of Peaceful Jury.
May he never rest in peace!

I sent Nicolas Rogers back to town to fetch John Roberts. Doctor John, as he was called, was the only doctor left in Jury. He had arrived, serendipitously, just two days after the death of the elderly surgeon who had treated the townsfolk for many years. John was a young man in his late twenties and had just started his internship when the hospital he was assigned to was victimized by bombs. Though not destroyed, it was condemned. Other doctors stationed at the facility had searched out other workplaces, but John had heard of Jury through a friend, and had gathered his belongings, left the city, and made his way to town.

After John had studied Burnwell where he hung, the three of us worked to remove the nails, then carried the dead mayor to John's home office, where we rested him gently on the examination table. Nicolas Rogers left us to spread the word.

"Does this mean our job is mute?"

"It's moot. And, yeah, I'd say so," Tim answered.

It was early evening, and they were back in the park again, under the spreading branches, smooching from time to time. Voices in the near distance, quiet laughter and secretive whispering in shadowy small groups, both women and men who in the growing darkness appeared to be in uniform and carrying weapons. The birds had fallen silent, and even the distant gurgling of the river was absent.

"Who do you think would do such a thing?"

He turned her face and kissed her on the forehead.

"I don't know," he said. "But I think we'll soon find out. And then ... I don't know."

They could hear percussive sounds in the far distance in the flatlands, then a burst high in the mountains, on the other side of town.

"Night bombing," she said.

"But far away," he said.

"Do you think it will ever get here?"

He squeezed her hand. "It hasn't in human memory. I doubt it. Don't worry."

"Okay," she whispered, then leaned her body against his.

The delegation arrived at my bookstore the day after the

funeral. Many in the town had attended, but not one of those who came to see me. There had been no tears, and the mayor had been buried in an elevated site that he had set out for himself, prominent in our small cemetery. With his death, Jury was without governance, and since I'd supposedly found and removed the body, and since I held a significant place in the community, it was left to me to take the reins, though there seemed to be no horse or other vehicle before me. I became the de facto spokesman until a proper election could be held, though I soon found out there would be nothing of the kind.

There were six of them. The Bollinger sisters, Edna and Emma, George Papadopoulos and his strapping young son, Bemus, Petra Kovack, an accomplished seamstress in charge of the clothing "factory", and Epson Wolf, the local barber. All carried weapons, even Edna and Emma, their sidearms in broad western holsters that appeared somewhat ludicrous, hanging from broad hips that were covered in billowing, flowery dresses. We repaired to the ice cream parlor next door and arranged two table so that they became one. Jane Zane turned the door sign to read "closed" then took our orders, ice cream cones and sundaes, and for me a chocolate malted. Then, when we were settled, she took her place at the head of the table, clearly the one in charge. She had removed her apron and little white hat, revealing herself in tight jeans and a brown shirt with epaulets at the shoulders. Her dark hair was cut short, pageboy fashion, and her eyes were steely where they glared out from under her long bangs.

"Let's get right to it," she said, glancing round the table, then fixing her eyes on me. "There are at least a hundred of us, all armed, and we're taking over this town."

"But Jackie Burnwell," I said. "What about him? That note. Did you kill him?"

"Kill is not the word." The start of a snarl played at the

edge of her lips. "The king is dead. Long live the king. And I'm the king."

"He was innocent."

"No! He was weak, and he made the town weak. In his graft and rules and stupidity, he had to go."

"But, to be crucified?"

I could feel a bit of discomfort in Papadopoulos and his son. The sisters and Petra Kovack drew themselves erect, smiling at their leader. Epson Wolf ran his fingers through his neatly trimmed hair.

"We are Christians," Zane said. "And this is war. Jury must be armed for war."

"What war?" I said. "There's been nothing here for centuries."

"But it will be coming. A first, not a second coming. Let me explain."

The others settled back in their chairs, spooning their sundaes and licking their cones, ready for the monologue they had heard many times before. Silence had fallen, and under it we could hear the hum of the ice cream freezer.

"War is at the heart of all religions. Most especially it is the engine that drives Christianity. And the war that surrounds us is a religious war. We are at war with Islam, Buddhism, Hinduism, whatever."

"But here in Jury we are at peace!"

"Don't interrupt!" Wolf smacked his hand on the table.

"War must be accepted as the Christian way. We must reject the defensive posture at the heart of Mayor Jackie Burnwell's cowardly and corrupt ways.

"Christ's crucifixion is an emblem of war. Yes, he died for our sins, but he was killed in a war against Christianity even before it was a religion. Burnwell's mock crucifixion was aimed at the old order, to put an end to it, both symbolically and actually. We can no longer sit by idly while others, many of them our brothers and sisters, take part in Christianity's destiny. Thus have we gathered the faithful here in Jury. We are a hundred strong, at least. And I, Jane Zane, am the boss, though I prefer the more modest appellations of Captain or Leader, even Prophet will do.

"Now, my dear Freddy Rush, you who loves guzzling malteds, I wish to designate you as mayor, the one who I will manipulate from the shadows. I'll be the controller, the war preparer, and you will keep the town's books, will oversee rules of the new order. 'Hold everything close?' Ridiculous! Buy and sell, forge weapons, distribute the fine war-art sculptures fashioned by Edna and Emma, batten down the hatches, prepare for the war to come to us, even go out into the flatlands to engage the enemy!

"What do you say, Freddy? Are you ready?"

In the next few days and into the evenings the bombing was severe and came close enough to shake many buildings in the town. Some of the explosions were deafening, both out on the flatlands and high up in the mountains beyond. Many in the town stayed sheltered in their houses and businesses, but many others, weapons at the ready, roamed the streets, park, and the river's edge.

For the first time in a long time I eschewed my malted and went at nightfall to have a talk with Doctor John.

"This is nuts," I said. "Insane. Who in the hell do they intend to fight? There's nobody, just the bombs. They can't even see the planes or whatever they are that drop them."

"I hear that with the help of Jason Brats, the steelworker guy, who's one of them, they're building rockets back up in the hills."

"And I hear that's bullshit. Something Zane in spreading around in order to urge them on."

"Ah well, what you gonna do?"

One of the sisters' sculptures, a phallic-looking cannon of some sort, sat on the end table beside my chair. Emma had come in for a checkup and had presented it to the doctor.

"I don't really know. I hate to be a front man for Crazy Jane Zane, but somebody has to try to keep order. People are frightened, even those who are her followers. I've spoken to a few. They seemed bewildered by the whole thing."

The sculpture on the table rocked in place as an explosion close by in the flatlands shook the town.

"Anything I can do. Just come and get me."

She wore blue high-top tennis shoes, white sox turned over at the cuffs. She was going to be blue this evening. On the shoes' rise, a salvaged "Converse" emblem had been sewn in at the "factory". A powder-blue sleeveless blouse, with a frilly, broad tie-like structure draped between her breasts. The tie's folds glowed faintly red under the blue. Her squaw skirt was knee-length, midnight, and loose. And she saw in this deep color, in the candle-lit space, dark possibilities, things to come. She was wet. He was tan.

He wore khaki pants, and below that, argyles, tan loafers. His shirt was the same burlywood chambray as always. Cologne, Old Spice. There was a special presence pushing at his underwear.

"Is the end coming?" she asked, whispering the words of her plaintive question into the candlelight, but beyond that to his half-shadowed face.

"I hope not," he said, taking her hand and leading her to the couch, where she sat beside him. His hand crossing her stomach, coming to rest on the attractive rise of her behind. He could feel the seam of her underwear below the folds of fabric at her thigh.

"But I think the good guys will prevail. Jane Zane is clearly a lunatic who has found a way to enter the almost forgotten fears of a number of people in Jury, to drag them to the surface. But I think that once these deep-seated fears fade away again, her followers will have the strength to leave her."

She turned toward him. "I love it when you talk like that." She smiled, the tip of her tongue briefly touching her lower lip. The faintest of blue lipstick. She leaned toward him, his face, her lips slightly parted and swelling a little, reaching out to him. He kissed her, deeply and long, their tongues intertwined and active, then boldly grasped her right breast and held it. He could feel the thin fabric slide over the ribs in her brassier.

And, as boldly as he, she reached over and grasped his erect penis – she thought of it as his cock – through his pants and underwear, squeezed it, and delivered her mouth for another long kiss.

Then his hand was between her legs, closer than it had ever been before. His index finger touched her through her panties, tickled and moved. She opened her legs. One hung over the couch arm. Her panties were, of course, blue, turquoise, made from the finest cotton. And through these panties he caressed her vagina, that was how he thought of it, and she squeezed and slid the fabric back and forth, again and again, over his member. They did these things for a very long time, and when they fell apart, soaked in satisfaction, he looked at her, her skirt hiked up and her legs spread. She was looking into his eyes.

"Good God!" was his deep groan.

"We were *so* close," she thought. "We almost did it."

He slid a finger into her mouth. She bit it.

In the following months, change came to the town of Jury and those within it. Zane put a curfew in place in order to display some personal control over our already instituted blackouts. The barter system was ended, and though there were those who tried, secretly, to continue using it, stiff penalties were put in place.

A currency was fashioned, then doled out to the towns-folk in exchange for old bills and selected goods. The money consisted of thin chips of balsa wood, one side not-ing the denomination in confiscated nail polish, the other branded with a symbol of authentication, an intricate one, hard to counterfeit. The branding iron was locked up in a safe.

Guards were, for some reason, placed at the doors of important businesses, and women, including Petra Kovack who had closed the repair and creation of clothing "fac-tory", were sent out in shifts to watch the sky and the flat-lands below. Epson Wolf, now weaponized, no longer worked hair in his shop, but home clipping, produced a certain heady wildness in the population. There was man-dated exercise and weapons training. The Bollinger sisters' sculptures were urged on the community, and Edna and Emma collected a good number of chips. The ice cream parlor was closed down, and this produced a deep sadness in Jury, one that I shared.

The bombing had lessened, until there were no more than a few daily percussive blasts heard at a far distance. Still, the crazed Christians, and those infected by their demeanor, were nervous and vigilant in their fear.

But for Zane's followers, their weapons always at the ready as they strutted about, the streets became, for the most part, empty. People stayed in their homes, leaving only for food and supplies, and in the evenings the park, the path along the river, the woods above town, and the edge of the flatlands were mostly empty of all but the occasional cat and nocturnal raccoon.

"A sad state of affairs," Doctor John said. "How are you handling it?"

"Okay, I guess. Various records to keep and edicts to formalize. But it really pisses me off. Carrying out the orders of that lunatic. But I have to do it, have to try to prevent chaos. She doesn't know what she's doing, and she doesn't know how to do it."

We were sitting in John's living room, drinking the rough whiskey the stills continued to produce. Jane Zane liked to drink and had left them in place. The street beyond the windows was silent, and in the blackout, shades drawn, we sat in candlelight, sipping the foul substance.

Then there was a pounding at the door. We lurched in our chairs. What in the world could that be, something that idiot has cooked up? The pounding continued. Doctor John crossed to the door and yanked it open, and a small young man in torn and dirty clothing rushed into the room, grinning and nodding his head.

"What do you want?" I said.

"Are you the boss, the Mayor, something like that?" He was staggering, breathing hard, his eyes flashing between us.

"Not exactly," I said. "Something like that? Yes, I guess so."

"Great! Then you're the man I'm after. I've come a long way. With the news."

"What news is that?" John asked.

"It's the wars!" he said. "They're over! There's a treaty and a common surrender! No more war! I have this official paper." He reached out with it, his hand shaking, and I took it and quickly read it. It held an official government stamp. He was right. This was all the evidence I needed.

I moved to the door, hearing John offering a chair and a drink, and headed quickly down the street to the church. "Curfew!" someone yelled out behind me, but I ignored him.

The Congregational Church was one of the few places Jane Zane hadn't commandeered, and I opened the heavy door and rushed inside to find only a smoky darkness and a dim light on the high altar. My voice echoed in the somber space as I called out. I received no answer. The church was empty, so I turned and headed across the street to the bar, the only one still active in Jury. I knew that the minister was a drinker. Maybe he was in there. The blackout shades were drawn, but I could hear voices inside. When they left, they'd violate the curfew, but it was only ten o'clock, and they wouldn't be leaving for a good long while. Heads turned when I entered. A few nodded greetings.

"Is the minister here?" I called out over the loud conversations, and Tunis Lingerlonger rose from his stool at the bar's end.

"Hey, Freddy," he said. "What's up?"

Tunis was a small, chubby man, who looked nothing like the severe Scandinavian ministers of old. In the pulpit, in his ill-fitting, baggy raiments, he was a comic figure, though a jolly and forgiving one. His sermons were always upbeat, bringing an optimistic view of things to Jury's watchful and anxious population. Now on his feet, he waddled toward me, his street clothes, like his vestments, askew.

"Come with me," I said. "Right now!" I guess I spoke sternly enough, for Lingerlonger didn't linger, but waved off his drink and his bill and followed me quickly through the door.

"What's going on?" he called out behind me.

"I'll tell you, right away," I called back. "But we must get the codes. Hurry!"

He couldn't believe it when I told him. He thought I was joking. But when he saw that I was serious, he began to hop around, throwing his arms in the air.

"Dear Lord!" he said. "This is amazing! Are you sure?"

"Yes," I said. "But we must get the bell codes."

The codes were a list of a good number of bell rings, many of which had been memorized by the townsfolk. Codes for church suppers and services, for the end of the school day, for barter and clothing at the "factory", for bomb warnings, and for twenty or more other things that had been forgotten, since they were rarely rung. And there was one for the end of war. It had never been used, and in time had been dropped from the list.

"There's a file of old lists," Tunis said. "I think I know where it is!" And he left me standing before the altar and rushed behind it and into the vestry. He was gone for a few long minutes, then returned, grinning and waving a paper.

"Here it is!" he said.

It was simplicity itself: three long gongs on the big bell and a tinkle on one of the smaller bells between them. We went together to the pulls, and Lingerlonger, still grinning, grasped the two ropes and leaned into them, squatting as he administered the sequence.

We could hear them. They were loud, not somber but joyful. At least we heard them that way in our enthusiasm, as Tunis continued with the task, and when he seemed to be tiring, I took over. We rang out the news for a good long while, and when we thought it was enough, we dropped the ropes, then left the church and found ourselves standing in the street in a gathering of those who had exited the bar. Most of the drinkers seemed bewildered, but a few had grasped the significance and were slapping one another on the back, laughing and passing the word.

And the streets and the park were beginning to fill, figures, some in night clothes, hugging each other, weeping joyfully, calling out the obvious, "The wars are over!" Weapons of most of the followers were dropped to the street or cast into yards, and I saw Jane Zane moving frantically through the crowds, followed by two diehards, their rifles at the ready, heading toward me.

"Freddy, this can't be! We must stop this!" She was yelling, her pageboy bouncing.

"It's over, Jane," I said, when she reached me.

"No! No, it's not! It will begin again! It must! This is the Christian way! It's mans' destiny!"

She began to strike me about the head and shoulders then, waving her hands and fists frantically, and a couple of bar frequenters stepped in and grabbed and held her. The men behind her lowered their weapons then and dropped them to the pavement, where they landed with a clatter. I turned to the sound of Jane's hysterical screaming, and saw those stalwarts carrying her away. A loud "Yahoo!" rang out in the group of jubilant drinkers, and I made my way through the crowds to Doctor John's house for another powerful whiskey.

It's been a year since the wars ended, and Jury in some ways has changed and in other ways has remained the same. The old spirit is back, minus that deep-seated underlying fear, and people go about as in any old town, greeting passersby, whistling newly recovered tunes. Yet we have TV and phones too, though the latter are rarely used. Jury's people like to converse face to face.

And a new monetary system has been put in place, bills and change, all stamped with the emblem of the new republic. In time, the town may become even more modernized, as newer technologies creep in.

I'm the mayor now, and I've been abroad, to Washington for consultation, returning to Jury with news and great box-of-chocolate images of past presidents and cabinet members for the children. I've replaced the power that was Jane Zane's, but I have not and won't use it. All I do is monitor Jury's finances, make announcements, greet townsfolk at various venues. Jane Zane, for her part, was exiled, taken away screaming to that same psychiatric clinic in Cleveland that was itself still in recovery, and like that past president of old, her delusions of power would take a long time to cure, if curing were even possible.

Things move along. The streets are newly paved; new businesses have opened on Main; lawns are freshly cut, and a good many dwellings have been painted. There are church suppers, community gatherings, yard sales, and children play in the park without a care. Epson Wolf is back at his chair, cutting and trimming. The Bollinger sisters are working on less aggressive sculptures. Petra Kovack is constantly at the task of constructing refined clothing, but out of fresh, new fabric now, and has even opened a dress shop. I haven't seen hide nor hair of Papadopoulos and his son. But the young lovers are still here.

Though not yet married, Sandy has quit her cramped apartment and has moved into Tim's larger but no less modest one. And Tim has taken a job as manager of the new florist shop, next door to my bookstore, where I now sell and buy books rather than lending them. The florist owner welcomed Tim, whose knowledge of flowers, learned from his mother, was vast and particular. She had taught him flower arranging as well, and he was able to produce lovely, and at times haunting, bouquets. I'd seen both of them on the street and in the newly reopened ice cream parlor. They each seemed happy. They moved about insouciantly, but when I caught sight of them together, strolling, holding hands, I noticed a hitch in their behavior, an itchiness, and on a bright winter's day, billowy drifts of snow on streets and awnings, I found them, bundled up in thick coats and wool caps, standing before my shop window, looking in at the books on display there. I went out and greeted them. It was close to Christmas, and there were wreaths pinned to doors, jolly Santas in their white beards and red suits chuckling along with children on the sidewalks. There were lights and decorations in the trees, and down the way I could hear carolers singing, and above that the sounds of bells playing a Christmas tune. I imagined Minister Tunis Lingerlonger joyfully pulling the many ropes.

"How are you two?" I asked them. I was wearing no coat and was shivering a little.

They nodded and beamed and pressed against each other in their winter garb as an answer.

"But I've noticed something," I said. "Are you planning to leave Jury, to get out in the world? I'm guessing you might be."

"We were," Tim said, smiling down at her.

"Do you really want to stay here?" I asked Sandy, whose smile broadened, her rose lipstick the color of real roses.

"Why not!" she said, grinning. "I think this might be paradise!"

A Brief Encounter

LARRY HAD MANAGED to push out thirty-nine of the condoms, but when he got to the last one he had some trouble. He forced and grunted, and finally it broke free, plopping into the toilet bowel among the others. Each condom contained its portion of black tar heroin, and all but the one came clean in the toilet water. He lifted them out, letting that last one soak, and wiped them dry with toilet paper, then stuffed them into his pockets. The remaining one wouldn't give up its stains. It was gummy with fecal matter, and the more he wiped the stickier it got.

It was quiet in the airport men's room. Nobody in the stalls beside him, and he heard only what he thought were two men at the urinals, a cough and a groan. So he decided to head out to one of the sinks, where there was soap.

"What ya got there?" an old man two sinks down called out. The place had quickly filled; probably some plane had arrived. All the urinals were in use, and men were going into the stalls to piss.

Larry mumbled something as he soaped up the condom, then heard a shuffling of feet behind him.

"Looks like drugs to me. You one a them coyotes they talk about?"

He turned and saw five men, shoulder to shoulder, looking into his sink.

"Not coyotes, man," a tall, tough-looking guy in the back of the growing gathering called out. "Coyotes are people smugglers. These guys are called mules. They use balloons or condoms. Right up the ass. You a mule?"

Larry had finished washing the condom, and when he turned to head to the towel dispenser to dry it, he saw that the crowd had tightened and was looking at him suspiciously.

Quick thinker that he was, he held up the condom and waved it at the gathering.

"This," he said, "is not a balloon or a condom. This is a colostomy bag." He held it out and shook it. "And what's inside here is my shit." He glared at them, forcing them back just a little.

"My mother had one of those," a man a few sinks down called out.

"Mine too, but it was a hell of a lot bigger than *that*."

Larry addressed that man, a short fellow, maybe forty, going bald.

"They come in various sizes," he said, "depending on the medical issues. Okay? Now that y'all have violated my privacy, God damnit! – back off!"

"Let's see it," somebody said.

"See what?" Larry answered, his voice full of anger.

"That hole place where you slip in on."

There was no hole, of course, and Larry thought to brazen it out. But now he saw that the men, though still suspicious, were curious as well, and he had to come up with something else.

"The hole closes when the bag is detached for washing."

"It never did on my mother."

"Mine either."

"This is new," Larry said. "A new medical technique. Now if you're finished with your questions, you can step aside."

Not one of them did.

"Okay, okay. You wanna see it? Okay, for God's sake!"

He turned back to the sink, unbuttoned his shirt, and worked the gum he'd been chewing out of his mouth and into his hand. Then he hunched over and opened the condom and tried to connect it. He found a way, then turned and faced the gathering. Using the gum, he had attached the condom to his right nipple. It hung there, the weight of the black tar causing it to sway.

"Good God!" one of them said. "That's your nipple!"

"Yes, it would seem so," Larry answered. "But this is the route the intestine takes to get to the surface."

"Why d'ya say 'root' instead of 'rowt'? Ain't that from a tree, some bushes?"

"Because my pronunciation is correct, that's why. Your pronunciation of route as 'rowt' has the word referring to a successful storming of a castle, a Chicago Bears game in which that team has lost by forty points or more, not a direction between places. Route is properly pronounced 'root'. Hey, I hope there aren't any Bears fans in here!"

The men laughed and punched each other on the shoulders.

"What about the nipple?" somebody said.

"Boy, do I like a good discussion."

"Oh yeah, me too."

He gazed down at his nipple and the swaying condom full of heroin. Then he looked up at them and spoke.

"Three years ago, the Mayo clinic in Minnesota began a secret series of tests, using cadavers, to try to invent some new ways with bowel resections, one that would account for the differences between people. And people are different when it comes to their vital insides. Their discoveries bore fruit, and my operation was the product, an application of science to real life.

"What looks like a nipple to you is really a doorway to a tunnel, one that expels and renders half of the fecal matter into a liquid form. You see how it's attached? The nipple itself is really a miniaturized pump. It drawn the liquid parts of the fecal matter into the bag. What's in *this* bag – he caressed the hanging condom – is part of the other half of the fecal deposit, that which remains firm."

"My Lord, a medical breakthrough," said an awestruck voice.

"You can say that again."

"I'll sure as hell remember this for a long time."

"What's your handle, stranger?" A young man said in a cowboy twang.

All the men laughed and punched each other on the shoulders.

"It's Jessie, just Jessie."

"That's a corker!"

"Now would you please get the hell out of my way? It's time I rode out."

Larry was buttoning up as he stepped forward, and some caught a glimpse of the oscillating condom before the shirt, that was a curtain, hid it from view.

They part like the Red Sea, he thought, and soon he was out of the terminal and on the sidewalk in the sun.

He stood there smiling for a few moments. He could feel the smooth surface of the condom traveling through the hair on his chest.

"I think I'll wear it for a while," he said out loud, then walked away.

Too Young to Go Steady

WILL THE BURGER King marry the Dairy Queen? And will they live happily ever after in the White Castle?

A man's home, he thinks. Then a finger under her chin, a pirouette, that grin, and the passing poodle. Something at the door reflected. Her ankle bracelet? And then she's gone.

Christ, it's 1955. Modern Times. He's thirty-six years old, but he'd have a go at her too, were she not his daughter. What a thought! He'd never think about that.

On the bed, that evening, in her little pink room ... On the bed in a secret chamber in that opulent mansion ... In the castle, on a bed, far far away from Bleak House, near Canterbury, in "A Tale of Another Country". The King, the Queen, and the Dark Lady (that's her, though in a poodle skirt). She rises, spins again, turns on the light and draws the curtains. She doesn't use the new phoneline. Study time.

He likes a boilermaker, though it's not the same at home. The smell of ground beef still on his fingers. She should be back from the dairy by now. Give it a few minutes, then he'll call. Pay bills in the meantime: the mortgage, her birthday telephone line, for calling him? Present of the poodle skirt. Would that he were that young again. Sixteen a week ago. He gave her a red rose. He never studied like that. Even in love, she's hard at it. Even without a mother. He lifts the phone.

Whan that Aprille, with his shoures soote / The droghte of March hath perced to the roote. When April came with his sugar suit, the March Hair of Drought got perky to the root. That's Angie, goofing around. It's not funny, to her anyway. But she's got to memorize this for Mr Lumbson. And she likes it, Chaucer, Dickens too. She's a very good student. And mathematics. He says we're not ready. But she's sixteen! I'll bet he's talking to the Dairy Queen.

A plan for a picnic at Starved Rock, just the three of them on a day trip. She'll bring dairy ice cream, strawberries and whipped cream. She likes his daughter, can see herself younger in her bright eyes, somewhat tortured because of that older boy. Older? Well, he's eighteen anyway, a senior, but that's all she'll say. They've talked at least that much, though she's almost a total stranger. What's to become of me? Is he serious about this, a new mother? She'll be gone before he knows it. Curious. They were high school sweethearts too, for a while at least, in 1935.

Lights out (vocabulary), and the Dark Lady has risen to gaze at the gibbous moon, convex, from the parapet, her diaphanous gown penetrated by this recapitulated diffusion. Every night, lachrymose, she muses over the Prince and his reluctance. Is he made of stone, impenetrable igneous rock, pyrogenic? Too young to go steady? Pshaw! Her ebullient trousseau is ready, a portmanteau in which she savors the most diminutive trinket: her Solstice Ball dance card. Full, of course. There's a plethora of other Princes; score of the minuet he'd composed for her; a pressed flower from some perennial; his letter and the Petrarchan sonnet; and a lot of other stuff. He rings the coach's bell to summon her. The Burger King doesn't like that. The Queen has departed, looks like forever, on that interminable journey of hers. Someday he'll be sorry. Yet the Dark Lady muses on his machinations, stepping lightly along the dark battlements. Then the moon sidles behind something cumulus. To be continued. Goodnight, my Prince.

He blows the goddamned horn, that annoying toot, then just sits in the MG. She doesn't take her time. A car like that, he's got money and the whole damn school year ahead. Then off to what? He'd heard a mention of Stanford, and in two more years she'll wind up at the JC. Smart as she is, smart as he thinks he is. Why not let her go? Is he making her, in that car of his? Isn't it too small? He can't believe that of her. She seems desperate in her first love, but not that desperate. Good Lord, I remember it all from his side. The Dairy Queen, her father's dairy. We did it in the forest preserve, under the stars. Her body was like heavy cream, firm but compliant. Those scents, that thrill, and the mastery! He's made a romance of it all, the memory. It was furtive, messily ejaculate, embarrassing. But she's back now. The same high school. He blows the goddamned horn.

Oh, God! I've got my period!

Blood between his fingers at the butcher shop.

Milk, cream, and butter. Always the same thing. Milk, cream, and butter.

Can't he see he drives me wild? The Beautiful Child, that Prince, and the Hungry Lady. The Queen is dead, or at least gone on some interminable journey. Entourage of the King defeated. The creak of languorous coach wheels at a distant border. Perhaps in the White Castle, something reflected. Shined shoes, the ankle bracelet, knees. Must he always treat me like a child, having changed into other garments aggressively? Retirement of the poodle skirt, not really the fashion, back in the dark closet. Too much waiting on absence, these muscles under the muscles like curdling cream. Someday, just wait and see. The sumptuous board, the poised mendicant, that's me. Under a habitat of crystal teardrops in a chandelier: bright light at the butcher shop, the dairy. Having filled the basin with bloody water. Certainty of invisible instruments at the ready. Someone hanging from a showerhead. He drowns in a moat, lake, or river. The Beautiful Lady, the King, and the Hungry Child. Won't he ever own up? Coach wheels under a chassis, rubber, a certain vehicle. Someone watching from an MG at the water's edge. The knees, always the knees, and above the knees. He says we'll have to wait. Don't say it. Certainty of cunning instruments at the ready. This dark dream. Is it hers, his, or the Dairy Queen's?

Little white five-room house. Cinder block, green trim, a little crenelated filigree in the eaves, a faux turret. Steps down to a gravel path, two stunted trees, a gate in a white picket fence, break your mother's back sidewalk, crabgrass in the verge, then the road. He'll blow the goddamned horn. He doesn't blow the horn. Daddy? He's late again, this time very. She flops down on the kitchen chair. Just a light bourbon for the Burger King this evening, that smell again as he lifts the glass. Let's talk, he says. There's nothing he can tell her. The nature of her underwear, those hearts? She tries to talk about the way she feels. It's hopeless. Saddle shoes and turned down sox, hair like butter, tied back with a red ribbon. Oh God, it's high school and the Dairy Queen again. Is she like what she was? His imagination. Was she ever like that? He'll wish he'd gone steady. She's petulant for a moment, like a child. With me. Of course, it's just a pin, a ring, his letterman's sweater, lugging her books, holding hands in the hallway conspicuously, secretive whispering in public places, his initials, DP, on a charm on her ankle. Could have been BK, had he gone steady with the DQ. Why not? he thinks, and troubles it like a teen. Good God, I'm thirty-six years old, and she's back again. It's not the same thing. I'm grown up. This can be serious. But then why am I feeling this way? Well, he's not coming at all, I guess. It looks that way. I'm very sorry, he says, formally and with effort. It's okay. I'm off to study now, and bed. Then she's gone. The pink room, the desk, the carefully made bed, her posters on the wall: a country garden in Britain, Starved Rock, dairy cows in a meadow. She's a very good girl. He lifts the glass. Outside, the street is dark now, and quiet.

Lights out, and the Lady is dressed now in a white, virginal gown. But it complements her dark tresses erotically. Oh, I wish I could dye my hair! Once again on the battlements. Or parapet? Look that up. After the ball, at which he did not make an appearance. The Wife of Bath, her servant, comes out with a cloak, something woven, but of soft fabric, dark as her hair. The Wife bows and scrapes in a slightly ribald way, which is her nature, then retreats. And she's alone again. Why wait 'til it may be too late? Only a year now and he'll be off to the university, at a far distance, near the sea. She fancies she can taste something of it, salt in water, but it's only tears, lachrymose again. Her own life, she thinks, her hair lifting now in the breeze, to stand out in the air behind her like a dark flag. Friendly bats are black spots against the black sky. No moon tonight, only a few faint blinking stars. She looks so mysterious and passionate here, she can't stand herself. Too young, I hear him say, but he doesn't show up. If I am as such, I must be tender, a child? And yet he treats me like an adult, one who can handle broken promises. Too young, so he tells me. Well, enough with him. But she is still lachrymose. Tears

fall – of regret, betrayal, or is it relief? She turns, a pirouette, walks back across the terrace to the glass doors of her
pink room. Her hair blows free in the night. She undresses
in the dim light, casting away her heart-embroidered
panties, stained lightly with blood from her period, then
accomplishes her toilet. After that, she enters her bed,
crawls down between the cool sheets and their comfort.
Will sleep come, as usual, almost immediately? Goodnight,
Daddy.

The months limped slowly by, or skipped, depending upon
weather and the engagements of the perceiver. By late
October the grills were set aside. Ground beef mostly for
meatloaf then, very few patties. The blood on his apron
congealed more quickly come November and the cold, and
as his knife sliced into the roasting meat and he spread the
flesh, he thought about her hands at the Dairy where she
was measuring, dipping cream, thinking about the coming
need for eggnog and about him. At Christmastime, the
Prince went off with his family to warmer climes, and the
Dark Lady thought only briefly of that Floridian indul-
gence. She was hard at Shakespeare now, puzzling out the
poetry and was fussing with the idea of torts, the advanced
student mini-law-course she'd been admitted into for the
coming summer. The days skipped by. Christmas dinner
with the Dairy Queen, an exchange of gifts. She'd gotten
some books she'd wanted, had given aftershave, a wallet
for each one, and perfume. Then back again into her little
pink room, more study and the fun in such imagination.
Was she getting too old to go steady? He was there, it
seemed only a few times. He blew the goddamned horn.
And when he wasn't there, he was gone out of mind.

At the start of March, after the pressures of college applications and return replies. Halfway through the year-book planning stages, getting ready for the prom and graduation.

At the end of the basketball season, but before final examinations and those following goodbyes that will seem no more than temporary, the body was discovered under the waterwheel at the Old Mill, a place where steady lovers went for adolescent groping, just a few hundred yards from the road.

He had been dead for a few days. Hung and not drowned, but not there. He'd been a basketball player, not a star but a stalwart, a senior on his way to California and Long Beach State College. It wasn't Yale, but a good if imperfect venue. He was of average size and a little awkward in his bearing. Of less than average intelligence, he talked a lot, told loud jokes about girls. He was arrogant slightly beyond the reach of his abilities. He wasn't well-liked.

The school closed down for a day of meditation and mourning, and the students mourned in the drive-in restaurants, at the movies, in shops at the town center, in convertibles with their tops down in the cool weather, even drinking beer in the forest preserve. Some actually did mourn. Even wept. Not so much for him as for the vague feeling of a dark veil fallen to snuff expectations of joy in the coming endings, the final year, high school itself, the prom and bittersweet partings.

They were outside the satellite ring. It held a few clusters of chatting students, just three or four in each, at an equal distance from the fountain, which spewed a great geyser of water that fell in a dull, almost subliminal roar.

They watched and held hands. His friend, his fellow teammate, dead now, both of the same social class. Did he actually say that? I know, I know, she said, I understand. But she caught his pretentiousness and wasn't thinking right then about going steady. I can be his girl then, just for another month or so. Straight As this semester! He never studies. Nor does he talk about ideas. Jesus, he says, we were friends! As if saying that can make feelings come true. What's the use? Summer school's coming soon for the fun of it. Part-time work at the Dairy. The Queen arranged it. They're getting very close, she thinks, not a bit like us. Hey! There are some teammates! he calls out as he sets off, leaving her standing there.

A funeral was held at the Episcopal church, family, invited guests, and parishioners. That left her out, as well as ninety-nine percent of the community. The principal, no fool, scheduled a secular service in the gymnasium. There was a stage there, accessible once the baskets were cranked up. Hundreds of people came. They played his favorite songs, Pat Boone, The Four Aces, Patti Page. *The Great Pretender* seemed ominous. The color guard lowered the flag. The principal, the police chief, even the mayor gave speeches. Each one too long. The entire basketball team, in full uniform, stood with their heads bowed, a conspicuous void in their ranks, a coat rack draped with a black cloth. It looked very much like the grim reaper, a rising specter. He was there, of course, as somber as all the rest.

Life goes on. The police placed his death in a shower stall at the high school. He'd been hung from the shower-head. His own hand? Didn't seem likely, since he was found miles away. But at the high school! The whole town was up in arms, hysterically, having no clear idea at all of the implications. The police had. Someone at the school. The best bet a staffer, even a student. Could it really be a student? They picked up a drifter, questioned him awkwardly, then let him go. They took fingerprints most every-where, ran a great variety of chemistry-set tests. They came up with very little, actually nothing.

He had been in the presence of others into the afternoon, on a Wednesday. Then he was seen heading from the weight room to the showers at about four-thirty. His parents knew of the team dinner and party a week before the last game. He and some others would be staying over, for a few days, at a cabin in the woods. Signals were crossed. They hadn't missed him. But he was not present with the others. He was found under the waterwheel after three days.

He had no enemies. The police interviewed his friends, even the Prince, but learned only that he was a nice guy, easy to get along with, a stalwart on the court. They were stuck, would have gone back to the drawing board had they had one.

Dinner. She brought the whole thing. Hamburger casse-role, sweet potatoes, even a hotpot of little braised onions. And she brought dessert. Ice cream and whipped cream, various sauces, bananas, chopped nuts, and maraschino cherries. Oh my, he thought. This is it. This has to be it. Her smile, her skin still milky. What was it? Her lips pecking lightly at his in the forest preserve. A starry sky! Okay, she said, let's chow down. The Dark Lady was hungry. Conver-sation, like a family, between bites. Is he getting over the death? It's the Burger King. I don't know. He's acting so strange, kind of numb? she says. Passing the onions, the Dairy Queen poses the question formally. Was it a student, do you think? Well, actually, the Dark Lady answers demurely, I think it's him. The Burger King falls back into his chair, his fork still at the ready. Are you serious? Why? The police! Whatever the hell they can do, says the Queen. I've been thinking, says the DL. She's ready for the law course now. Oh, oh. It's the King. That we could look into this on our own. Are you serious? The police! But the Dairy Queen doesn't balk. Are you kidding? That's insane! Why not? the Queen thinks. This is a way to get closer, involved with each other. How can it hurt? We can make a list, the Dark Lady opines.

1. Alibi: he doesn't have one.
2. All their classes were taken together.
3. Similar grades on the SATs. They'd both bragged about it.
4. Basketball.
5. The Prince and his family sat to the far side at the funeral.

Were they really friends, then? I don't think so, the DL says, but they did have secrets. The Prince had been awkward in his good fellowship. The guy was quite dull, after all. But then, she'd been wondering about the Prince himself recently. Then there was basketball. They'd spent a lot of time talking, over to the side. Plotting? Neither one had ever studied. Good God, this is insane. What exactly is it you want to do? Invite him to Starved Rock, the Dairy Queen says. Oh, Jesus. And then there's the MG, says the DL. That should be on the list too.

The Dark Lady walks again on the ramparts. She's dyed her hair blond. It catches the moonlight. No shawl is necessary this time, it's warm, and the day birds are still up, although it's past their sunset bedtime. Gee, that's early! Blue jays, sparrows, and red-winged blackbirds: an incessant chatter that might have destroyed another mood, but not this one. Forget him. Her shift is almost transparent, her figure blah blah, and her thin ankle, bound with the bracelet on which dangles his charm. She raises her delicate foot high up to the rampart wall, hopping a little on the other to keep her balance. She's searching for the clasp. She finally finds and unhooks it, removing herself from this once acceptable bondage. Then she flings out the bracelet beyond the battlements, into the dark night. Goodbye to him. And goodbye to the charms of those other attachments, but for the serious ones that require no such trinkets. She steps away from the wall, pirouettes, then walks to the glass doors of her bedroom, her new hair bouncing, blond to the very roots. The light's on, bright over her desk. That's it. Just study now, very hard. No more fantasy nonsense.

This is completely crazy! But that night in the forest preserve. The stars! Her lips! Their bodies in glorious union for long moments! God, she's gorgeous. Who does he mean, the Dairy Princess or the Queen? He blows the goddamned horn every night now. She skips to the gate. Some sort of undercover agent? This may be madness. That burger-smell again as he lifts his glass, club soda with a twist of lemon, now that it's getting serious. His wife, the escapee? He hasn't thought of her but for the papers he signed recently. Should he kneel when he offers the ring? She likes his daughter. It's mutual. Thank God the dairy keeps limping along. She earns about as much as he does. It's perfect.

Milk, heavy cream, and butter. Get me out of this! But there's no chance. Not many good men around. In high school, he was handsome enough, but awkward. Pleasantly, without guile. She thought she wanted something else, even had it for a while, much too long, until divorce. He'd asked her to go steady in their junior year, after six months of courting, stars in his eyes. They'd faded away when she declined. What was it exactly that she'd wanted? They'd joined again briefly for the junior prom, went once to the forest preserve, where it rained lightly and he displayed his prematurity. Wasn't that something! Funny for her, both then and now. But not for him. This isn't the point. He drinks, his hands smell, but he's steady and simple, and a damned good butcher. And he loves his daughter intelligently. That's special. She'll say yes!

They arrived at Starved Rock late in the morning, the rock itself a massive hulk at river's edge, wide at that point. It looked like a mound of ground beef that had been frosted with a mixture of brown sugar and stiff whipped cream that had then been festooned with pralines, mint leaves, and chunks of peanut butter fudge. They found a cookout meadow. Tables and benches and grated fire pits, set among hickory and red oak, and below their branches, witch hazel, black huckleberry and bracken fern. Then the Burger King prepared the burgers and hot dogs, while the Dairy Queen covered and set the wooden table. The fire, to be proper, would take a while, and David Prince, tall, stiff and lanky, a basketball player, and the Dark Lady, five-two and some said perky, Mimi actually, Miriam, the old testament, took a walk, circumventing other rock formations, stopping for a moment only to gaze out at Lover's Leap overlook, then wandering into wooded glades, accompanied by nuthatches and chickadees. Gosh, this is beautiful, she said, though she had other things on her mind, her creamy blond hair tied back with a blue ribbon. Gosh, this is nice! It's okay, he said. So when are you leaving for California? Next week, he said, giving up nothing more, reaching down in the thick undergrowth, into what she knew from Botany was poison ivy, to pull up a delicate purple flower and raise it to his cheek and nose. She dipped under a low branch brushing the tail of her hair, then looked up at him. You never studied, you know. She was acting coy.

Well, maybe I'm just smart, he said. Stanford, after all. Plenty of girls there, I bet. I suppose so. But math, Shakespeare, how did you manage that? I paid attention in class. Your friend, she said, he was going to California too. Yeah, he said, but not Stanford. Did he study? I can't really say. I guess so. But you were together almost all the time. Yeah, he said, right. She kept needling him, among the red cedar and white oak.

And at the cookout she continued. They had eaten their burgers and dogs and the Dairy Queen's slaw and were now getting into the ice cream. It was mid-afternoon, just a light warm breeze and a few tree shadows on the ground. Well, I just can't understand it, she said, calculus, Chaucer, the Mystery Plays? That's all fun, but it's very hard, and you never studied. Look, he said, finally completely frustrated, I cheated a little, okay? She rested her bowl on the table and reached down for her Poo Bear shoulder bag. With these? she said. She had lifted the fat sheath of copies, test answers and cheat sheets, and was waving them in the air. He was shocked, though not profoundly, having no such depth. How in the world did you get those? he said. Easy. Work-study. I was assigned to clean out his locker. I got myself assigned. What a fool, he says. I told him to destroy things. He was going to give it up, guilt or something, like a girl. Now just a minute there, says the Dairy Queen, oaks sending their shadows down upon them as the day wanes. Come again? The Burger King had fallen back into his chair. Well, it was an accident, kind of, says the Prince. But he was hung from the showerhead! says the Dark Lady. That's the "kind of" part. That's witty, surprisingly, given the circumstances and his dull way with language. Am I getting this right? The BK. Are you saying what I think you're saying? You killed him, says the Dairy Queen. Well, yes, I guess you could say that, but an accident. And Stanford. And then moved him? says the DL, in the MG? Of course, he says. I don't have another car. And it wasn't easy. Now wait just a damned minute, am I getting this right? Yes, Daddy. Well, it's Stanford, you know. The grades. There was no other way. He was going to give it up! In English and math, she says. I could have tutored you. Are you kidding? he says. A sophomore? My social class? Come again? says the Burger King. He will go down as the sun goes down over Starved Rock. He hasn't a clue. Jesus, whispers the BK, his face in complete shadow now. Shouldn't we be going? says the Dairy Queen. It's a long way back.

July came to its ending with a burst of scandal, and then betrothal, neither producing difficulties that the community at large couldn't handle. Ninety-nine percent of the populace didn't much care, about either, the two boys and the butcher. Yes, a few whispers of gossip about the remnants of mucus and blood found in the MG, and the Burger King actually down on his knees!

I guess Stanford is out now, he said through the bars, scratching at the rashes on his arms and cheeks.

She'd dragged the poodle skirt from the closet for the occasion.

But you can study here! she said. It's fun! I'll bring you the books!

Fat chance, he said.

The proper plea was insanity.

Brochures and reservations. The new suitcases, the clothes, the underwear. Her camera, broad-brimmed hats, feminine

items, prophylactic medicines and swimsuits. It's off to
Mexico for the honeymoon! But first the marriage, then the
reception, the former a private affair, just the three of them
and the dairy and butcher shop witnesses. But the reception! Her schoolmates, twenty at least, his few acquaintances, and the Dairy Queen's entourage of multitudes: relatives, workers, friends. And the food? The finest cuts of
beef, pork, veal, and lamb. Even geese and quail, even
pheasant. And cream: whipped, clotted and heavy, laced
with nutmeg, mint, strawberry, mango, lime. And fine
milky cheeses, rich sour cream and sweet butter. And
somebody brought sauces, nuts, and shortcake. And there
was joking, a few tears, and some testimonials and a lively
band: the Dictionaries.

Exhausted from a night of dancing, and stuffed with
food, they slept all the way to Acapulco, while the Dark
Lady watched as the earth moved away below them
through the plane window.

Swimming, sightseeing, a mariachi concert, good Mexican dinners at outdoor restaurants, a little TV. Then,
Daddy? Can I go out for a walk? I mean, alone? To the
library? Too much time on the beach in the first few days, a
little burned. Of course, he says, wanting to get back to the
Dairy Queen. And he trusts her. You're sixteen!

So she walked the streets of the small, vibrant city, just
Mimi now, in a nice new skirt and a white blouse, her hair
held up with combs, appropriate she thought to this prom-
ising foreign experience. She passed shops and restaurants, dipped into a few bookstores, even stopped for coffee at an outdoor café, red-checked tablecloths and blue
china, the waiter in a blue uniform. She found a small
museum, Mexican art and artifacts, and she lingered in it,
looking at paintings, tin retablos, and ceramic pots, read-

ing the small bilingual placards, even taking notes in the new book she'd brought along for that purpose.

Hola, señorita. Are you a visitor?

They stood side by side, before a painting of an elegant dark lady wearing a tiara, her shoulders draped in a fine, dark shawl, something woven of soft fabric. My age, she thought. He was a bit taller than she, dark and lean, and he'd spoken without guile, just friendly and a little curious. He's quite handsome too, nice eyes.

Yes, she said. From America. Oh, I mean the United States, of course.

Is okay, he said, a common mistake.

Very good English.

No, he said, not college, just high school.

Me too.

They drank coffee in the museum cafeteria. She had to pee, and when she returned to the table, he asked her to the dance. Something weekly, for young people. Just down the way from her hotel. Is tonight! he said. I could come and escort you. Or we could meet there. In front. There, she said. Is somewhat formal, he said. Not too much.

It was ballroom dancing. She'd taken a brief mini-course, no credit, for the fun of it, and he had taken one too, Alejandro. His parents were wealthy, and the skill was necessary.

They danced the night away. Not into the wee hours, of course, just eight to ten. He wore a blue suit, she her pink dress, yellow lilies on cotton over the crinoline, a rosebud in her hair. Am I a woman? she thought, in the middle of a slow foxtrot. A mirrored ball turned above them, flickers of light on her bare arms and the little white hand he held out in his soft, darker one.

And the next evening they went to an amusement park at the city's edge in his sporty little car. They threw darts at balloons and from the top of the ferris wheel saw lights blink on along the shore as darkness approached and the city came back to nightlife once again after siesta.

And the next day he showed her the city, the parks, cafés, and museums, some lovely houses secreted on flower-laden streets, and they wound up at the central library, an elegant old building in which study took place as in ancient times. Old men sat under private lights in the reading room, dressed quite formally in suits and ties, and children were quiet and attentive, alone, or beside mothers who tended to their explorations.

Do you study? she whispered.

They were standing close together in the stacks, beautifully bound books all around them, rising in neat order to the ceiling. Of course, of course! he said. Mathematics, all the great writers, Dickens, Octavio Paz, Chaucer. I love it all! Then he turned and kissed her carefully on the lips, right there in the library. Oh, God, she thought. I could really go steady with him!

Their two weeks came to an end, as all things will come to an end. They flew home, and the Dairy Queen moved her belongings in. And after that they went out on the porch, just the two of them. Mimi was in her room, writing a letter. Well, here I am, she said. You're welcome, he said, then lifted and carried her across the threshold.

And they lived happily ever after in the White Castle, the Burger King, the Dairy Queen, and the Dark Lady with her authentic blond hair. Until she went off to Stanford on a full scholarship, English Literature, then Harvard and law school.

The Yacht

THE WOMAN WHO owned the yacht went south in the winter, even before winter began, and the upkeep and guarding of the thirty-five meter tri-deck mega-yacht, the Enchantress, were left to him, who was otherwise unemployed.

He had been an accountant at a bank in this small Mediterranean village, and when the bank went under and the patrons moved their meager savings to one in a larger town nearby, he had lost his job, and finding nothing clerical there, had accepted this strange wealthy woman's offer.

The one thing he knew, besides figures, was boats. His father had a motor launch, and he had worked on it in his youth. And though there were many in the village more qualified than he, for some reason this tall, stately woman had taken a shine to him, a very strange one that troubled him, something in her smile or in her eyes. Her short hair was jet black and oiled. Fixed tight to her skull, it resembled a helmet of some kind. And each time he met with her, she was wearing the same formal attire, a masculine-looking gray suit, high heels, a subtle rose-patterned tie.

He was provided with a cabin under the aft deck. It was small and imbued with a scent reminiscent of his mother's bedroom at home, and he avoided it, using it only for sleep. His house in the village stood empty, and he was pleased to be away from it.

His responsibilities included taking the yacht out into the Mediterranean every so often to check its seaworthiness, and on this day he had carefully maneuvered the yacht, with its deep, thirteen-foot draft, away from the dock and headed out into the more serious waters, though they were not so serious on this cloudy day.

The sea was flat calm, hardly a ripple, and he dropped anchor, then examined the gauges and oil pressures. Everything seemed fine, and he lifted his eyes to the curved windows that looked out from the bridge. Beyond the bow and across the calm waters, he could just make out the village church steeple, a slim needle at this distance. There were no other boats in sight, and he climbed down the ladder and moved to one of the lounge chairs on the foredeck, sat back, looked up into the slightly overcast sky, and thought once again about the locked hatch. There had been no key. "Not for that one," the woman had smiled. But there was hard steel in her eyes.

He was fifty-three years old, small, thin and slightly stooped, and though he had been quite handsome in his youth, the death of his mother, whom he had lived with, had brought him down a notch. She had been the love of his life, his only love, and the loss of her had left him alone, friendless, and deeply depressed. Even now, looking up into the cloud cover, he could see only sadness, that same sadness he saw in all things and people. It was his sadness, of course, and not theirs, and yet he projected it onto the world around him, and everything was alienating.

His mother had sewn clothing for the village poor, and he had supported her in her life and this endeavor, and when she died he had inherited the small house where the two of them had lived for all of their lives. His father had died when he was only twenty.

He was wondering what it would take to get into the locked hatch. And if I broke the lock, he thought, I can fix it. She'll be gone for three months. He sat there for a while. A light, warm breeze had come in and there were now gentle ripples, light green at their curls, on the otherwise flat sea. He took in the pleasure of them before rising.

The hatch was amidships, down below the bridge, toward the stern. It was accessed through a narrow passage to the portside of the galley, tucked in between the massive refrigerator and the six-burner stove. A prep counter blocked the way, a section of which could be lifted to allow access. The passage seemed to narrow even more as he moved down it, the green bulkheads pressing in against him. The hatch itself was small, and even someone of his diminutive size would have to squat down to enter.

He saw that the lock was large and complicated, and he had no chance with it, so he moved to the hinges and worked to drive the pins out with his punch and hammer. They were tight, and it took him almost an hour, but finally he was able to pull the hatch toward him, where he was squeezed down in the passage. There was enough space there, and he was able to climb through.

His mother had been tall and fit, athletic before her long illness, and she had urged him into exercise in the basement of their house where there were old machines, a treadmill and a stationary bike, and he was agile even at his age. Still, he was as careful as an old man as he stepped slowly down the steep ladder that moved off at a slight angle to the left as he descended.

The ladder ended at the foot of another passageway, this one brief, its bulkheads festooned with various tools: giant wrenches and hammers, together with other, more exotic elements that in another context might be seen as instruments of none-too-subtle persuasion: pincers and heavy hemostats, long, vicious-looking knives, all hanging from hooks affixed to the walls which were dampened with some oily substance, sticky to the touch. He figured he was well below the center of the vessel now, just above the hold. Could it be some illicit cargo, then? The woman had seemed capable of such duplicity; this questionable judgment garnered in their three brief meetings.

He looked down at his feet, his thin deck shoes. Just ahead was yet another hatch, this one in the middle of the deck floor. How deep was he now? The draft was thirteen feet. It must be a shallow hold, he thought.

He got down on his knees, reached out and opened the heavy circular hatch. A faint light greeted him, sending a cylinder of luminescence that was hanging with slow, dancing dust motes up to the passageway ceiling. He bent over, moved his head into the light shaft, and looked down.

The room below was lit by six wall sconces containing low-power bulbs. Two of these flanked an ordinary door at the room's end. Bookshelves, a few nautical prints, a couch and two upholstered chairs, and to the side of a heavy, mahogany coffee table, a large, sturdy crib that was made of metal and looked very much like a cage. Impossible, he thought. The walls must be ten feet high. This is yards below the draft. Could something have been added at dry dock, a kind of tumor protruding from the hull? A battery-powered clock, between two prints, ticked out the time.

There was no ladder, no stairway. He was looking down from the room's ceiling. There was only a fragile-looking chandelier, teardrop crystals hanging from a thin wire enclosure.

It seemed the only way, and so he moved his legs until they hung down through the circular opening, then lowered himself, his hands gripping the hatch edges, until he was hanging, his arms extended above his head, holding on and swaying. The drop was a long one, and he feared for his ankles and knees. I'm too old for this, he thought, then he reached out for the bottom-hanging teardrops, grabbed onto the wire rim they were attached to, and dropped, taking the entire chandelier with him. He landed on the upholstered couch, wires and broken glass inundating his torso. Nothing was broken but for the tears scattered across both his body and the couch, some also having fallen to the oriental carpet upon which sat the coffee table. Yet once he had removed the wires and glass, and struggled to his feet, he found that he had injured his knee, the right one, and he had to step gingerly.

He examined the room. There seemed no way out but for the one door. No papers, coffee cups, or other evidence that the room had been put to use. But there was that crib, and surely a story involving people and their actions could be constructed from that. He touched the thin mattress, bent over and smelled it. Nothing. If it had been put to use, that must have happened a while ago.

The room was quiet, the only movement came from the advancement of time registered by the clock. He looked over at its face. Eleven o'clock it said. Five hours? He'd dropped anchor at six in the morning. How could it have been that long?

The door beckoned, his only exit but for the hatch high above, which was impossible to reach. It was an ordinary wooden door with a brass knob. The sconces were slightly above the edges of the frame, and their dim light cast shadows that seemed to be sliding down to the floor across the panels of green-painted wood. And the key, attached to a rabbit's-foot fob, protruded from the knob.

Beyond the door was yet another descending stairway,

this one circular, and as he climbed down he gave up on the impossibility of the depth.

The stairway seemed endless as he turned in it, but it was no more than eight feet to its terminus. He expected pressure, but his ears were fine, and when he reached the lower deck he could feel no movement at all. The sea was still, and the yacht itself was still. At the end of the small chamber where he stood, a heavy, dark curtain blocked the way. It seemed to flutter, its folds exchanging spaces with one another. There was nothing for it now, so he pulled back the curtain and entered into a small compartment, to the side of which was a tubular opening large enough to accommodate a small, stooped-over man, which he was and became as he moved through the tube that curved off to what he thought was the starboard side of the boat. He wasn't sure of that or much else just then. The tube opened onto parquet flooring, a small room, its walls decorated with the pasted-on images of clouds and suns and cartoon figures. He saw a laughing Mickey Mouse, Casper the friendly ghost, a few dancing rabbits. Then his gaze moved to the room's end, to the steel bars and the metal door, and beyond them to what was surely a cell.

The girl sat erect on the single bed, an open book and a large doll, dressed very much like she was, on the thin coverlet beside her. There was a toilet in the cell and a sink, a small refrigerator and hot plate, a storage cabinet, and a bookcase full of various volumes. A gathering of wilted roses, a few petals having fallen to the surface of the storage cabinet, upon which stood the glass vase that contained them. The girl didn't rise, nor did she seem surprised by his presence.

"Who are *you?*" he said.

"Who are *you?*" she responded. "Come to rejoin us?" She shuddered slightly as she spoke her last words.

She's a teenager, he thought. Fourteen or fifteen. But she was dressed in the raiments of a much younger child. Her long blond hair fell in two thick braids, red bows tied at their ends, one to each side of her head, framing her lovely, though blemished, face. The braids touched the fabric of her blouse, a pattern of bonneted babies frolicking below the stiff white collar that closed just under her chin. A short, pleated seersucker skirt, yellow and red vertical stripes on a field of blue, white stockings ending in bright black patent leather shoes. The yacht tilted, and he shifted his weight to his damaged knee, felt the deep pain, then recovered. It could be another craft passing, even a bit of a storm. The girl gave no reaction at all, as if she were familiar with such subtle movements.

When he was a young child, his mother had insisted on his long, curly, baby hair, though his father often told her he looked like a little girl. And she had dressed him as she had when he was just emerging from babyhood: jumpers held up by suspenders, and snowsuits in the winter, though it never got that cold. And because of the way she had dressed him, she treated him as the younger child he appeared to be. There were books read to him in the evenings, even though he could then read them for himself; soft foods, when what he required was the same fare that graced the table for his mother and father. "Chicken Little," she would coo, chucking him under the chin before kissing him. It ended, of course ... or perhaps it didn't. At times he still felt like that costumed child, inauthentic and helpless, until his father insisted on his growth. With this girl, it was much more extreme. She was a sexual being, dressed even before puberty, dressed as a little child, strange as the architecture of this yacht that contained her.

"No," he said. "I'm not here to harm you. But what is this rejoining all about?"

"The mother," she said.

"But why here?" he asked.

"The mother says I'm trouble and must be locked away while she's gone."

"What kind of trouble?"

"Fire," she said. "I like fire. But I've never done anything, actually. Well, a few bonfires in the yard, a couple of old toys?"

"When you were younger?"

"Oh, no. Not back then." She caressed the babies on her breast, to demonstrate the past. "More recently."

"Would you like to stay here?" he asked. "Or would you like to go up on the deck, see what's going on up there?"

"Yes," she said. "Up on the deck. In the sun. I don't want to see the mother though."

"She's not here."

"Good," she said.

A key was hanging from a hook on the wall, just out of reach of she who was, perhaps in ceremony, locked up. It seemed a kind of tease. He lifted it and stepped to the metal door and opened it. She stood up from the bed, then, and moved to him and hugged him. She was taller than he was, and her scent was reminiscent of the talcum powder of his childhood. He was embarrassed by her closeness, the touch of her braid against his cheek, her warm body pressing into him, her quiet cooing. A child, he thought, and pushed her gently away, and waited while she scooped up her doll then searched out and lifted her heavy bag and slung the strap over her shoulder. She turned her head for a moment, considering the desiccated roses. Then she just stood there, bright-eyed and expectant.

"Okay, okay," he said. "Let's figure this out."

They could go back up to the room, but what good

would that do? The hatch in the ceiling was far too high. He looked around her cell and the room they were now in, but he could see nothing that might help.

"Wait," she said. "I know a way. I've seen them use it."

When he cared for his mother in the last years of her terminal illness, he treated her much in the same way as she had treated him when he was just a child. She wore a bib, and he fed her and wiped her lips, and when she became incontinent, he removed her diaper and cleaned her and spoke to her in a kind of baby talk, and she seemed to like this, to be treated as a vulnerable child, which in a way she was.

And now he was faced with another woman, though just a teenager, who had been thrust back into the position of a child as well. Before fire, he thought, cleansing by retrogression, though in the case of his mother it had more to do with his own early days. It was as if he were paying her back, putting her in the same position she had put him in. Well, not exactly the same. She had desired to fix him in place, to forestall his growth beyond childhood, his hair, that ludicrous clothing, while he had worked to send her back there, to cleanse her of the tribulations of adulthood and old age. That way she would be pure and innocent again when she entered the earth. Yet that baby talk, those smiling, whispered words, were of a kind that was spoken to small animals, a dog or a cat, for though her responses had been grateful, she was still an old, dying woman and not a child, and now he realized, standing beside this woman-child, that he had not addressed his mother's final conditions with dignity.

She touched him lightly on the shoulder. "This way," she said, and he followed her in her braids, her short, frilly skirt, her shiny shoes and her ludicrous blouse, back beyond the curtain and through the brief, curved tunnel and up toward the door that was the entrance into the room where he had dropped down from the ceiling.

She paused at the door, then pointed to the right. To port side? He wasn't sure anymore. The yacht had become an impossible maze, and he had little idea of where they were and where they might be going.

She bent down, felt along the bulkhead to the door's right, found the indented latch, and opened yet another, very small door. There was a sucking of wind, the smell of the sea, and she got down on her knees, her doll tucked under her arm and her bag slipping to the deck, and entered. And he followed her, hopping slightly on his good leg, dragging the other behind him.

Another tunnel, this one leading down and to the left. She said she'd seen them use it. But how could she have? Her cell was out of sight, somewhere below and to the right. Could there have been some sort of window, a porthole providing vision from her chamber? Impossible, he thought, though he was unsure of most everything now but for the breeze echoing in the tube and the scent of the sea.

A final turning, then fresh air and the lap of water against the hull, and they were now able to stand, she in front of him, wind gently blowing, her braids dancing on her shoulders. They were in the large anchor housing, links of the huge chain descending down the yacht's hull, then entering the calm waters of the Mediterranean far below their feet. There was a metal ladder attached to the yacht's side at the edge of the anchor housing, and she climbed up ahead of him. Following her, he could see her white, unspoiled, stocking tops, and what he thought was a white diaper hugging her behind under that short skirt. Could her mother have gone this far? Near the end, his mother had worn a diaper too.

The girl disappeared above him, and when he reached the ladder's final rungs and stepped over, he found he was standing beside her on the broad aft deck, and there was her mother, his boss, and three tough-looking men all glaring at them from the port rail. The mother was dressed in her gray business suit, the same rose-patterned tie, the collar of her starched white shirt tight at the neck. She held a pistol in her right hand.

"Mother!" the girl cried out, then began moving toward her, walking at first, then running, the doll, held by a blond braid, bouncing against her leg, and her heavy bag held tight at her hip. She had something in her free hand, and he saw a flicker leap out of it as she reached her mother and touched it to her bag.

An explosion of flames, then, the smell of gasoline, and they were both engulfed. The three men ran to the side as the doll rose up, a figure of lost childhood, cooking in the inferno. And out of the tower of flames and the smell of burning flesh, a fiery arm extended, the gun in a charred hand.

Mother, he thought. Then he turned and leapt over the deck rail, hearing the muffled report as he fell into the sea. The yacht was aflame behind him. He could smell it as he stroked out toward the church steeple, the village, and his home.

Journey on a Dime

There was a man who had plenty of money and could spend it freely and without worry, and he did. He had a fine apartment in the city, a new car parked in an expensive lot, invitations to exclusive parties to which he brought elegant gifts and left early – he was not sociable – a charming country house paid in full, more money than he could ever spend, time on his hands. And yet he valued none of his possessions very highly, these things money could buy him – take it or leave it – except for his shoes. In the past he had been a poor man and couldn't afford good shoes. Then he found his efficient broker and the stock market, and he could.

Crockett & Jones, John Lobb, Testoni, Martin Dingman, and of course Adidas Micropacers, Hogan, Bottega Veneta, a hundred pairs at least, for the man was a walker in this city, he couldn't sit still. He walked in the parks, along both rivers, around the lake, down boulevards, into narrow back streets, through aisles in the supermarkets and the massive specialty food shops out on the docks. He tried never to retrace his steps, and so he went. And once he went to a podiatrist on the far side of the city, walking there, because his feet had begun to ache from walking, only to find out his feet had become flat feet, the arches fallen, and he needed orthotics. So he was fitted for a set, which felt good; then, because money was no object, he bought a set for each of his hundred or more pairs of shoes, but for the one he valued above all the others, which for some reason didn't seem to need them. It's ironic, because he'd purchased these shoes at the end of a flea-market Saturday, when the prices fell drastically, for one thin dime. A lark to buy them at that cost, but in a way pragmatic, for he could then tell the story of his purchase, which might be worth much more.

They were goofy shoes, old-time tennis sneakers, black, with red flames on the sides, a little ragged, but when he worked his feet into them, dancing in place before the seller's table, then laced them, they fitted perfectly and he was sure they would deliver him wherever he wanted to go, at any time. Of course, they were magic shoes. Well, not magic, actually. They didn't do anything. And yet at times they did seem to have a mind of their own, taking him places without his conscious volition involved. And yet walking had often been like that anyway, the mindless perambulation of a rich man with nothing to do.

Then, one day, out walking, he was approaching an uptown bar, and his shoes turned and took him down steps into a darkness in which he had to squint until his eyes became accustomed to the dim light, and he found the story. It was an old-time tavern, like his shoes, and when he shuffled up to the bar he saw a woman sitting where the bar turned at the end. He ordered a beer. And by the time the beer came, he had smiled at the woman and she at him. So he lifted the frosty mug and moved down the way to join her.

At first she seemed an old woman, then she seemed a young one in her old woman's disheveled hair, clothing, and the demeanor he found in her face, which was slightly soiled by what he took to be experience. There was no money on the bar beside her half-full glass, so he ordered a second round for both of them, though he guessed it was not drink or poverty that had brought her to this condition.

They talked, his shoes resting on the bar-stool ring, about the hot weather, not good for walking, though they soon heard rain on the street above, about life on the city streets in both rain and sun, about music, painting and the stock market, small talk leading to moments of silence, and in one of these she asked if he might like to come to her place for more. His shoes shuffled on the ring, for he had no desire for her, but he agreed.

Her place was a hotel room, only a few doors down, but it was raining hard and they were soaked through by the time they got there. He sat in the couch across from the bed, and she went into the bathroom and then came out in a robe, carrying another. Her dark hair had been toweled dry and looked fresh and clean as it fell around her face in soft waves, and her face had been scrubbed into a glow and seemed no longer soiled by any care. He took the offered robe and went into the bathroom too and removed his wet clothing, even his shoes, and got into it. And when he came out, carrying his shoes, she was sitting at the bed's edge, her legs crossed, the robe fallen away to reveal her knees. They were long, lovely legs, and he placed his shoes on the floor and sat down in the couch again, facing her. Then they talked.

They talked for hours. She had a slight accent, and in this talk of politics, finances and travel, of history and the uprooting of settlements, even of cabbages and kings, they came to a place that seemed to him an oasis, and he told her his life's story, which ended too quickly because there was so little in it, that going from being poor to being rich, like walking mindlessly through the city streets, but for the realization in telling it that it might not even have started yet. She told him almost nothing about herself, but that she had been born in Italy. Then the talking ended.

It was very late, still raining cats and dogs, the rain beating hard at the window making the room seem a shelter from the storm, which it was, and she asked him if he'd like to spend the night there, what remained of it. She'd take the couch; he could have the bed. He said the couch was fine, and she handed him a pillow and a blanket she'd fetched from the closet, then smiled at him and turned out the light. He slipped out of his robe and got under the rough blanket. It felt good against his skin, and he left the story and fell asleep almost immediately, only to wake in the morning to bright sunlight in the room and the empty bed. She was gone, and so were his shoes.

What can happen now, but anything? For this man, like all men, is nothing but a figment of his own mind and has now come out of it, much in the way he might have come out of the mind of a writer sitting before a keyboard who has no idea where the man might be going, or even walking, next.

Sitting on the bed, the man is nothing, might as well be among the dead, but should he move or should his mind move, he'd come alive in a story, experienced or lived through or thought about, which is the only living to be counted on.

What should he do? What should his mind make himself do, or observe himself doing? All that walking around with all that money, getting nowhere, might well have been a searching for a story; but to find the start of a story implies its ending, and the man had only his shoes and the woman to get him there, and now they are both gone.

This is not a problem, he thinks. I have money, the rain has stopped, my socks are still here, and my clothes are dry. I can call a taxi, then walk the few yards in my stocking feet. I'll be home in under an hour, then under a hot shower, then drinking good coffee.

Okay, fine, but what will he do then, where will he and the story go? He has no shoes and he has no woman. Suddenly, he's exhausted, and he crawls back under the blanket to forget everything and goes to sleep.

The woman left the hotel room bright and early, with nothing but a large shoulderbag and his shoes, which she wore, having stuffed her own worn and flimsy ones down into the bag. He'd told her he had money. It had been there in his life story and she'd seen some of it in the bar. So how could he miss such raggedy tennies? She didn't have even a thin dime, but the sun was warm on her face, and her feet felt light and delicious in these new shoes. They were magic shoes. Well, not magic, actually. They didn't do anything. And yet at times they did seem to have a mind of their own. They were dancing shoes. They had once been worn by a mysterious dancer in practice sessions, and the woman herself felt like a dancer in them.

So she began to dance. At first it was on the street near the bar, for dimes, then after long walks through the city, reconnoitering, in discovered places, in front of museums and downtown art galleries, where she was thought of as some sort of artist herself, and quarters and dollars were forthcoming. And she found out, through the dancing, that she was quite good at it; even better than that, thought the man who approached her one day and offered her a position in a new avant-garde company he was forming.

She danced there awhile, awkwardly at first when she had to take her shoes off and put on more conventional ones, then better as she regained her recently acquired dexterity and picked up movements and routines that stood her in good stead when she moved up to dance with an established troupe.

And soon she was out front, the other dancers only a chorus behind her. She danced her way across the country, in places to great acclaim, and after a few years of this she was invited to dance alone in Italy, accompanied by a full symphony orchestra, in Rome. Many important dignitaries were in attendance, though not the Pope, though her dance numbers did have a religious flavor, one that seemed even more universal than Catholicism.

After the concert, photographs, the flowers and the reception, she slept like a log, and the next morning, refreshed, she slipped on the old shoes and went out for a long walk through the ancient city. She walked for hours, and in the afternoon she stopped for an espresso at a breezy outdoor café. She was not tired from all the walking, and was enjoying the coffee and her new view, when a well-dressed older man came to her table and introduced himself. He had been at the concert and was an admirer, and he asked her quite formally if she might consider coming to his villa for dinner the following evening. It would be no more than a small gathering of friends. She might enjoy their company. She liked the look of his clothing and his demeanor, and she agreed.

At the party, the guests were generous in their praise of her dancing, though only two had been to the concert and they were not among the royalty in attendance. She counted a Conte and Contessa, a Principessa, a couple of young Ducas and an ancient Marchesa, and her host revealed in private that he himself was a Visconti, seventy-six years old, and that his wife, the Viscontessa, had died just the winter before and that he was lonely in that magnificent villa of fifty rooms, marble staircases and fountains, paintings by famous artists, a ballroom with a mahogany floor fit for dancing, and numerous ancient vases and figurative sculptures placed casually throughout the rooms.

After the other guests had departed, he took her to sit beside him on one of the many tile terraces overlooking fields and stately rows of junipers marching down to the sea. They drank brandy there and talked into the early morning, until she grew tired and told him that, and his car and driver arrived to take and deliver her back to her hotel. She was hardly back in the room when the phone rang. He'd called to ask if she might wish to accompany him on an evening cruise on his yacht the next day, and after a few months of conversation, cruising, eating fine meals among friends and royalty at his villa, and attending concerts and other theatrical occasions, she agreed to marry him, and she did.

Their marriage lasted a full year, and then he died without other heirs, and she found herself in possession of the villa, the yacht and all his money, which was a considerable sum, most of it invested in the stock market. She had all this, and yet she valued none of it very highly. Take it or leave it. The only thing she really valued were those shoes that had carried her along all the way and had brought her to where she now was. She felt she owed them something, but how can one provide recompense to shoes? So she wore them often, regardless of the weather or the occasion, and because of this she became in the eyes of others at best curious, at worse eccentric. She stopped dancing, and while not a recluse, she kept to the villa on most afternoons and evenings, after her long walks through the city and through that beautiful countryside near the sea, where the villa was so perfectly situated.

Then, one afternoon, while she was sitting in her lounger on that same terrace on which her husband had keeled over and died a year earlier, she saw a figure approaching who seemed no more than one of those occasional country walkers that caught sight of the villa and moved closer, though they were never bold enough to intrude on her privacy. It was a man, and he seemed familiar in his posture, which she really couldn't discern properly at her distance from him. His feet hurt, for he had been walking all over Italy, looking for his shoes.

They were magic shoes. Well, not magic, actually. They didn't do anything, and yet why else would he set out on such a seemingly impossible journey? Years ago he had awakened finally, called a taxi and gone home, took a hot shower, then drank coffee. Then he had just sat there. Nothing to do. What could he possibly do without that woman and his shoes? Well, he could go out walking, as before. He had plenty of shoes, and orthotics in all of them, after all. But where exactly would he go, and for what reason? He'd been everywhere in the city, and there was no untold story to be entered into there. But wasn't the woman Italian? Hadn't she spoken with a slight accent? He'd never been to Italy, and he supposed he could walk into something new there. So here he comes.

And shuffling through the story in her memory, she recognizes him at about the same time he recognizes his shoes, resting on the tile beside her chair, where she had stepped out of them before settling in, legs crossed at the ankles, with her tea and cookies. There's another chair beside hers, and she smiles and gestures toward it, offering him respite in his journey, which will be over when he sits down, the shoes on the tile between them.

He sits down.

Is this *closure*? They have come back together after separate journeys in which they have both walked and danced their way through the world, or parts of it, and surely this reconnection and stasis is some kind of closure, if that word can hold any meaning at all in its current popularity. Which is much like the popularity of the word *hero* – both words standing as markers of time's passage from a time, in that uptown bar perhaps, when they were not popular.

Now it's the man stepping from the twisted wreckage of a train who is a hero, searching for closure as the sole survivor. It's the brave writer who makes an heroic choice of subject matter, risking the difficult journey to closure. It's people leaping to their deaths from tall buildings, rather than burning in the inferno; all heroes. It's the President sending children to their death, uselessly, in a foreign country, his heroic decision. One might wish for some closure when it comes to that, perhaps as a rope closing around an offending throat to close off blather. Still, in each case, even the writer's, there's travel.

So they sit there beside each other, talking, as shadows come down over the villa, the marching junipers, and finally the sea. She tells him the story of her travels and successes, and he speaks of his journey in search of his shoes, which was a meandering, and no story at all. Perhaps the stock market has crashed back in America. Maybe her yacht is sinking out there on the dark sea, her dead husband's investments dissolving into dust. There may be a crucial fault in the villa's foundation, and it will break free of this terrace and slide down the hill into ruin, taking everything she now owns with it. Maybe that uptown basement bar has been set aflame by an arsonist. She doesn't care. He doesn't care. They are both tired from the talking, from lack of motion, from the telling of stories rather than living them. The shoes sit on the tile between them, and, as in a story, continuance might depend on which one of

them falls asleep first. But as luck would have it, they both
nod off at the same time, and there's no motion or thought
or motion in thought anymore. And this is where the story
begins, and where it ends.

Also available from grand**IOTA**

APROPOS JIMMY INKLING
Brian Marley
978-1-874400-73-8   318pp

WILD METRICS
Ken Edwards
978-1-874400-74-5   244pp

BRONTE WILDE
Fanny Howe
978-1-874400-75-2   158pp

THE GREY AREA
Ken Edwards
978-1-874400-76-9   328pp

PLAY, A NOVEL
Alan Singer
978-1-874400-77-6   270pp

THE SHENANIGANS
Brian Marley
978-1-874400-78-3   220pp

SEEKING AIR
Barbara Guest
978-1-874400-79-0   218pp

BONE
Philip Terry
978-1-874400-81-3   150pp

Production of this book has been made possible with the help of the following individuals and organisations who subscribed in advance:

Peter Bamfield
Chris Beckett
Lillian Blakey
Andrew Brewerton
Ian Brinton
Jasper Brinton
Peter Brown
Mark Callan
Robert Caserio
John Cayley
cris cheek
Claire Crowther
Rachel DuPlessis
Ian Durant
Allen Fisher/Spanner
Nancy Gaffield
Susan Gevirtz
Jim Goar
Giles Goodland
Penny Grossi
John Hall
Andrew Hamilton
Robert Hampson
Peter Hodgkiss
Peter Hughes
Kristoffer Jacobson
Howard Jones
Steve Lake

Alison Lambert
Stacey Levine
James McDonald
Richard Makin
Michael Mann
Askold Melnyczuk
Joe Milazzo
John Muckle
Richie Nice
Jim O'Brien
Françoise Palleau
Sean Pemberton
Dennis Phillips
Pablo Seoane Rodríguez
David Rose
Lou Rowan
James Russell
Maurice Scully
Steven Seidenberg
Valerie Soar
Lloyd Swanton
Eileen Tabios
Robert Vas Dias
visual associations
John Wilkinson
Tyrone Williams
Tamar Yoseloff
anon x 2

www.grandiota.co.uk

CPSIA information can be obtained
at www.ICGtesting.com
Printed in the USA
FSHW010734280121
77981FS